Catherine Walsh was born and rais___ ___ ___
in Popular Literature and the only ___ ___ ___
was at the age of 14 in school (but ___ ___ ___ ___ ___).

She lived in London for a few years where she worked in Publishing and the non-profit sector before returning to Dublin where she now lives between the mountains and the sea. When not writing she is trying and failing to not kill her houseplants.

ALSO BY CATHERINE WALSH

CATHERINE WALSH

The Rebound

bookouture

SPHERE

First published in 2022 by Bookouture, an imprint of Storyfire Ltd.
This paperback edition published in 2024 by Sphere

1 3 5 7 9 10 8 6 4 2

A CIP catalogue record for this book
is available from the British Library.

ISBN 978-0-3491-3282-2

Printed and bound in Great Britain by
Clays Ltd, Elcograf S.p.A.

Papers used by Sphere are from well-managed forests
and other responsible sources.

MIX
Paper from
responsible sources
FSC® C104740

Sphere
An imprint of
Little, Brown Book Group
Carmelite House
50 Victoria Embankment
London EC4Y 0DZ
An Hachette UK Company
www.hachette.co.uk
www.littlebrown.co.uk

CHAPTER 1

Where are you?

I finish the last of my sandwich as I stare down at the text. My hands are so numb I can barely move my thumb across the screen.

Where am I? Where am I, Tyler?

Right back where I started from.

Or close to it anyway. And not to be dramatic, but I'm pretty sure I'm going to die here. Here on this freezing cold bench in this almost empty parking lot. I'm going to die wearing yesterday's clothing with six percent battery left and one bar of signal.

I swipe the message away, my stiff fingers protesting the movement, and try calling Louise again. The time on my phone tells me it's ten p.m. local time, which means I was supposed to be back hours ago, which means my sister is going to kill me.

I listen to it ring as I watch the remaining stragglers board the bus to Galway. I landed in Dublin this afternoon, naively thinking once I did it would be relatively easy to get to where I needed to be. But what should have been two to three hours on the road has turned into half a day trying to navigate the Irish public transport system. Or rather the lack of it. And now after managing to make it all the way across the country, I have a feeling that if I'm not careful, I'm going to have to walk the rest of the night.

I get to my feet, brushing away crumbs as I look around. In the tourist brochures, the west of Ireland is usually portrayed as a lush, windswept vista. Full of rugged cliffs and green fields. They do not show places like this. And for good reason. When I arrived, the small crossroads town had been full of people making their way home for the weekend. Now it's quiet, the surrounding businesses closed, leaving the streets eerily empty, and I'm left staring enviously as the final bus pulls away, leaving just me and a girl in a bright orange vest talking to another customer.

Louise doesn't answer, so I hang up and drag my suitcase over to her, trying to make eye contact. I'm not used to being ignored, but she does a pretty good job of it, oblivious to my existence as she peers up at the man in front of her.

"Katie says we might finally win this year," she tells him as I do a "please pay attention to me" smile.

"Without you?" he replies.

She giggles. She actually giggles.

I drop my luggage at my feet. I don't have the energy for this.

"Excuse me," I interrupt. "Could you—"

"Just a second." She barely spares me a glance. "I'll have to come back and support," she says to him.

"You'll probably just make them nervous."

"*Me?*"

I roll my eyes at the delight in her voice and step between them, forcing the man to move back. "Sorry to butt in," I say, making sure I don't sound sorry at all. "Could you tell me when the bus to Clonard is coming?"

She looks as if I just pushed her. "Where?"

"Clonard. There was one due forty minutes ago but it didn't show. I've been waiting for an hour."

It takes so long for her to answer that I wonder if I've simply vanished into thin air.

"I think you might have missed it," she says finally.

"Missed it?"

"By about eight years. It only runs on Wednesdays now."

"On *Wednesdays*?"

"Didn't you check the website?"

"Yes!"

"The new website?"

She can't be serious.

"I can call you a taxi," she continues when I don't respond.

A taxi. I'd laugh if I didn't want to hit something. The one credit card I have left still worked when I checked it at the airport, but I doubt the local taxi company will take it and there's nowhere open to exchange money. I can only imagine the look on Louise's face when I show up at her door asking for cash. "How much will it cost?"

The girl shrugs.

"Well, can you go and check?"

Her lips part in indignation, but when it's clear I'm not budging she scowls. "Sure," she mutters, storming into her little hut as I check my phone again. Two percent battery. I'm doomed.

"Do you need a lift?"

I almost jump at the deep voice behind me. I'd forgotten the man was there.

"I'm fine."

"There's a match down in Hollybrook, so you'll be waiting awhile," he continues, ignoring me trying to ignore him. "They'll hear that American accent and double the price."

"I don't have an accent. I'm from here."

"Okay." He sounds amused. "But I'm going that way now if you're stuck."

"I'm not stuck. I just need your girlfriend to do her job."

"She's not my girlfriend."

"Whatever. But I'm still—"

Fine.

I don't get the last word out; it dies on my lips along with my annoyance as soon as I turn around.

He's older than I thought. Early thirties maybe? And handsome. Very handsome. His hair is cut short, almost shorn on his head with a face that's blessed with, and let's be real here, some outstanding genetic luck.

His eyes are green. I know his eyes are green because I'm staring into them as he stares into mine.

We look at each other in silence, neither of us saying anything, and I realize with supreme embarrassment that my mouth is hanging open. I shut it and stick out my hand.

"Abby," I say. "I'm Abby."

He doesn't respond at first, an odd expression flickering across his face, and I instantly regret the handshake thing. Years in the corporate world have made me formal. But before I become too self-conscious, he thankfully returns it, his palm large and dry against mine.

"Cold hands," he says.

"Oh, sorry."

His grip slackens and I force myself to let go. "Bad circulation," I babble. "But you know, warm heart and all that. Mam always said I'd make an excellent pastry chef."

"A pastry chef?"

"Because you have to keep the dough cold."

He blinks at me. "Right."

Because you have to keep the dough cold. Jesus Christ, Abby.

"So you're heading home?"

"Who said it's home?" I hedge but he only smiles.

"There's not a lot of other reasons to go to Clonard."

He's got a point. But before I can respond the girl stomps back out of the hut, pausing as she takes us in.

"It will be eighty-five euro," she says, her attention flicking between us like she doesn't know who to focus on. "But you'll be waiting awhile. There's a—"

"Match in Hollybrook," I finish. "I heard."

If looks could kill. "So?" she asks. "Do you want me to order one?"

I hesitate, looking back at the man. I'm not usually one to accept rides from strangers but...

He catches my eye. "Offer still stands," he says.

The girl's eyes narrow. "What offer?"

Thirty seconds later I follow him across the parking lot, feeling only a little smug as she stares furiously after us.

"I'm Luke, by the way."

"It's nice to meet you."

He glances back at me as if I said something funny but doesn't say anything as he opens the trunk of a small red car.

"Do you live in Clonard?" I ask as he takes my case, fitting it in between a pair of muddy running shoes and an empty cardboard box.

"I sleep there. That's about it."

I don't miss the way he keeps a respectful distance between us, as though careful not to crowd me. He offers me a choice of the front or the back seat, keeping the lights on when I slide in beside him.

It's a nice car. Worn but clean and smelling strongly of coffee, though I can't see any evidence of it.

I need to learn to drive. Dad gave me a few lessons as a teenager but neither of us had the temperament for it and he was terrified I was going to hit every wall I saw. I toyed with the idea of getting my license in college, but there were always friends to take me where I needed to go and then I moved to cities with plenty of functional public transport systems and never had any need to.

Maybe I could get cheap lessons while I'm here.

Maybe I just found my teacher.

I glance at my mystery savior, now cast in shadow as he pulls out of the parking lot. He's smiling to himself, a slight tilt of the lips that I find insanely attractive, and I wonder what someone like him is doing in the middle of nowhere.

"Been living in the States?" he asks. I look away before he can catch me staring.

"New York. I had a job over there."

"Had?"

"Had."

He takes the hint. "So you *are* coming home."

"I'm visiting my sister for a few days." Weeks. Months. Oh God. "She would have picked me up but her husband's a nurse. He's working late shifts this week and they only have one car. I thought I'd be fine getting the bus."

"This is the problem. We haven't had a decent bus route in years. The government want us to cut back on our emissions but won't give us the proper resources to— What?" He breaks off, catching my look. "What did I say?"

"Nothing. Sorry. It's just you sound exactly like her."

"Your sister?" He frowns. "Is that a bad thing?"

"No." Sometimes. "So were you at the match in Hollybrook?" I ask, eager to change the subject. "Is that why you're driving around so late on a Friday night?"

"I'm coming back from Sligo."

It doesn't tell me much. Sligo town is a two-hour drive from Clonard and most of the village commutes there for work or to shop.

"Visiting your girlfriend?" I ask, super casually.

"No."

"Do you have a girlfriend?"

He shakes his head.

"A boyfriend?"

"I was studying," he says. "I'm doing a physiotherapy course there."

"Good for you." I immediately wince at the condescending tone in my voice. Thankfully he doesn't seem to notice.

"Better late than never. What about you?"

"Oh, I'm single."

"I meant your job," he says with a small smile.

"I don't have a job, remember?"

I meant it as a joke. It doesn't come out like one.

"Well," he continues after an awkward beat. "You know what they say. When one door closes another one opens."

"I think I'm going to have to kick it down actually."

"That bad?"

"I used to work for MacFarlane."

His reaction is what I expected. Or one of two I expected anyway. It was going to be a look of surprise followed by either pity or anger. Thankfully it's the former.

"I'm sorry."

"Yeah." I sigh. "Me too."

MacFarlane. My home for the past five years. As of December, it was the ninth biggest investment bank in the world. As of three weeks ago, it was nothing at all. On a cloudy Sunday afternoon, while I was dropping too much money for a facial, it filed for bankruptcy and my entire world, along with thousands of other employees, came crashing down with it.

Everything in my life was tied to that company. Everything I'd worked for. Not just my salary but my investments, my savings. Everything I had I put into its hands because that was what we were encouraged to do. Now all of it was gone.

And I don't know how I'm going to get it back.

My chest tightens as I sink into my seat, drawing my jacket around me.

"Are you still cold?" He doesn't wait for an answer, leaning over to adjust the heating on my side. I breathe in as he does, catching the scent of him. Coffee and paper and soap.

Tyler always smelled of cologne. The same expensive cologne day in and day out. He'd go through two bottles of the stuff every year. It used to give me a headache.

Where are you?

It's the fifth text he's sent me in as many days. I haven't replied to a single one.

Childish? Yes. But forgive me if I'm not thinking straight.

"Apologies about Ava."

I push Tyler from my mind, focusing on the here and now. "The charming girl at the depot?"

Luke grimaces. "I think she was having a bad day."

I think she has a giant crush on you. "Is she a friend of yours?"

"An old student. She graduated a while back."

I glance over in surprise. "You're a teacher?"

"A coach. I volunteer with the girls' under-seventeen football team in my spare time."

"Oh yeah? How are you guys doing this year?"

"Terribly," he says with a self-deprecating grin. "But it's the taking part that counts."

"I'm sure."

My hands now thawed thanks to the heating, I try my phone again, only to find it officially dead. I stare at it for a second, angling the screen to try and see my reflection but it's too dark in the car. Then again, knowing how I looked the last time I saw it, I don't think I even want to check. I hadn't given much thought to my appearance when I boarded the plane at JFK. But now I wish I'd at least brought a comb.

"Do you need to call someone?" Luke asks.

"It's okay. My sister's going to be mad but she's always mad. I'm hoping she'll go easy after the day I've had."

"How long have you been traveling?"

"About fourteen hours. I know," I add at his glance. "I think I'm growing delirious."

"A good night's sleep and you'll be grand."

I hum in semi-agreement, straightening as we pass the entrance to the local forest. We can't be more than ten minutes from the village.

It'll be my first time back in years. Five of them, to be exact, and before that it was only ever brief visits, a few days at Christmas spent working from the back room where the Wi-Fi signal is best. When my salary went up, I started flying my parents out to New York, but the furthest Louise ever traveled to see me was Dublin, when I'd schedule in brief layovers that always ended in the two of us arguing over lunch before stiffly exchanging birthday cards or early holiday gifts.

Clonard itself has never been somewhere I've missed. Has never been anything other than the place where I happened to grow up. But still. I suppose I should feel *something*. Some sentimental tug of the heartstrings, some unexpected well of emotion, even if it is misplaced. Instead, all I feel is an increasing dread.

"Is this a bad time to tell you I also charge eighty-five euro?"

I turn to Luke in alarm as he snaps me from my self-pity.

"Plus tip," he adds, sounding so serious that I believe him for a whole other second before I catch his smile.

Mother of— "You're an asshole."

"College isn't cheap."

"It's not." I sit back, playing along. "Would you settle for the ten dollars I have in my pocket?"

"With this exchange rate? You got anything from duty-free?"

"I took some of those little bottles of alcohol from the plane."

"Throw in one of those travel pillows they give you and you've got yourself a deal."

He winks at me and I feel a rush of gratitude. It's the first time in weeks someone's tried to cheer me up in a way that didn't involve drugs or a pyramid scheme.

"Seriously though," I say. "At least let me help with gas money."

"*Gas* money."

I roll my eyes. "Petrol."

"There you go. And your suitcase is in?"

"The boot," I answer. "Not the trunk." I hold up my phone. "Mobile."

"You're good at this game."

"I've had a lot of practice. And I don't have an accent."

"You have a little twang."

"A *twang*?" I stare at him in mock horror. "And what do you have? A lilt?"

"A brogue. It's completely different."

"Now you're definitely making fun of me."

"Ah, only a little bit." His eyes slide to me. "I got you smiling though."

He did. For the first time in I don't even know how long.

"What?" he asks when I don't say anything. I'm watching him fully now, not even pretending to be discreet about it.

"Nothing."

"I got something on my face?"

I shake my head as his gaze flicks between me and the road. Once, twice, three times and I wonder if he feels it too. That spark of attraction I felt as soon as I turned around.

I'll admit it's a little surprising because (a) I've only just met the man and (b) the only other person I've felt about this way recently is Tyler and he's probably off sleeping with someone else this very second. Maybe before he even— No.

I shut that thought down before it can go any further. He never gave me any indication he cheated on me.

I'm feeling this way because I've barely slept in the last few weeks. Because I lost my partner and my job and I'm one step away from rock bottom and so, of course, I gravitate to the first bit of kindness I'm shown. Of course, if I'm in close confines with a handsome, nice-smelling stranger, I'll start to get a little... smiley.

My friend Jess would be thrilled if she could see me now. She always moaned about how boring I became once Tyler and I got together. That I wasn't any fun anymore.

But I can be fun. I can be... well, not impulsive. Intuitive maybe.

The car slows as we reach a red light and Luke pulls up the handbrake.

"Back to serious," he says, catching my eye. "What are you thinking about?"

I go to answer but something tugs at the back of my mind, a flash of déjà vu that vanishes before I can grasp it.

I'm definitely delirious. Delirious and exhausted and losing my mind because all I can think about is... what? What am I going to do?

Ask him out for a drink? Do people still do that? He'd probably laugh in my face. Or kick me out of his car.

Except the way he's looking at me now makes me think he wouldn't do either of those things. The way he's looking at me now makes me think if I showed the slightest inclination, he'd do whatever I asked. Whatever I wanted.

"Abby?"

My heart stutters at the familiar way he says my name. "Ask me again."

"What?"

"Ask me again what I'm thinking about."

He looks surprised. "Are you flirting with me?" he asks instead.

"A little."

"You're good at it."

I'm pretending to be good at it. I'm pretending to be cool and suave and not start giggling like that girl in the parking lot, that girl who I now completely understand, by the way.

He smiles when I don't respond, jumbling my thoughts even more. "Is that it? I thought you were flirting."

"I am!"

He laughs. "You've got to keep it moving! You've got to be quick."

"I'm tired."

"That's a terrible excuse."

"Well, you flirt then. Since you're so confident."

"I don't think you're ready for that yet," he says seriously. "It's pretty powerful stuff."

"Now who's— Jesus!"

I jump as a car horn blares behind us, sending my heart racing in a way that can't be good for my health.

It sounds again, angrier now, and Luke twists in his seat, giving whoever's behind us the finger as he shifts us into gear. "I'm going," he calls, as we stutter forward through the now green light.

Barely a second later the other driver overtakes us before pulling rapidly away, the engine roaring into the distance.

"Dickhead," Luke mutters, glaring after him. "Are you okay?"

"I'm fine."

"They're going to hurt someone. That's— You sure you're okay?"

I nod as he checks the rearview mirror, almost like he expects there to be a line of traffic behind us. "Are *you* okay?" I ask. He doesn't look okay. He looks rattled, still a little mad.

"Yeah. It's late," he adds, as if that explains everything, and before I can respond he presses down on the accelerator and the world outside blurs by again.

Still feeling a little skittish, I force myself to turn back to the window as the forest gives way once more to fields, the odd farmhouse and then, before I know it, the graveyard marking the boundary of the village.

It's not the most welcoming of sights and it's only made weirder by the tourist sign outside. FÁILTE GO CLONARD it says in flowing Irish words. Welcome to Clonard. They didn't include the THANKS FOR STOPPING BY. HERE'S WHERE WE KEEP THE DEAD PEOPLE. but that's probably for the best.

We zoom past both it and the elegant church where my parents were married and, just like that, I'm back.

Home.

Except it's not my home. Not anymore.

I start to panic as the roads grow increasingly familiar, even in the dark. In five seconds we'll pass the pink house with the butterfly sculptures on the wall. After that, the playground and then—

"Left."

"What?"

"You can take a left," I say, louder now as I direct him the long way around the village. Luke looks at me, confused, but I'm not ready to see everything else just yet, so I simply point to the turn up ahead until he thankfully does as requested, driving down the older narrow road. The only time I talk now is to tell him where to go until we eventually reach my street and stop in front of a small two-story house.

My sister's place, my childhood home, sits quietly in the darkness, one lonely light on in the upstairs landing. The driveway is empty. Her husband, Tomasz, still at work.

"You sure someone's in?" Luke asks.

"She's probably in bed."

I know I should thank him for his help. I know I should get out of his car. But I don't move. I can't move. Not because I don't want to leave him, but because I don't want to go inside. Now that I'm here, I'd rather be anywhere else.

I don't know why I thought this would be a good idea. Why I thought I could actually *do this*.

And he must sense something's wrong because though Luke turns the engine off, he doesn't push me out of the car, doesn't try to hurry me along even though he must be tired.

"Listen," he begins, sounding oddly guilty, but I don't let him finish.

"Thanks for the ride. Maybe I'll see you around."

He seems torn, but he lets it go as he nods.

"I can get my stuff," I add.

He ignores me, getting out with me and retrieving my luggage from the trunk. Boot. "Good luck" is all he says when he places it on the curb.

I give him a final, polite smile and wheel my case up the short driveway. He doesn't start the engine until I'm standing on the porch and even when I do the stupid "okay, bye" wave he doesn't leave, no doubt playing the gentleman and waiting until I'm safely inside. There's a lengthy pause once I press the bell, long enough that I think Louise actually is in bed, and I'm just about to turn around when the porch light snaps on, blinding me.

"Finally!"

My sister throws open the door, dressed in her pajamas. "I was about to call the guards!"

I open my mouth to explain but don't get a chance as she pulls me inside, berating me the entire time. The engine starts behind me, but by the time I extract myself from her grasp, the car is driving off, leaving me behind.

CHAPTER 2

I wake with no idea where I am.

I haven't woken naturally in a long time. My haphazard sleep schedule means I rely solely on an alarm to let me know when to get up and I'm used to being jolted to consciousness by ABBA or ACDC depending on the kind of day I plan on having. It's strange to wake naturally, floating in and out for what feels like hours but what is probably only minutes before I finally open my eyes.

The world comes back to me in pieces. My job, Tyler, Ireland. Crap.

I stretch, craning my neck and pointing my toes, but I'm unused to the narrow single bed I slept in as a child and when I roll over to check my phone I almost fall straight to the floor. I save myself just in time and with a groan, push myself up, throwing the lumpy duvet off of me.

The room feels smaller than I remember. The pale lilac wallpaper is pockmarked where my posters used to hang, the carpet dotted with nail varnish and hair dye stains. My desk is still here, polished and looking a little sad. It used to hold a million textbooks and stacks of essays. Now, Mam's ancient sewing machine takes up most of it, along with a bag of clothes marked for charity.

My old digital alarm clock, if still correct, tells me it's eleven in the morning. It's the longest I've slept in in years.

Stiff-limbed, I climb out of bed. My suitcase lies open on the floor, my gym gear and shoes folded on top for easy access. I lay them out on the mattress and get to work unpacking the rest. There are only a few odd-sized hangers in the closet, so I drape most of my clothes over the back of the chair, trying not to think about how much they cost and how much I could sell them for.

At the bottom of the case, wrapped in tissue paper in a small plastic bag, is my engagement ring.

I take it out carefully, holding the silver band between pinched fingers. I'd picked it out myself from a swanky boutique in Chelsea after days searching for the perfect one. Afterward, Tyler treated me to a champagne lunch by the pier and teased me because I refused to put it on. I'd been too scared to wear it, sure I'd scratch it against something. He never told me the price of it. But I knew it was a lot.

I'll have to return it to him. Or try to return it. Maybe he'll tell me to keep it.

Maybe I could sell it too.

I stare at it for a moment longer, twisting the diamond so it catches the sunlight before dropping it back into the bag.

One thing at a time.

I take out my planner, one of dozens I've had over the years. Tyler used to make fun of me for being old-fashioned, but the expensive "time management" apps that he used just never did it for me. There's something about recording my tasks in writing, with pen and paper and the occasional coffee stain, that helps cement things.

I got into the habit during my exams at school when my mother gave me an ordinary spiral notebook to start recording everything I needed to do each day. I carried on the habit through college and then at MacFarlane, where the intensity of the internship meant I switched from recording my work to reminding myself to go for a run or pick up my dry cleaning. In the early months, I even carved out time to "eat" and "shower." It sounds ridiculous now but it was so easy to lose track of yourself with the hours we worked. And once something was in my planner, I tended to stick to it.

My current one falls open easily in my hands, already broken in. I'd recorded my flight yesterday, the booking reference, departure and arrival times carefully noted down. Today is blank. And so is tomorrow. Monday, I was supposed to get my hair cut, an appointment booked weeks ago, but I've already crossed that out.

For the first time in years, I have no plans. Nothing to factor in. Nothing to do. And the sight of the blank day freaks me out so much that I snap the thing closed again, tossing it into the suitcase.

I keep an ear out as I pull on my running clothes, knowing it's the only thing that will clear my mind.

I can hear the radio on downstairs but no other noise in the house, no footsteps on the landing, no voices drifting up the stairs.

With a lot of financial help from me, my parents packed up and moved to Portugal just over four years ago, determined to spend their twilight years in a sunnier climate. If I knew then what was coming down the line, I maybe wouldn't have been so generous with my savings, but I don't regret it. It meant everything to me to do that for them and because of the move, they were able to hand this place to Louise and Tomasz, who have lived here ever since.

Louise didn't hesitate to say yes when I asked if I could visit. She'd heard the news of MacFarlane like everyone else in the world and, though surprised by the request, seemed to accept my reasoning that it was a great excuse to spend some time with her. I didn't tell her I had nowhere else to stay. I didn't tell her that my fiancé had dumped me and I'd moved out of his apartment and lost another apartment and that because of the mass layoffs I couldn't even get a rejection for a job, let alone an interview. Instead, we had a polite conversation on the phone, followed by an equally polite email confirming the details.

Even still, I stay as quiet as I can as I tiptoe down the stairs. I was so tired last night I barely spoke more than a few words to her. It was all I could do to shower and collapse into bed and the thought of bumping into her now while I'm still getting my story straight makes me wince. It's not that I'm scared of my sister. It's just that we—

"Are you seriously sneaking out?"

I whirl to see Louise standing in the kitchen doorway, dressed in black leggings and a pale pink sweatshirt. Her brown hair is pulled back into a bun, her arms crossed over her chest. Like me, her face is covered in freckles, but instead of my dull hazel eyes, hers are a brilliant blue that now stare at me accusingly.

I try not to look as guilty as I feel. "I'd use the back if I were sneaking out."

She clicks her tongue off the roof of her mouth, an action that reminds me disconcertingly of our mother. "Are you hungry?"

"Not really," I say, edging toward the door. "I'm going for a run."

"You can't run on an empty stomach."

"I do it all the time."

"You'll faint."

"I've never fainted in my life."

"She made you breakfast," Tomasz yells from the kitchen.

I stop in surprise. Louise scowls.

"I didn't make *you* breakfast," she says. "I simply *made* breakfast."

"You made me breakfast?"

"I just said—"

"Can we eat the pancakes now?" Tomasz calls. "Please?"

Avoiding my eye, Louise spins back into the room, looking like she's going to kill him.

"Well?" she says, a warning in her voice, and with a sigh, I follow.

The kitchen is exactly how I remember it, but with a few upgrades since my parents moved out. A new coffee machine sits on the countertop and our childhood drawings on the fridge have been replaced by an impressively detailed schedule of work shifts and bill reminders, her system unnervingly similar to mine.

Tomasz smiles tiredly at me from the table. "She said we weren't allowed to eat until you woke up."

Originally from Poland, Tomasz met Louise during a, by all accounts, very messy night in Dublin celebrating the end of her college exams. It was drunken love at first sight. Other than a few family video calls, I haven't seen him since their wedding in Gdansk, but I've always liked him.

"She thought you were dead," he says as I take a seat.

Louise huffs by the stove. "She wouldn't answer her phone."

"There was no signal," I say, repeating the same curt conversation we'd had last night after her initial relief turned to annoyance. "I tried to call you a dozen times."

"And you said you were getting a taxi."

"It all worked out in the end," Tomasz says pleasantly.

Louise mutters something under her breath and a moment later puts a plate of pancakes in front of me.

Well. This is weird.

We were never a family that ate breakfast together. Breakfast was a slice of toast on the way to school or a bowl of sugary cereal on the weekends. We certainly didn't sit at the table like a family in a sitcom, not even on special occasions. Not even at Christmas.

"Thanks," I say, picking up a fork. "This is nice."

She nods, squeezing half a lemon over hers.

"You should have made American pancakes," Tomasz says, already several bites into his.

"I love crêpes," I say quickly as Louise glares at him. Tomasz doesn't notice. Or maybe he's just used to it. God knows I am.

Louise and I have never gotten along. We're only three years apart but might as well have been from different planets. While I was studying between house parties and imagining a life beyond the border of my town, Louise was writing letters to local politicians and begging our parents to drive her to Dublin for the latest protest. She was an ecowarrior before it was cool, driven by some grave sense of injustice since birth. I don't know where it came from. Definitely not my parents, who treated it all with bemused indifference, buying organic food at her urging and dutifully recycling. I took no interest in her marches or her petitions. Saturday mornings were for sleeping in, not standing in the cold collecting money for a seal sanctuary.

I know she resents me for leaving like I did, straight out of school without so much as a "see you later," but the real knife in the back was going on to work at a place like MacFarlane, which in her mind did nothing to help the world and everything to ruin it.

I mean, she wasn't wrong.

"What's the plan for today?" Tomasz asks when neither Louise nor I attempt conversation.

"I'm not sure yet," I say. "I'm still pretty tired. I might just relax and catch up with some people tomorrow."

Louise's eyes flick to mine at the last bit as if to ask "like who?" but she takes a sip of her tea instead. "The Baileys are coming over for lunch if you want to join."

Pat and Susan Bailey from next door. They've lived beside us since before I was born. We've always been on friendly terms, but her tone makes it clear she neither expects nor wants me to be here. Probably because I'll be the focus of attention. And even though it's the exact opposite of what I want, the younger sister in me rears her ugly head. "Sounds great."

"You don't have to if you're too tired."

"I'm not," I say, smiling sweetly at her. "I'd love to see them."

"But you just said—"

Tomasz clears his throat.

"Great," she says smoothly. "They're coming at one-thirty."

I nod down at my plate, trying to hide my smirk. But Louise always knows when to strike. Even when she doesn't mean to.

"How's Tyler doing?"

I shove a forkful of pancake into my mouth, eating far quicker than I usually would. "He's good," I say. "Busy."

It's not a lie. He probably is busy.

"Is he still planning to meet you here?"

I nod, poking around the plate. "As far as I know. Depends on his workload." She'd asked almost as an afterthought whether Tyler would be coming, probably not expecting me to say yes. But I did say yes. The word popped out in my hurry to convince her everything between us was alright and now it was just one more lie to keep track of.

"It would be nice to finally meet him in person," she says. "At least before the wedding."

"You will."

"Do you have a date yet? We'll need to book time off work."

"You'll be the first to know," I say, even as I start to feel a little ill. It occurs to me only then that they're probably saving up to go to the wedding. Neither of them has much money. Tomasz is on a nurse's salary and I know Louise takes on a lot of seasonal work like everyone else in the town, meaning the charity she works for must not pay very well. I had tried to help them when I first started at MacFarlane but Louise had been very insulted and flat out refused during a very heated argument one Christmas.

The only time they go overseas is the annual trip to visit Tomasz's family. Of course they'd need to save for the wedding. The wedding that isn't happening.

I swallow my last bit of food, barely tasting it. "All done," I say a little louder than I meant to. "Thanks, Louise. We're doing this every morning, right?"

"I think that sounds like a good idea," Tomasz says, transferring one of Louise's pancakes to his own stack.

She watches me as I put my plate in the sink. "The Baileys are coming at one-thirty."

"Got it," I say, backing out the door. "I'll be here."

"*Not* in your running clothes."

"I was thinking a ballgown actually." I flash her my best smile, escaping outside before she can reply.

Okay, so I do have something for my planner.

Tell Louise about Tyler.

Tell everyone about Tyler but start with Louise.

Start with Louise so she can tell my parents and they can tell everyone else and soon everyone will know how monumentally destroyed my life is.

I close my eyes, trying to banish the thoughts before they overwhelm me. Try, as Jess always says, to focus on the now. And the now isn't so bad. It's a relief to be outside. There's a nip in the air despite the sunshine, but it's unusually warm for late March and I breathe in deep before starting a light run on the road.

I ran every morning in New York. Or at least every morning when I wasn't called in early. I'd loop around Central Park, under the towering buildings and thick canopy of trees. I never entered races, I never did marathons, I never timed myself or tried to go farther than I wanted to. I just did what I felt like, content simply with the steady beat on the ground, the delicious stretch in my legs.

I'm not a pretty runner. I like that too. I like that my face goes bright red and I sweat and I puff. I like that I can fall apart only to return to my apartment and piece myself together again with a shower and coffee and makeup and clothes. It's more than a routine, it's a ritual, and it's one I intend to keep.

I pick up my pace, following the river into the village, past the garage and the tired gas pumps, past the garden center and the primary school and over the ancient greystone bridge that leads me to the place that was the center of my universe for the first eighteen years of my life.

Clonard is either a small town or a large village, depending on who you're talking to. It's really just one long road, spread out over a series of hills. This road splits off into smaller ones, all with the same terraced buildings and the odd stable yard. The layout of the place hasn't changed much since the fifties, though the population certainly has, most of its inhabitants moving on to newer housing developments closer to the offices and industrial parks farther out.

The only reason the village has even survived as long as it has is because of the summer tourists who come in droves for the surrounding lakes and mountains. In a few months every shop, restaurant, and B&B will be bursting, but for now the storefronts are boarded up for the off-season, the streets empty. The barbershop is still open though, along with the butchers and the newsagent. Pete's pub is still there and, to my relief, a new café that would look more at home in Brooklyn than Clonard. But other than that, there's not much to see and a part of me is almost relieved I don't have to drag Tyler out here so he can pretend to like it.

I can picture it perfectly. The polite smile, the pleasant inquiries, all while he plans our escape route.

Tyler and I dated for three years, partners in every sense of the word. And though the unspoken agreement between us was that for now our careers came first, we hit each relationship milestone exactly on time. We met each other's parents, we moved in together, we had weekends away and dinner parties with friends.

A few months ago, a little before Halloween, he arrived home for our scheduled date-night dinner and halfway through the second course the conversation turned to the topic of marriage. Specifically, marriage between us. There was no down-on-one-knee moment. It wasn't Tyler's style and, to be honest, it wasn't really mine. We discussed the pros and cons, we went over timelines and next steps, and after a few minutes, it was decided. We would get married. We opened a very expensive bottle of wine and made love twice and it was like all the pieces in my life were coming together exactly as I hoped.

And then, just a few weeks before the *New York Times* released its damning exposé on MacFarlane, a few weeks before our offices were raided and my career fell apart in the space of a few hours, Tyler sat me down on a cold February evening and explained calmly and somberly that he was having second thoughts about our engagement. That between his job and... well, his job, he was re-evaluating the important things in his life and that re-evaluation had made him unsure if our relationship was as strong as it should be.

He wasn't sure if he loved me anymore.

Not that he *didn't* love me. Just that he wasn't sure. And for Tyler, who made every move, every decision with a confidence that sometimes awed me, that was enough. I cried and he stayed with me while I did and then I yelled at him and then I left. The next day I moved into one of MacFarlane's apartments. They're supposed to be kept for new starters as a perk, but it's not unusual for a good chunk of first-year analysts to drop out over the holidays, so I was able to stay there until that was taken from me too.

Something catches in my chest and I stumble, barely halfway into my planned route as a familiar pressure starts in my chest, a rising panic I try to shove down as I double over, hands on my knees. It's been happening a lot the last few weeks and I don't need to go to my therapist to know that it's stress. Which is fortunate, seeing as I can't afford my therapist anymore. I can't afford anything anymore.

I straighten, my breathing strained, and catch the eye of a young woman across the street who's watching me with a concerned look. Embarrassment rolls through me and, before she can cross the road, I turn to jog back, my legs sluggish beneath me.

Once home, I take a long shower and make a note to pick up some conditioner. My curls will quickly spiral out of control if I go a few days out of routine. Louise knocks on my door twice, reminding me of the time, and I toy with the idea of showing up in sweatpants just to annoy her, but instead pull on jeans and a nice blouse and try my best with my makeup.

When the bell rings I'm already halfway down the stairs, intercepting Louise with an overly friendly "I'll get it!"

I have an image fixed in my brain of Pat, my potbellied, friendly neighbor, so when I open the door to a man who is most definitely not him, I am very confused. My head is level with his Adam's apple and for a second all I can do is stare at it before the stranger clears his throat. Only then does my gaze snap up, not to the face of Pat Bailey, not to Tomasz who for a moment I thought must have popped to the village for supplies, but straight into the eyes of my nighttime savior.

CHAPTER 3

"Hi." The word comes out as a high-pitched noise but it's all I can manage in my surprise.

He cracks a smile. "Hello."

"I'm okay," I continue, thinking maybe he's checking up on me.

"Glad to hear it. I brought a cheesecake."

My eyes drop to the tin foil–covered package he's holding. "Oh." Weird. It doesn't diminish his hotness but still weird. "You didn't need to do that."

He's grinning now. "Ah, you know. I didn't want to appear rude."

"Abby?" Louise's voice calls from the kitchen as my mind struggles to piece together what is happening and what should be happening.

"Thank you," I say. "That's really kind. I'd invite you in but—"

"There she is now." Pat Bailey climbs the porch steps, his voice booming. "Abigail Reynolds, you haven't changed a bit."

"I've changed a little bit," I say, my eyes flicking between them. "Pat, this is—"

"It will be nice for you two to catch up," he interrupts, stepping past me into the house.

Catch up?

"He didn't believe you were coming back," Pat continues, slapping me on the shoulder as he heads to the kitchen. And then it hits me.

It's less like two pieces of a puzzle fitting together and more like two cars crashing into each other as I look back at the man on my porch.

The gorgeous, sex-on-legs man holding a cheesecake is not some anonymous newcomer to town. He is not some mysterious horny fever dream I created in my mind. He is...

He's...

"Luke?" Louise appears behind me. "Did you bring the hedge clippers?"

"I did," Luke says. "Left them in the garden. Do you want me to make a start?"

"No, I can do it. We've got a stepladder in the shed. Abby?" Louise frowns at me. "What's wrong?"

"Nothing," I say, my voice faint to my ears.

He's Luke Bailey.

Wimpy, weedy, next-door neighbor Luke Bailey. Luke Bailey who I used to play in the mud with, who I went trick-or-treating with, who I'm pretty sure I *shared baths* with. Luke Bailey who was by default my best friend growing up until I grew breasts and learned how to use eyeliner and he remained looking like he was twelve years old.

He no longer looks like he's twelve years old.

"Abby!" Susan's here. His mother. The whole Bailey family. They're all here, crowding me and confusing me. "Louise said you were visiting. Now, aren't you glad you came?" she adds to Luke. "You wouldn't have seen her otherwise."

"I saw her last night," he says, handing me the cheesecake. "Brought her home."

Louise turns to me. "You didn't tell me Luke was the one who dropped you back."

"I didn't?" I glance around the curious faces. "I thought I did."

She's instantly suspicious but before she can say anything else Susan steps in, kissing me on the cheek.

"Look at you," she says. "I'd barely recognize you if it weren't for that hair."

"Dad says she looks the same," Luke says, shrugging off his jacket.

"Did he? What do you think?"

I freeze as his attention flicks to me but Luke only smiles.

"Come in before you freeze," Louise calls, and Susan closes the front door, following my sister into the kitchen.

For a moment we're alone. Luke's still looking at me with a glimmer of amusement and I'm hovering like a weirdo clutching his cheesecake.

"I..." It's as far as I get. I don't know what else to say. Thankfully he doesn't seem to mind.

"Come on," he says, taking pity on me. "I'm starving."

He walks in ahead of me and my eyes stray to the way his jeans cling to him before I realize what I'm doing.

Luke Bailey?!

I force my feet to move under me, my thoughts scrambled as I follow him into the now cramped kitchen.

Louise has pulled the table into the center of the room and the chairs are set so that she and Tomasz are at either end while Pat and Susan sit opposite.

Luke sits in the chair beside mine.

Luke Bailey who knew who I was this entire time.

I'm Luke, by the way.

He was probably waiting for me to recognize him. But I didn't. Because who in their right mind would? I picture him as the kid I once knew, pale and skinny, all elbows and knees as we chased each other around the playground.

There should be an automatic report when you visit home, some kind of newsletter detailing all the changes you need to know about. All the marriages and all the glow-ups, so situations like this don't happen.

Louise is still looking at me like I've lost my mind and maybe I have because when Luke pulls out my chair it takes all my willpower not to simply stare at him.

"This looks delicious," Pat says, pulling the butter dish toward him.

"It's nothing. Just some leftovers." Louise motions for us to start eating and I sit, tucking my chair in as Luke does the same.

I wonder if it's too early to ask for wine.

Susan smiles kindly at me from across the table, her face more lined than I remember. Her hair is no longer honey blond but a light silver that she still wears down to her shoulders. A good soul, Mam used to say. I spent my childhood in her house while my parents worked. Some weeks I had dinner in her kitchen more often than my own.

How funny to think one day I left it for the last time and didn't realize it.

How funny her son turned into a freaking Adonis.

The Baileys dig into their food while Louise, Tomasz, and I pick at ours, still full from our pancakes.

"How did you two meet yesterday?" Susan asks. "I thought you had your course, Luke?"

"I did. I found her on the way back, waiting for a bus."

"What bus?"

"Exactly," he says, and I force a smile as they laugh.

"That was lucky." Susan watches us for a moment, her chin propped on her fist, before turning to Louise. "When's that new couch of yours coming?"

"Not for another few weeks," she sighs. "They keep pushing the delivery date back. I'm starting to think it would just be quicker to cancel and order from somewhere else."

"Did you try that new Danish place in Sligo?" Pat asks. "Cliona Mitchell got hers from there."

Susan frowns. "I thought it was Norwegian?"

"I'm sorry," Luke says quietly as the others talk around us. "I couldn't resist when I knew you didn't recognize me."

The sound of his voice makes my stomach dip and I concentrate on pushing a piece of chicken from one side of my plate to the other.

"It's okay," I say. "It's funny. If not deeply humiliating."

"It was dark. And you were exhausted."

And you look like a completely different person, I want to add, but don't.

"I haven't changed at all?" I ask instead.

"Well, your eyebrows have grown back."

I glance over to find him smiling at me. "Shut up. I overplucked one time."

"You walked around in a beanie hat for a whole summer."

"See, this is why I don't visit. Everyone knows me before I was incredibly glamorous."

"Is that what you are now?"

"Could you not tell when I was lurking by an abandoned bus stop?"

"It's not abandoned on Wednesdays."

Susan's eyes flick to me as I laugh but otherwise she doesn't falter as she describes her sister's new curtains.

"I am sorry though," I say to him. "I was in a bit of a weird mood last night."

"You mean a flirting mood?"

"I wasn't flirting," I whisper, embarrassed. "I was delirious from traveling. And if I was, you were flirting too."

"Hmm. No, I don't think so."

"Oh really? Then why did you—"

I break off as his knee touches mine under the table. Luke picks up his water glass, the innocent expression back on his face.

"Now I'm flirting," he murmurs, taking a sip. He doesn't move away and it's like all the heat in my body focuses in on that one spot. "It's much more fun when you know who I am."

"You're never going to let this go."

"Nope."

I turn my gaze to my plate. It's impossible to keep the smile from my face. "You live in the village?" I ask in normal tones because this is a normal conversation.

"I do. But I'm usually at college. I'm not here a lot."

"Oh." I grimace inwardly at the obvious disappointment in my voice.

"I'm thinking about moving to Sligo full time," he continues.

"By yourself?"

"With Sean."

Sean. Sean... Sean Higgins? I have a faint memory of a tiny, dour boy doodling in the back of the classroom. "You two are friends?"

A faint smile appears on his face. "We've been best friends since we were kids."

"Right," I say quickly. "Duh."

"Don't worry. You didn't pay much attention to us back then. I wouldn't expect you to remember."

"I paid attention," I protest even though I know it's a lie. There's a reason I didn't recognize Luke last night. It's because even though we went to the same school, even though we were neighbors, I barely gave him a second thought for most of my teenage years.

It wasn't personal. I barely thought about anyone but myself back then.

"Hey." Luke frowns as though sensing the direction of my thoughts. "I mean it, Abby. Don't worry about it."

"Yeah." I spear a green bean with my fork but can't bring myself to eat it. "Sean's still around then?"

He nods. "A couple of people are. Or they come back to visit during the summer when everything's open."

Unlike me. Would I recognize anyone if I saw them again? Would they recognize me? Or was I forgotten about as quickly as I forgot them?

"Rory comes back now and then," he continues, and I start at the mention of my old friend's name. Rory and I were stuck together like glue. I haven't thought about him in years. "You should tell him you're visiting."

"I should," I say, even though I have no idea how to contact him. Luke must realize this the same time I do because he swiftly changes the subject as he adds more salad to his plate.

"Of course, the most important thing you should know about is the new doughnut counter in Dessie's place."

"Now you're lying to me."

"I'm serious. He has three different kinds. Sugared, plain, and red."

"Red?"

"That's what he calls it. I'll bring you down tomorrow," he adds casually. "Or maybe we could—"

"I was sorry to hear about the job, Abby."

I jerk back in my seat as Pat speaks. I hadn't realized how close Luke and I had been leaning into each other.

"It was on the news over here," Pat continues. "Awful stuff. I didn't even realize it was yourself until Louise mentioned."

"Thank you," I say, hoping he doesn't ask for any insider information. Most people just want to hear the gossip, as if a cog in the machine like me would have had a front seat in the boardroom when it all went down. "It was a shock to everyone."

"Have you found somewhere else? A smart girl like you, they must be knocking down your door."

"Dad," Luke protests.

"What? She always was the best thing to come out of this town."

"Not yet," I say as Louise's gaze falls to her plate. "I won't lie, it's pretty tough out there, but I'm sure things will calm down."

Pat chews thoughtfully, a small frown on his face. "I'll give my cousin in Dublin a ring. His neighbor has a son in your line of work. I remember him because he got caught having an affair with some young one a few years ago."

I force a smile as Tomasz chokes on a potato. "Thank you, Pat."

"Wife threw his electric scooter into the canal. The council weren't too happy about that."

"Do we have to talk about work?" Luke asks, pouring himself more water. "It's Saturday."

"Not the best lunchtime conversation," Susan agrees, sending a warning glance to her husband. "Are you staying long, Abby?"

"She's leaving at Easter," Louise says. "Right, Abby?"

"Right," I say. *Right.*

"Three weeks!" Susan smiles. "That'll be a nice break. You should take her to the beach, Luke. Before the schools are out."

"Great idea," he says, and I perk up some more.

It *is* a great idea.

Luke Bailey at the beach. Luke Bailey in swimming trunks. Luke Bailey stepping out of the ocean with water running down his presumably chiseled chest.

"You know that hotel got planning permission," Louise says, interrupting my fantasy.

"You're joking," Susan gasps. "The one by Castlebay?"

"They want to seal off the south beach."

"Honestly," she says with a shake of her head. "You won't be able to go anywhere in this country in a few years. I'm sure you'll be fighting it?"

"If we have to." Louise works for the Irish Oceans Association, a charity dedicated to the conservation and protection of our waters. A few Christmases ago, she gave me a certificate informing me I'd adopted a whale. The year before that it was an eel, so I like to think I'm slowly moving up in the marine world.

"It's a pity you're not here for the summer, Abby," Susan says. "The town is so quiet at the moment. Are you sure you can't stay longer?"

"I doubt she'll even make it to Easter," Pat says, pointing his fork at me. "She'll be bored out of her mind in two days. I guarantee it."

"It's okay," Tomasz says. "Her fiancé will come and rescue her."

My knife slips from my grasp, falling with a clatter to my plate as everyone turns to me.

"I didn't see a ring," Susan says.

Oh my God.

I bring my left hand to my lap as five pairs of eyes drop to my fingers.

Oh my *God*.

"Actually, yeah," Louise says, peering at me. "Where's your ring? Mam wouldn't shut up about that picture you sent her."

"I don't like wearing rings," I say after a moment. "It's on a chain upstairs."

"You're engaged?" Pat wipes his mouth with his napkin. "But that's brilliant news. Who's the lucky man?"

My eyes dart to Luke but he's looking at his plate, his expression calm even as his knee moves from mine.

"Tyler Olsen," Louise says when I don't answer. "He's some lawyer."

"He's a senior associate," I say automatically, his little beige business cards flashing through my mind. TYLER OLSEN. BENTON, DWYER, AND BARNES. One of the top law firms in New York. We'd been together only a few weeks when he got the job. I thought he was the most impressive man I'd ever met.

"He sounds wonderful," Susan says, finding her voice. "When's the wedding?"

Louise pokes at her salad. "They haven't set a date."

"Louise," I snap, clenching my fork so hard my fingers start to ache.

"What?" she asks. "Have you? Or did you just forget to tell us?"

"Would you be having it in the States or over here?" Pat asks.

"We don't know yet," I say, and there's a slight edge to my words that shuts everyone up.

It's Susan who saves me, changing the conversation to the new supermarket that's opening two towns away. She somehow manages to make the topic last until the cheesecake, which is when Louise starts talking about the rise of plastic pollution in Malaysia and Pat talks about a documentary she recommended to him and still Luke won't look at me. He doesn't even acknowledge my presence, even though I'm sitting right beside him and all I want to do is tap him on the shoulder and say, *Hang on a minute, buddy. Let's rewind here. This is nothing but a big misunderstanding.*

After what feels like hours, Pat and Susan make their excuses and get up to leave. Luke offers to bring everything to the sink and I volunteer to help as the others move to the porch with a chorus of goodbyes.

"Can we talk?" I ask as soon as they're gone.

"About what?" He clears the table with the efficiency of someone who's worked in the service industry, balancing the plates and cutlery with ease.

"About what Louise said. About Tyler."

"Who?"

"My fiancé. Or my—"

"Right."

I stiffen at the edge to his tone. "It's not what you think."

"I don't think anything."

"But you do," I say. "And I—"

He turns abruptly, wiping his hand on a dishcloth. "Do you have a fiancé?"

"I..." What do I say? *No, Luke! I don't have a fiancé! He tossed me to the curb right before I fell off my pedestal. What I do have is an inferiority complex that makes me lie to my friends and family so they don't think I'm more of a failure than I already am.*

"Abby?"

"Yes," I say. "I have a fiancé." I cross my arms and immediately hear the coach at my women-in-business seminar screaming about how my posture is too defensive. But I can't help it. I feel defensive. This feels like my last freaking defense right now.

"I don't know what the big deal is," I continue, regretting the words as soon as I say them. But before I can even begin to backtrack, he dumps the cloth on the countertop.

"No deal at all."

"Luke—"

"Welcome home, Abby," he says, walking past me into the hall. "Enjoy the cheesecake."

CHAPTER 4

Born a few months apart, Luke and I were friends for most of our early childhood. We didn't really have a choice in the matter, the two of us forced together by sheer proximity. Both my parents worked and Louise and I were often deposited with Susan after school. Being that bit older, Louise would disappear to do her own thing while Luke and I watched television or ran around doing whatever it is seven-year-olds do. I don't know when that stopped. Maybe when Louise became old enough to look after me in our own house. Maybe because that's just what happens when you grow up. People change. And it takes more than living next door to someone to be friends with them. We grew apart and the only time I ever saw him was glimpses of him mowing the lawn in the summer. Honestly, between studying and navigating my own teenage drama, I rarely thought about him.

And now I can't stop.

I exit Dessie's store, picturing the tight look on his face as I unpack the suspiciously cheap Irish cell phone I just bought. It's Tuesday. Three days since the lunch. Four days since I came home and I still haven't told Louise the truth. To be fair, I was very tired for most of that time. Once the Baileys left I more or less collapsed back into bed, where I stayed for the rest of the afternoon and all of Sunday.

I woke in a panic yesterday and spent the morning applying for every job I could find back in New York and the afternoon making endless to-do lists of all the steps I'd need to take to get myself back to normal. As bizarre as it sounds, it made me feel a little better seeing my life broken out into color-coded sections and bullet points within bullet points. No more "get a well-paying position, pay off your debts, and move back to New York." Now I dealt in the granular. Get up. Get dressed. Buy an Irish phone. Offer to help Louise make dinner. Smile pleasantly when she says no. Get a job here.

I wasn't too sure about the last part. But I needed money and I wasn't above taking grunt work to get it. But where? Clonard isn't exactly full of opportunities at the best of times and during the off-season it's even worse.

I stare down the town's main street, trying to count the businesses that are still open. The Irish tricolor bunting and posters are still up from St. Patrick's Day two weeks ago, making the town look cheery and welcoming and completely at odds with my sour mood. Without a car I can't commute anywhere, but short of knocking on doors, I don't know what else to do. I don't even have my own computer to work remotely.

I watch a skinny tabby cat slink across the road, brooding as a phone starts to ring. It takes me few seconds before I realize it's my American one, tucked into the pocket of my fleece. I answer it quickly in case it's a recruiter.

A mistake.

"What the hell did you do?"

Jess.

"Why did I have to find out from Alicia—*Alicia*—that you left New York? I thought you were just sulking."

"Sulking? Losing my job and my apartment is sulking?"

"I mean, God, if you're going to be dramatic about it." She pauses. "What do you mean you lost your apartment?"

"It was one of the MacFarlane lofts."

"I thought you were moving out of—"

"I said I was *going* to," I interrupt as her voice rises with each word. "But I didn't see the point of tying myself to a lease when I was up for a promotion. They might have relocated me. Obviously, in hindsight, it was not the best decision."

"But why didn't you ask *me*!" she exclaims. "You could have stayed with me!"

I don't have an immediate answer for her. Why didn't I ask Jess if I could stay with her? Stay in her beautiful Upper West Side apartment with her red brick walls and her many green plants and her expensive furniture designed to look cheap. She would have said yes in a heartbeat. But even now the thought makes me embarrassed. I'm not used to relying on other people for help. Even when I need it.

"How long are you staying there?" she continues when I don't say anything.

"I don't know. A few weeks? Or until my sister kicks me out. I'll find some temp work to keep me going."

There's a long pause on the other end of the line. And then: "Oh my God, Abby."

"You're making it sound worse than it is."

"You're going off the rails. I'm going to have to call an intervention."

"I'm visiting my sister! That's allowed!"

"Your sister who you *hate*? In the town you *despise*? To do some *freaking temp work*?"

"I don't hate her. We're just very different."

"Screw Tyler," she says suddenly. "Screw him. This is all his fault. I'm going to beat him up."

"Please don't."

"I'm going to punch him in that smarmy face of his. In that goddamn perfectly symmetrical face."

"Did you call just to yell at me?" I sit on a nearby bench, suddenly tired again.

"A little bit," Jess mutters. "I don't suppose I've magically convinced you to come back, have I? You can stay with me, I mean it. I'll put in a good word for you at work."

"I don't want to work in real estate."

"But you want to work *somewhere*, don't you? You've gotta keep moving."

"I am moving. Do you seriously think I haven't applied for everything under the sun? There's too much competition. It's like the Hunger Games out there."

"Maybe Alicia can get you a job," she says, sarcastic. "Seeing as you two are so close."

"She found me crying in the ladies' room, okay? That's the only reason she knows."

"Whatever. The point is I'm coming to get you. I'm coming to get you and take you out of there even if I have to drag you by that pretty brown hair of yours. Why didn't you call me?"

She sounds genuinely hurt.

"Because I was embarrassed," I say. "I was upset and I was embarrassed and I panicked. That's why. I needed to get out of the city."

She silent for a moment. Then she sighs. "A few weeks?"

"That's the plan."

"I'll come visit."

"No." I can't think of anything worse. "You don't need to."

"I do need to," she says flatly. "And I want to. I want to see you and I need a vacation anyway."

"You vacation in Bora Bora."

"But unfortunately for me, that's not where you fled to. I spoke with your sister, by the way. I looked up that dolphin website you mentioned and called her. She did not sound happy to speak to me."

"That's just her general tone." I smooth back my hair as a cool breeze whips a few curls from their hairpins. "You talked to her?"

"Is that not allowed?"

Not if Jess let slip about Tyler. I stare down at my left hand, where my ring glints tauntingly. I'd put it on the other night when Louise kept asking questions and it freaks me out every time I look at it.

"I needed to get her address because I knew you wouldn't give it to me," Jess continues. "I'm looking at it on Google Maps right now. Tell her she needs to retile her roof."

I put the Irish phone into my bag and sit on my free hand, trying to keep warm. "I have to go," I say. "I have no idea how much this call is costing me."

"Are you serious?"

"I was on MacFarlane's cell plan. I had to buy a separate one to keep the phone working."

"The year 2002 called. It wants your—"

"Goodbye, Jess," I interrupt. "And... thank you. I'm sorry I didn't tell you about Ireland. Believe me when I say it was a last-minute decision."

"I forgive you," she grumbles. "I guess it's like that time I didn't tell you about my rhinoplasty."

"Yes, you're right. It's exactly like that."

"Just come back, okay? Come back and we'll fix it like we always do."

"That's my plan." I gaze at an empty restaurant space across the street. "Bye, babe."

"Bye, idiot."

I hang up with an ache in my chest that wasn't there before.

Jessica Darcy. Deceptively smart and not afraid to work hard, my best friend was punctual, wild, and wealthy. We started as analysts together at MacFarlane and she took a liking to me. I'm still not sure why. Maybe she saw me as a bit of a side project. Help the intensely serious girl with the cheap shoes and the odd accent. Whatever it was, I'm grateful for it. I don't think I would have survived the first few months without her. At least not socially. She'd grown up in the world I was trying to break into and, as they say, imitation is the sincerest form of flattery. I copied her confidence and her poise. I ate where she ate and shopped where she shopped until I knew enough and earned enough to find my own way. She ended up dropping out after the first year, unable to balance the sixteen-hour days with her penchant for nightclubs, but even after she left we remained close.

And now she wants to come here.

She wants to rock up in her designer jeans and her four-inch heels to see what? This? Me? I barely recognize who I am anymore. And what if she—

"*Are those Red Dots?*"

I turn at the shriek by my ear to see a woman in a long padded coat standing beside me. She's tiny, her face round and pale, her nose tinged pink from the wind. Her jet-black hair hangs in a blunt bob around her chin as she stares at me, or the bottom half of me, with something akin to awe.

"Um..." I glance down at my clothes. "Yes."

"They charge two hundred euro for a pair of leggings."

I wince. "Do they?" I ask as she continues to stare unabashedly at my calves before seeming to realize what she's doing.

"Sorry," she says. "It's just that they're my happy place."

"Your...what?"

"You know, some people watch TV bloopers, some read comics. I go on the Red Dots website, fill my basket with all the things I want, and then pretend I'm going to buy them. Plus, if you wait long enough and pretend you don't want them? They email you a discount code. Not that it makes them actually affordable. Would it be weird if you let me touch them? It would be weird. I'm sorry. Forget I asked. Sorry." She snaps her mouth shut, clutching a takeout coffee cup to her chest. "I'm Beth," she adds.

"Abby."

"Abby? Abby Reynolds?"

I'm about to reply when panic strikes. Is this another Luke situation? She might have been my best friend at school, for all I know, but both her name and face draw a blank.

"Oh no, you don't know me," she says, reading my mind. Coffee sloshes through the lid as she gestures wildly. "But everyone's talking about you."

"They are?"

"Well, no. But a few people are. They said you were moving back."

"I'm just visiting," I say as she sits beside me, tucking her coat under her.

"From New York, right?" Her eyes are big and bright, framed by blue eyeliner. "I'm not a stalker, I swear. It's just so rare we get someone new. Not that you're *new* new but I'm the newest person here and I moved a year ago."

"You did?" I'm unable to hide my surprise. People don't come to Clonard. They leave Clonard. "Why?"

"True love, of course." She grins. "My boyfriend wanted to be a farmer. He bought some land on eBay. I'm still not sure it was entirely legal but they showed him this boundary map? So I dunno. It looked fine. We don't have it anymore." Her smile fades. "Ross did *not* like being a farmer. Turns out it's actually really hard. He's also not a morning person, which you kind of have to be for that line of work. We broke up."

"I'm sorry."

"Don't be. He wanted to move back home but I was tired of following him around all the time. Plus... I liked it here."

"Here?"

"I know." She laughs. "My friends thought I was just going through that breakup phase where you change your hair color and maybe get a cat but sometimes you just connect with a place, you know? I got a job at the library in Manorhamilton and then sold my apartment in Dublin and now I'm a local business owner!" She raises her hands, spilling the coffee again. "I love it. But sometimes, *sometimes* I wonder what it would be like to be a little more stable with my income so I could walk around in a pair of those."

Her eyes drop to my legs again and, honestly, I'm two seconds away from just giving them to her when she speaks.

"So you lost your job, huh? At McDonald's?"

"MacFarlane."

"Right. Sorry. I meant that one. You're not going to jail, are you?"

"Not that I know of."

"Good! *Phew*." She shakes her head. "You know it was on the news? It was the number one headline. And you *lived* it. That must have been so hard. I bet you just..." She trails off, her mouth twisting into a guilty frown. "Hate people talking about it," she finishes. "I'm sorry. I don't know when to shut up."

"Don't worry about it."

"I talk and talk but I don't think."

"Honestly, I don't mind," I say. And strangely, I don't. At least not with her. She doesn't seem to have a filter of any kind, but after years of coded language and reading between the lines, she's like a breath of fresh air.

"It's nice to talk to someone," I add. Or have them talk at you.

"Well, I'm always around," she says with a sigh. "How long are you here for?"

"I'm not sure yet. Depends on the money."

"The money?"

I nod, trying to guess her reaction before deciding to try the whole "honesty" thing. "I don't have any. I'm going to need to get another job soon if I want to—"

"You're joking!" she exclaims. "Why didn't you say? We need someone at the café to do marketing. Setting us up on social media, flyers around town, that kind of thing."

"The café?"

"Coffee!" She holds up her cup, which I now see has the café's logo on the side.

"Your café is called Coffee?"

"That's right." Beth beams at me. "This is perfect. Why don't you come in and I can tell you about it. You can meet the team!"

"Oh, that's so kind of you but that's not actually what meant when I..." I trail off when I realize what I'm doing. Who the hell am I to be turning down any opportunity? I'll take what I can get. "Like right now?"

"Sure. We're not very formal. Unless you want to—"

"No," I say quickly, rising as she does. "Now is good. Now is very good."

"Amazing. You see? *This* is the power of Red Dot leggings. They bring people together." She gives my legs one last wistful look and then, like we didn't just meet five minutes ago, loops her arm through mine and brings me down the street.

CHAPTER 5

Beth's café sits between the funeral home and a boarded-up retail space that looks like it used to be an ice cream parlor. It has a small front door and a large square window that reveals wooden countertops and a complicated-looking coffee machine. It's nice. But cramped. The room isn't particularly large and, as well as the counter at the front, there are bookshelves to the left of the entrance, with no indication of whether it's a shop or a library. A corner at the back seems to have been cordoned off for a yoga studio, and an abandoned slushie machine takes up a chunk of wall space next to a unisex toilet. The only place to sit is at a brightly painted bench that looks awkward to climb in and out of.

It should be charming on paper. A multiuse space for the village, a cute little coffee shop that locals will love and tourists can discover. Instead, one glance inside tells me it doesn't know what it is yet. It's too busy. Just not with customers.

In fact, the place is empty except for a twenty-something girl behind the counter, scrolling through her phone. Her bleached-blond hair is scraped back into a bun, revealing dark roots and a multitude of glinting piercings in her ears. She brightens when I enter but that quickly diminishes when Beth comes in after me.

"This is Ollie," Beth announces cheerfully. "Our barista."

At the sight of her boss, Ollie reaches toward the coffee machine as if to wipe it down or fill something up only to realize that there's nothing to do.

"Do you want anything?" Beth asks, rounding the counter. "It's on the house."

"Don't be silly," I say as Ollie's eyes flick to Beth in a silent protest. "I'll pay. I'll take a double espresso."

A little mollified, Ollie starts up the machine.

"All our cups are one hundred percent compostable," Beth says over the noise. "And the coffee is Fairtrade certified. Napkin. Loyalty card..." She lists off each item as she places them on the counter. "Your tenth one is free. That will be three eighty-five."

Three... "Great." I glance at the prices overhead. This place is expensive. Especially for Clonard. But I hand over the few euros Louise gave me that morning ("Wouldn't want you to be stuck for the bus again," she'd muttered only a little sarcastically) and drop another into the tip jar.

"And *this* is my big blue binder," Beth says, taking out a messily indexed folder. Labels of varying colors and sizes stick out and I watch as one loose piece of paper slips free as she dumps it on the counter.

"I have a marketing plan in here somewhere," she mutters as my fingers itch to grab it from her and organize it. Or possibly burn it. I know some people find order in chaos but... yikes. "I was even working on a job description. Do you have any social media experience?"

I think of my defunct Facebook page and the Instagram account I set up so Jess could stalk an ex. "Yes."

Ollie hands me the espresso and I sip the bitter liquid as a door slams somewhere above.

"My landlord," Beth explains as footsteps sound loudly on a staircase opposite me. "He lives in the apartment overhead."

That must be calming during yoga class.

"Maybe you can tell me a bit about the business," I say, distracted as even more pages spill free from her binder. "Or I could—"

"Beth?"

I still at the familiar voice, watching as two long legs appear halfway down the staircase.

Oh no.

"I called Harry about Wednesday and he said—" Luke breaks off when he catches sight of me, bumping his head off the low ceiling as he stops two steps from the bottom.

"Ouch," Beth says as Ollie snorts. "Are you okay?"

"I'm fine," he mutters, rubbing his forehead.

"It sounded—"

"I'm fine."

I smile weakly as he frowns at me.

"Hello," I say when he doesn't. If he can't get it together then I will. "You didn't tell me you owned a café."

Beth straightens from where she's hunched over the counter. "You've already met?"

"We live next door to each other," I explain. "Or we used to."

"That's crazy!"

"The craziest," I agree.

Luke ducks his head as he skips the final steps, landing with a thump on the polished concrete. His eyes drop immediately to the diamond on my finger, but his expression doesn't change, even when I hide my hand behind my back on instinct.

"He doesn't own it," Beth continues. "I do. But he owns the building and lets me rent it on the cheap."

"Until you start making your millions," Luke says, heading to the counter. "I thought I dumped that thing in the river," he adds, gesturing to the binder.

"Very funny. Abby's interested in the marketing job."

"What marketing job?"

"The one you told me I should set up so I can get more customers." She sounds exasperated. "You're grumpy today."

And I can guess why. "You know what? Now that I think about it, I probably won't have time for something like this."

"But I thought you said—"

"There's no point in hiring someone who's going to leave us high and dry in two weeks," Luke interrupts, his voice firm.

Ollie glances between us while pretending to type into her phone.

"I wouldn't do that," I say, my friendly tone beginning to strain.

"That's your plan, isn't it? Back to your fiancé?"

I stare at him. Okay, so he's still mad at me. That's fine. I'd be mad at him too if I was all knee-touching and sly-glancing and it turned out he was engaged. Only I'm not engaged. I'm just lying to everyone about it. Which is fine.

I mean it's not fine. It's the opposite of fine. But—

"You're *engaged*?" Beth gasps, clasping her hands together. "I didn't even notice the ring. Ollie, did you see the ring?"

Ollie shakes her head.

"She's just visiting," Luke says.

"She told me that." Beth rolls her eyes. "But we only need someone to start us off. Then Ollie can take over."

Ollie looks at Beth with an expression that tells me she will be doing nothing of the sort.

"Do you even have marketing experience?" Luke asks me and I feel a sharp spike of annoyance at his tone.

"I'm sorry," I say. "Are you the owner or the landlord?"

"I'm a friend," Luke says. "And we don't need the help."

I do a pointed sweep of the empty café. "You sure about that?"

Shit.

I feel terrible as soon as I say it, even more so when Beth's mouth pops open, her lips forming a little hurt *o*.

"Nice," Luke says, turning back to Beth. "You want to hire her? Be my guest."

Oh, for the love of— "I don't even want the damn job," I snap. "I was being polite."

Shut *up*, Abby.

Beth looks crestfallen. Luke looks furious. Ollie looks like she's trying to solve a puzzle.

"I didn't mean that," I say after an awkward beat. "I'm sorry."

"It's okay," Beth says. "We're new and I guess I haven't had the chance to—"

"It's not that," I say quickly. "Luke's right. I won't be staying around long. You should hire someone who can commit."

Luke huffs at the last word and it takes all my willpower not to glare at him. I tell myself I don't care. Let him think what he wants to.

Instead, I try my best to focus on Beth. "I think you have a lovely space here. Really. Small communities like this can be hard to break into but you'll win them over. It just takes time. Plus it will be tourist season soon, so rack up those online reviews and you'll be flying."

I knock back the rest of my espresso and slip the cup into my bag.

"Compostable," I say, patting it. "I'll have to tell my sister."

Beth looks miserable, but maybe for a different reason now. "Abby—"

"I'll swing by tomorrow," I say. "Try one of those pastries."

"Okay," she says quietly.

Luke just looks at me. Ollie is back on her phone.

"It was really nice to meet you," I say finally, and walk as quickly as I can out the door.

*

"You're on mute, Dad."

I keep my smile on my face as he searches for the right button, my mother frowning unhelpfully beside him. I'm sitting on my bed, using Louise's laptop to video-call them. The machine itself is a heavy industrial thing that's already starting to heat up from the strain of having to turn on, and I slide a plastic tray under it, not wholly convinced it won't set the duvet on fire.

"I can't hear you," I say as Mam's mouth moves. "You're going to have to—"

"—said you look very pale." I quickly turn the volume down as her voice blasts through the speakers. "Are you taking enough zinc?"

"Probably not, no."

"You should take more zinc."

"I'll get some. Dad?"

"What?" Dad's eyes snap back to me from where they'd been drifting to the iPad on his lap.

"Are you playing solitaire?"

A brief pause. "No."

"Well, could you continue not playing solitaire so you can pay attention to your youngest child? Mam?"

I watch as she takes the iPad from him, tucking it in between her and the armrest of the sinking white couch in their living room. Warm sunlight shines through a window to the left of her, the only indication of where they are. Otherwise it's like they could walk through my bedroom door at any moment. The thought of it makes my heart hurt. I'd avoided their calls when I lost my job, only sending them a few carefully worded texts to let them know I was okay. I couldn't bring myself to talk to them. Even though I knew it was ridiculous, the whole thing felt like *my* fault. Like if only I'd chosen another company or I'd worked a little harder, I wouldn't be in this mess.

"It's nice of you to finally call us," Mam says. She leans toward the screen, still examining me. "A week after you landed."

"I've been busy."

"Louise said you were delayed getting back. You shouldn't travel so late without a clear plan, Abby. You're supposed to be the organized one."

"Well, it's a little hard when... Dad!" I snap as his attention drifts again. "Put your phone down."

"I'm just checking the headlines," he says, defensively.

God help me. I know if we're all lucky to live long enough, there'll come a poignant moment in our lives when the parent-child relationship switches but I didn't think it would be this early because they're both behaving like toddlers over a video call.

"There," Mam says, taking the phone from him. "We're both here and we're both listening to our darling, disgraced child."

"You're not funny," I tell her, and she mimes zipping her mouth shut. My mother's sense of humor. Most people don't know whether to laugh or feel insulted when they meet her.

As they refocus on me, I glance at my planner, where I wrote the day's one task in large capital letters. "I have some news. More news. Ty—"

Mam gasps. "You got a new job."

"I... no."

"You got an interview."

"No," I say. "But I will soon," I add as her face falls. "No, what I wanted to tell you was that unfortunately Tyler and I—"

"You do look a little pale," Dad interrupts.

"It's probably the stress," Mam says to him. "Julie Connolly's son signed off work from stress. Though if you ask me—"

"We broke up!"

I sit back, waiting for the onslaught. But Dad only frowns.

"The signal's just fine," he says. "We had new Wi-Fi installed the other—"

Mam places a hand on his knee, silencing him.

"I mean Tyler and I aren't together anymore," I explain. "He broke off the engagement."

Mam's expression is carefully neutral. "You're not engaged?"

"We're not engaged and we're not living together. I moved out of his apartment. We're not getting married."

Dad crosses his arms over his belly and looks at my mother.

"It's a little surprising," she says. "Is this because of what happened at work?"

"No," I say quickly. "No, come on, Mam."

"It's a reasonable question."

"It's not like that. *He's* not like that." The looks on their faces tell me they don't believe that for an instant but I'm not really in the mood to defend him further.

"It's definitely over?"

I nod, nervous.

"I'm sorry, sweetheart." Her voice softens and for one relieved moment I think that's it. Then: "You've canceled everything? You know how these companies can get with their deposits. I hope you went with refundable choices."

"We hadn't booked anything yet. We hadn't even made any plans other than—"

"You hadn't booked anything at all?" She sounds personally offended. "You've been engaged for months."

"I was busy."

"Doing what?"

"Going down with a sinking ship, Mam. I don't know if you heard the news."

"There's no need to get so tetchy."

"I'm not getting—"

"I didn't like him," Dad barks suddenly, making me jump. "I never did. He was too clean."

I'm lost. "What does that even mean?"

"And the way he paid for dinner that last time we were over," he says, ignoring me.

"He was trying to be nice."

"He was being smug," Dad says. "There's a way you go about these things. And it's not brandishing a credit card about like you're the Queen of Sheba."

"What happened happened," Mam says as Dad's face starts to go red. "Better now than a week after the wedding."

Better not at all, but I suppose I should appreciate the positive attitude.

"You should have married an Irishman," Dad continues.

I try to stay patient. "Louise didn't marry an Irishman."

"The Polish are grand."

"You can't say things like—"

"What was his excuse?" Dad interrupts. "Some other girl is it?"

"He wanted to focus on his career."

"And he can't do that with a wife at home?"

"Dad!"

"A wife in the office then."

"This is why I didn't want to tell you," I groan, rubbing my face.

Mam's eyes drift to the right, getting that look that means she's thinking hard about something. "We'll come back."

I stare at the screen. "No."

"Just until you're back on your feet."

"I'm on my feet!" I say, beginning to panic. "I'm fine!"

"Your Aunt Ellen rents out a room in Dublin. I'm sure you could stay with her. She's fed up with those students."

"I'm not moving back."

"Well, obviously not to *Clonard*," she says. "I can only imagine how that would sit with your sister. But Dublin will be fine. You could—"

"I'm not moving to Ireland at all," I interrupt. "This is just temporary. I'm going home in a few weeks."

Mam looks confused. "Without Tyler?"

"*Yes.* I wasn't in New York because of Tyler. I moved there before him."

"I know that," she says. "But you said you're no longer living together."

"Yes. I mean, no, we're not but—"

"And you don't have an apartment or you wouldn't be with your sister."

"No, but—"

"And you don't have a job!" she finishes. "So why be so far from the people who can support you?"

"It's not that far," I protest. "And I have people there. I have friends."

"But what if this happens again, hmm? You're much better off back here where we can look after you. What does Louise think?"

"I haven't told her yet."

"What was that?" She leans into the screen. "Don't speak with your hand in front of your mouth, Abby. No one can hear you."

I drop my fingers to my lap. "I said I haven't told her yet."

Mam looks aghast. "She doesn't know you're homeless?"

"I'm not *home*—"

But she's already reaching for her phone. "I'll call your aunt."

"No, don't. Mam." I clap my hands to get her attention. "I'm going to talk to her. Stop freaking out."

"I'm allowed to be worried about my daughter, Abby."

"Not when there's nothing to be worried about." I straighten as the front door shuts below. Louise and Tomasz are back from their walk. "I'm fine. I've got everything under control. I'm just visiting her until I can get something new."

"But you said it was impossible to get anything at the moment."

"No," I correct. "I said it was hard at the moment. They also told me it was hard to get into the top colleges and hard to get into the top graduate schemes and hard to work such long hours but I did, didn't I?"

"Abby—"

"Didn't I?"

Mam sighs. "Yes. You did. And we are so proud of you for that, but this is different."

"It's not," I say. "I'm still me. I'll find a way. Look, I have to go. Don't say anything to Louise. We need to have a proper conversation about it and I haven't found the right moment for it yet. I love you guys. I'm sorry I didn't tell you before."

"We love you too," Mam says. "And of course you'll figure it out. But know that we're here to help you."

"I do." I glance at my father, who's still glaring at something off camera. "Dad?"

"You should never have dated a lawyer," he says, carrying on a different conversation.

"I'll remember that for next time. I'm hanging up now. I'll call soon."

"Abby?"

I pause, one hand on the lid of the laptop, one ear listening out for Louise. "Yeah?"

"Just..." Mam looks so worried that it almost breaks my heart. "Mind yourself," she says eventually.

"I will." I wave goodbye, ending the call. I'll try.

CHAPTER 6

Excluding the pubs and the man who drives around local events serving tea, coffee, and the occasional questionable sandwich out of his van, there are three places to eat dinner in Clonard that are open all year round. One is a small greasy takeaway that used to be the ultimate treat as a child. The second is the local Chinese restaurant that caused *great* excitement when it opened twenty years ago, and the third is a midpriced Italian place called Roman's, which used to be a shoe shop. It's the fanciest of the options as it has tablecloths and corked wine and this is where I now sit with Louise and Tomasz on what is clearly supposed to be their date night.

This is not a guess. About five minutes after I finished the call with my parents, I heard them talking about me in the kitchen from where I hovered in the hallway, like a child eavesdropping. Tomasz insisted on inviting me so I wouldn't be alone. Louise, as expected, wanted the opposite. I should have walked out of the house and pretended I was going somewhere. I should have announced breezily that I was fine and settled in for a night in front of the television. But I didn't.

Because the thing is, I'm not fine. I don't think I've ever been less fine.

I've never spent so much time by myself before. So much time with nothing to do. So when Louise knocked on my bedroom door ten minutes later and asked if I wanted to come I immediately said yes and chose to ignore the resigned look on her face.

I got dressed up, if not a little too dressed up, and now here I am, wedged between them, looking at six different kinds of pasta.

"The early bird is really good," Louise says as if challenging me to say otherwise.

Across the room, a young child starts to wail.

"What's the one I like?" Tomasz asks absently. "With the things?"

"The mushroom fettuccini," Louise says, her eyes on the mother opposite as she tries to calm the toddler.

"I don't think that's it."

"It is."

I glance around the small restaurant. "I wish we had something like this growing up. Can you imagine? Actual pizza instead of frozen ones?"

"A few more places would be good," she says. "We need some new businesses in this village that aren't just open six months of the year."

"What do you guys think of the new café?"

"Coffee?" Louise's voice takes on an odd tone while Tomasz sighs.

"*I* think it's nice," he says.

"What's wrong with it?" I ask. With all the organic compostable talk, I thought it would be right up her street.

"There's nothing wrong with it."

"Then why do you sound like that?"

"Honestly?" She shrugs. "It's expensive."

"Three-fifty for a croissant," Tomasz says gravely. "A plain one."

"Eilish does lovely coffees at the pub," Louise continues, looking back to the menu. "And soon you'll have all the pop-up places when the summer starts. I don't think it's going to last."

"Their hot chocolate is nice though," Tomasz adds at the look on my face. "They give you free marshmallows."

"Beth only opened it a few months ago," I say, feeling oddly defensive. "Give her a chance."

Louise turns to me. "When did you meet Beth?"

"The other day. She wanted me to help her out with some marketing."

"You're not in marketing."

"I know but she—"

"Did you say yes?"

"No," I say stiffening at the interrogation. "Like you said, I don't do marketing."

The one server appears with a basket of breadsticks and we all smile pleasantly until he leaves.

"Did you ask Abby about the stall?" Tomasz asks, reaching for a handful. "For the Easter Fun Day?"

I have to smile. "They still do that?"

"Andrew insists on it every year," she says, and I picture the unofficial but very dedicated village mayor.

"Last year they had the weather lady as the guest of honor," Tomasz says. "The six o'clock one."

"We rent a stall for the charity," Louise continues. "If you're still around, I could use your help signing people up."

"I'll be here," I say. "I used to love Easter Fun Day."

"When is your flight anyway?"

I pause, annoyed by this perfect opening to tell her. We're in public too, so it's not like it can go that badly. But she's not in a good mood. If anything, I feel like she's waiting for me to give the wrong answer so she can find a reason to be angry with me.

"I haven't booked it yet," I say with what I hope is a convincing smile. "I might wait until after the Easter break for the prices to go down."

She accepts this as reasonable excuse and returns to her menu while across the room a tired-looking man now tries to distract the toddler with a video of Peppa Pig.

"Will you remind me to give those hedge clippers back to Luke?" Louise says, reaching for her water. "I think he borrowed them off Sean."

Tomasz nods absently, twirling a breadstick in his hand.

"Does he often come for lunch?" I ask.

"Luke?" Louise shrugs. "Not really. He's busy. Pat and Susan come by every other week."

"I almost didn't recognize him."

"Well, that's what happens when you don't visit," she says.

Alright. Fair. "But he looks different, doesn't he?"

Her eyes flick up. "What do you mean?"

"You know."

"No."

"You *know*."

"I don't, Abby."

Is she really going to make me say it? "Like really hot," I whisper. "Right?"

She stares at me. "I guess."

"Come on. You can say it in front of Tomasz."

At his name, Tomasz drags his gaze from the pasta section. "Huh?"

"Objectively he looks extremely different," I insist.

They're both staring at me now.

"If you say so," Louise says finally. "He's always just been Luke to me."

I slouch back in my chair. "Never mind."

Tomasz flicks the menu closed. "You're right," he says to Louise. "It is the mushroom fettuccini."

"I know." Louise is still looking at me. "So any plans for tomorrow?" she asks in a "or are you just going to hang around the house all day?" voice.

"Not really."

"Maggie Breslin says she saw you coming out of the funeral home."

"Maggie..." I roll my eyes, picturing the village gossip. "Small town much? She could have said hello instead of spying on me from behind a lamppost."

"What were you doing there?"

"Applying for a job, Louise. Is that allowed? Or does Maggie Breslin think I'm having an affair with the funeral director?" They were the only place in town advertising any vacancies. I handed in my résumé feeling pretty confident but got a call twenty minutes later saying they thought I was too overqualified for what they were looking for.

I mean, duh. Tell me something I don't know.

"A job?"

"Yes."

Tomasz looks concerned. "With the dead people?"

"It was for the receptionist role and I didn't get it, so none of it matters. Tell Maggie to mind her own business."

A strange look crosses Louise's face. "I thought you were applying for jobs back in New York."

"I am. It's only temporary, so I don't go insane while I'm here. Don't worry," I add. "I'm not putting down roots."

"That's not what I meant."

Tomasz smiles encouragingly before we can launch into another argument. "I think a job sounds like a great idea, Abby. Maybe you could help Louise with the whales."

Louise and I glance at each other, silently agreeing not to pursue that ridiculous suggestion.

"I didn't know you were intending to stay so long," she says instead.

"I'm not."

"But long enough to get a part-time job."

"I told you, it's just so—"

"Okay," Tomasz says loudly. "Who wants to see me put my finger through fire?" He pulls the candlestick toward him before swiping his finger through the flame. "See?"

"Thrilling," Louise says flatly.

"Your turn."

"No."

"I'll protect you."

"You're such an idiot," she mutters but doesn't protest when he lifts her hand, doing the same thing.

My sister smiles in a way I rarely see on her, soft and sweet, and I glance away at the suddenly intimate moment, meeting the eyes of the still crying child, now with tomato sauce smeared all over their chin.

"I think I'll have the lasagna," I say, and turn to catch the waiter's attention.

The mood doesn't get better when the food arrives. Louise and I eat our dinner in silence, while Tomasz keeps up a steady stream of chatter about the dire fate of his football team back in Poland. Two scoops of surprisingly good gelato follow, but with nothing to talk about, we ask for the check and then we're back outside, lingering by the door as Louise puts the receipt away and Tomasz rubs her back and I stand there wishing I hadn't come. I wish I'd stayed home and given them an evening to themselves, especially when Tomasz works so many night shifts.

"I think I'll do a loop around town," I say, zipping up my jacket. "Get some fresh air."

Louise opens her mouth but Tomasz gives her a not-so-subtle dig with his elbow. "Okay," is all she says.

"I might go to Pete's," I add, glancing down the road at the pub. "See who's around. I promise I won't wake you."

"If you're sure."

"Positive. Don't wait up."

"If you find a rave, let us know," Tomasz says with a grin. He places an arm around Louise's waist and steers her in the direction of the house. I pretend to go the other way before slipping down a side street, instantly regretting my decision.

Now what?

A couple of people linger around the Chinese place a few doors down and I can hear music coming from Pete's, but I have no inclination to go there tonight. It's not the kind of place where I could drink anonymously in the corner.

But I can't go home. I want to give Louise and Tomasz some time together that doesn't involve me hiding in my room like a sulking teenager.

But I'm not used to this. This having nothing to do. I *always* have something to do. There was always work. Always life in between work. Always Tyler. Always Jess. Always parties and dinners and bars and co-workers and friends of friends. Being alone was never an option. Being alone with nothing to do was unthinkable. I don't even have laundry. Louise did mine the other day because she said she didn't trust me to do an eco-wash.

I stare down the street, feeling sorry for myself when my phone vibrates against my hip. I don't need to look at the screen to know who it is. Mam's already messaged me twice since I broke the news this afternoon and no doubt she's calling to confirm that Aunt Ellen would be *more* than happy to have me stay with—

"Abby?"

I clutch the phone to my ear, swallowing my automatic greeting. The person on the other end sounds as surprised as I am.

Not my mother.

Tyler.

"I didn't think you'd pick up."

The sound of his voice is jarring and I find myself glancing over my shoulder, almost expecting him to appear.

"Are you there?" he continues when I don't respond. The frustration in his tone snaps me from my surprise.

"I'm here," I say. "Why are you—"

"Where is here?" Tyler interrupts. "Where are you?"

"I'm in Ireland."

"Ireland?" The disbelief in his voice makes it clear it's one of the last places he expected me to be. "You went home?"

"What do you want?"

"To talk to you."

"Well, I don't want to talk to you. I'm hanging up now."

"Wait, Abby. Just… wait." He sighs down the phone and I close my eyes, picturing him in his suit, standing in his office. He has his own office. On the ninth floor at the back of the building. I never had my own office. I worked in a large, open-plan space and that was how I liked it. When you shut the door to Tyler's, the room got so silent I sometimes felt like we'd been sealed in. Trapped.

"I want you to stop contacting me," I say.

"I know you do. But I'm going to Shanghai for a few weeks."

"So?"

"So I won't be in New York. I thought you could stay at the apartment."

"I don't want to stay in your apartment. I'm visiting my sister."

"You can't stand your sister."

"And yet she's my preferred option right now."

"You're being ridiculous." I feel a spark of annoyance at his tone. He sounds like he's talking to a child. "Come back to New York. I have a friend at First Capital who might have an opening. Do you remember Hunter? He's—"

"You talked to Hunter about me?"

"Of course I did."

"What do you mean, 'of course I did'?"

"Abby—"

"No, don't *Abby* me. Don't talk about me."

"I'm just to pretend you never existed, is that it?"

"Pretty much," I say. "You broke up with me. Remember? Remember the whole 'I don't want to marry you anymore' conversation? Because I do."

"I know you're hurt—"

"You don't know anything!" I lower my voice, realizing I'm shouting. "You don't get a say in what I do anymore. You don't get to advise and you don't get to ask. So stop."

"I just want to help."

"And I don't want you to. Goodbye, Tyler."

I hang up, cutting him off as a surge of adrenaline races through me. Hunter? He called *Hunter*? Hunter with his trust fund and his Forbes Thirty under Thirty wife?

I'm so embarrassed I could yell. Or hit something. Or—

"Abby!"

I turn at the shout to see Beth jogging across the street, her hands shoved awkwardly into the pockets of her coat. "I thought that was you!" She comes to a stop in front of me, tucking a strand of hair behind her ear. "You going out?"

"Coming back," I say, trying to calm down. "I just had dinner with my sister."

"Nice!" She smiles at me, looking hopeful. "You didn't stop by. I was saving an éclair for you."

"Oh. Um." I falter, looking for something to say that's not *I'm avoiding you even though you were nice to me because I'm a giant coward.* "I've been really busy."

"Of course. Sure. I just wanted to say sorry about the other day."

I can only stare at her. "*You* wanted to say sorry?"

"Luke's super stressed with his course but there was no excuse to talk to you like that."

"But he was right," I say. "I shouldn't have said those things. I'm the one who should be apologizing."

"For what? Telling me the truth?" She smiles ruefully. "You think I don't know opening a café in the middle of nowhere would be tough? People have said a lot worse to me."

"Still," I say. "I'm so—"

"You're forgiven." She waggles her fingers in a downward motion. "Cleansed. Forgotten. I don't even know what you're talking about. So long as you can forgive Luke for being an idiot. Honestly, that man is like a child sometimes."

"It's not his fault," I say tiredly. *It was mine.*

Beth hesitates, sensing my mood. "Are you doing anything now? You want to get a drink? You'd be saving me from a night alone in front of the television."

"Look, this is... you don't have to—"

"What? Be nice to you?" She shrugs. "I can't help it. You look super pathetic right now."

"I would love a drink," I say truthfully. "A very large, very alcoholic drink."

"I think we can manage that," she says, looking thoughtful. "How do you feel about questionable merlot?"

CHAPTER 7

Beth brings me to one of the newer pubs in the village. It's small and busy because there's not much else to do in a place this size, and is aimed at a decidedly younger demographic judging by the underage drinkers sipping furtively in the corner. There's a slightly grimy feel to the place and, though we get a few looks, there's no one I recognize.

In New York, Tyler and I only went to upmarket bars, the kind without prices on the menu. Sometimes Jess would drag me to some new club everyone was talking about or I'd take her to a few of the Irish places I knew around the city, but it's rarely how I'd spend a free evening and I'm momentarily awkward when Beth returns to our table with two extra-large glasses of red wine.

"One for you," she says. "And one for me." She places them down with exaggerated care before noticing my expression. "Did you want a beer instead?"

I shake my head as she takes a sip. The glass is so full it's almost brimming over. "I haven't had a night out in a while."

"You live in New York," she scoffs, and I laugh.

"I'm usually very healthy."

"I thought you moneymakers were all work hard, play hard."

"Lots are. I just never knew where they found the time." And Tyler was never into that scene. He was a natural early riser and hated anything that messed with his REM. Nothing alcoholic, caffeinated, or spicy at least four hours before bed.

"Were you always in New York?" Beth asks, shrugging off her coat. She's wearing dark blue dungarees underneath and a white and black striped shirt. I'd look like an overgrown child if I wore something like that, but she manages to make it look chic.

I try the wine. *Questionable* is the right word to describe it. But it's cheap and needed and coats my mouth. "London first," I answer, taking another sip. "I was there for a year after I finished up at LSE. Then Paris for a few months on an internship and then New York."

"And now Clonard." Beth grins. "What's one more than a trifecta?"

"Quadfecta."

"No, that sounds made up."

"Let's just say I've come full circle."

"At least you tried," she says. "The farthest I ever got was here."

"There's always time."

"Nah, I've decided to lay down roots. Plus, I can't do long-haul flights. I get headaches. I will make an exception for New York however. Especially now I have a floor to crash on." She winks. "That was me inviting myself over, by the way."

"I'd love to have you. Unfortunately, I have no floor to crash on."

"What do you mean?"

"I had to give up my apartment. I had to give up everything."

"Everything?"

"Everything but what I brought in my suitcase."

Her smile fades. "You're joking."

I hesitate, realizing I said too much, but Beth picks up on it immediately.

"To be clear, I brought you here so I could get you drunk and pry into your life. You are falling for my plan perfectly."

I laugh. "I didn't mean to bring the mood down."

"You're not," she insists. "Tell me about the apartment. What happened?"

"It's less dramatic than it sounds," I say, uncomfortable. I think about changing the subject, but she just waits, folding her hands on the table. "I'd started renting from MacFarlane a few weeks before it went under," I explain. "On top of my salary and my savings, it was a perfect storm."

She's not quick enough to hide her shock. "They kicked you out of your home?"

"It wasn't mine," I say. "It was theirs and they could do what they liked with it."

"So when you say everything..."

I nod. "And I was one of the lucky ones. Some people had kids and college funds, houses... some lost millions."

"Millions?" Beth stares at me, her eyes wide. "How much did you lose? Wait! Don't answer that. That is such a rude question, ugh. Look." She pushes up her sleeve, showing me her bare arm. "I'm breaking out in hives just thinking about it."

"I didn't have millions to begin with," I assure her. "I wasn't that high up. I wasn't even close. I mean, yeah, I was doing okay the last few years, but..." I push down the queasy feeling inside. "Sorry. I don't know why I'm telling you all of this."

"It's because I asked," she says. "And because people tend to tell me things. I think it's because I tell them so much. Also this is like fourteen percent, so bottoms up."

I watch with a smile as she takes an impressive gulp. "I spent my money at the start," I tell her. "I used some early investments to pay off student loans. I gave some to my parents. Plus New York isn't cheap. But everything I did have I lost. MacFarlane encouraged us to put our entire lives into their hands. The more we gave, the more they promised to give back. It sounds so financially irresponsible now but everyone was doing it."

"Then maybe it's a good thing you got out. They sound awful."

"They do," I agree, rotating the glass slowly. "We all knew we weren't working for UNICEF. We took rich people's money and made them more money. That was our job."

"You make it sound so worthwhile," she jokes.

"I know. And I know how it sounds but I'd give anything to go back to how things were. I feel like I'm lost without the work."

"Can't you go somewhere else?"

"I'd love to. I just can't *get* anywhere else. Because the layoffs were global, there are thousands of us vying for the same positions and I don't have the family connections or family money to help me in the meantime. Coming back here was my only real option. At least that's what it felt like."

"I don't get it," Beth says. "What about your fiancé? Can't you stay with them? Or did they lose their job too?"

We both glance down at the ring on my finger. I keep forgetting I'm wearing it.

I just want to help.

"I don't have a fiancé."

A look of horror crosses her face. "Did they die?"

"No," I say, choking on my wine. "No, he broke it off."

Beth's forehead crumples. "Oh my God, Abby, I'm so sorry."

"I shouldn't even be wearing this. I don't usually. I didn't tell my family when it happened. I couldn't even *think* about telling them and then just when I was beginning to get back to normal everything happened at work and I couldn't hide that from them because the news was everywhere and it's bad enough losing your job, but the thought of everyone knowing about Tyler on top of that was too—"

"I get it," Beth interrupts. She reaches across the table to grab my hand, stopping me mid-breakdown. Something in my chest loosens as she squeezes my fingers and I take a large gulp from my glass.

"It's hard telling people when things go wrong," she says. "Even if none of what happened is your fault. You know that, right?"

"Sure." I can tell she doesn't believe me but I give her a weak smile until she lets me go. "Sorry to problem-vomit all over of you."

"Do you want to talk about him? Tyler?"

"No." *Yes.*

Beth turns serious, seeing right through me. "We're going to need another round."

And that's exactly what we get.

"So he's just like 'move back in with me'?" she asks with the exact amount of skepticism I needed her to react with. A fresh bottle sits between us, despite my reminders that I don't have any money.

"He said he'll be away on business."

"Still."

"I know."

"That's weird."

"I *know*. Right? Thank you."

"You think he feels bad?"

"I don't know. And I don't want to figure it out. It's too messy."

"Do you think he's still in love with you?"

"No," I say. "Maybe. I don't know. But that doesn't matter because I'm not in love with him."

"Not even a little bit?"

I shake my head, ignoring how my vision is starting to swim at the edges. "I can't be. Because of my principles."

"I completely agree."

"Plus we'd drifted apart," I insist, pouring more wine into my glass. "All of last year. Even before we got engaged. In fact, I think he proposed because he knew it too. Like he was trying to bring us back together."

"Too busy with work?" Beth guesses.

I nod. "There were redundancies at MacFarlane, hindsight now, of course, but back then we didn't think anything of it. But it meant I was working more than usual, and on top of that, Tyler signed this big client and it was just crazy. He was sometimes gone for weeks at a time. We became one of those couples who saw each other on the weekends but we thought it would be okay. I mean, we discussed it."

"Discussed it?"

"Yes." That was what we did. We talked. We were honest with each other and we got to the point of things. It was how we avoided petty fights, annoying "small talk" as Tyler always called it. We didn't waste time because we didn't have time. "It was part of our plan," I explain. "We both knew we were working hard now for a later payoff. We both had demanding jobs. That's why we worked so well together. Or at least that's what I thought."

"You don't think he cheated on you, do you?"

I shake my head. "He would have told me."

Beth makes a noise.

"What?"

"You think he would have told you if he cheated on you?"

"Not while it was happening," I say. "But if that were the reason for breaking up with me then, yes, he would have. Obviously, I've had some doubts but I don't think he would have done that to me. Hell, I don't think he had time to. But that still doesn't mean I'm going to step one foot inside his apartment. Even if he's not there."

Beth props her chin on her hand, thoughtful. "What about your friends? Can't you stay with them?"

"They're not doing much better than me. Nearly everyone I know worked at MacFarlane. They're too busy trying to rescue their own lives to help rescue mine as well. And others..." I think to Jess. "I just couldn't face crawling on my hands and knees to them."

"Asking for help doesn't mean you need to crawl."

"That's what it felt like."

Beth leans forward, almost toppling her glass as she does so. "Have you ever thought about staying here? I don't mean in Clonard. But Cork or Dublin. Up to Belfast. We've got cities on this island too, you know."

"No. It's too small. The whole draw of the rest of the world was anonymity. Some people love knowing everyone else," I add. "But it's not for me. I've never felt like myself here. Over there I found people who got it. Who got *me*. I never had to explain why I am the way I am or why I do the work I do. I liked my job. I loved my job. And I liked making money. I know you're not supposed to but I did. I liked buying nice things and eating in nice restaurants and I liked not having to worry about bills or rent or what I would do if something happened. I knew what I would do. I would pay for it."

"With all your money."

"Exactly." I flex my fingers, staring at the ring. "I liked being busy. It motivated me. I liked working at the highest level with people who were smarter than me because it meant I would get smarter. I liked solving people's problems. I really liked making reports. Some people hated doing reports but not me. I was good at it. I was *great* at it. And I worked for years to get to where I was only for it to be taken from me in the space of few minutes by a security guard with a cardboard box." The pressure in my chest rises again and I focus on Beth, pushing it back down. "I liked my life," I say. "I don't want another one."

"So that's your only goal?" she asks after a moment. "Get the hell out of Dodge?"

"And never look back."

She looks like she wants to say something but, whatever it is, she thinks the better of it, sitting back in her seat. "You know. At times like this I find there's only really one solution."

We get drunk.

Another bottle of wine turns to shots and I barely notice the time go by. Beth is... fun. A lot of fun. Less extreme than Jess, where I never knew what was going to happen when I was with her. Warmer than when I went out with people from work, when every conversation involved an undercurrent of one-upmanship. She tells me all about her ex's farm and the three weeks he lasted running it. She tells me about deciding to stay in Clonard, about the community she found here, and though her descriptions of this place are so at odds with my own memories, I bite my tongue even as the alcohol loosens it. Clonard needs people like her. I just hope everyone realizes it in time.

By the time they kick us out, we're holding on to each other, half because of the wine, half because Beth insists we're best friends now, and she's yawning as she leads me to the street.

"Do you want to split a taxi?" she asks.

"I'll walk. I need the air."

"You can't walk."

"I'm twenty minutes away." I urge her toward the short line of cars waiting outside the pub. "It's Clonard. I'll be fine."

She's too drunk to argue but sticks her head out the window when she gets in, her face open and earnest. "Don't be a stranger this time," she says, and she sounds so genuine that I don't know how to respond, only offering a small wave as the car drives off.

I watch until she disappears around a corner and only then begin to wander home, not wanting the night to end just yet. I feel lighter. And yes, that is probably the wine coursing through me, but I have a feeling it's also from seeing a friendly face and getting to talk about my problems even if I didn't solve them.

I twist my engagement ring from my finger and for one wild moment think about throwing it into a nearby rain gutter. I put it in my pocket instead.

I'll tell Louise this weekend. I chickened out at dinner but it wasn't so bad telling Beth. And maybe Louise will be a little nicer to me.

Or maybe not. But it's worth a shot.

I keep walking, past the funeral home and Dessie's store and am heading to the bridge when I hear a car slow behind me. I glance over my shoulder, pausing when it stops in front of the café, its lights switching off.

Luke gets out.

His course in Sligo. I remember him talking about how late he can be sometimes. And, of course, it's been exactly a week since he offered me a ride. A whole week I've been here.

It feels like much longer.

I should keep moving, but I don't, lurking in the shadows as he reaches into the back seat for something. I'm still hurt about what happened between us and unfortunately the wine only increases it tenfold, making me almost angry as I watch him. I know it's irrational, but I can't help it. I don't need to be frowned upon just because of some ridiculous misunderstanding. This is why I left this stupid town. No one understood me. No one even tried to.

I mean, who does he think he is? Judging me like that. He doesn't even know me. We've barely talked since we were kids. He's just jealous that I got out. He's jealous and petty and mean and—

"Hey!"

Luke jerks upright at my shout, almost dropping a textbook as he turns my way. "Abby?"

"Yes, *Abby*." My boots slip out from under me as I stumble toward him.

"What are you…" He trails off with a frown. "Are you drunk?"

"Obviously." I stop a few feet from him, holding on to a lamppost for support. Drunker than I thought. The chilly night air has done nothing to sober me, if anything I feel fuzzier. "I have a question for you."

"Alright." Luke grabs a plastic grocery bag from the back seat and flicks the door closed. "Ask away."

"What," I begin, momentarily distracted by how loud my voice sounds, "is your problem?"

"Right now it's deciding between the two microwave meals I bought."

"You—"

"Go home," he interrupts. "It's late."

"I can't go home." I follow him to the café. "I don't have a home."

"I mean your sister's."

"That's not my home."

"Then—" He breaks off as he turns, not expecting me to be so close. The grocery bag swings, banging sharply into my hip as we collide and he grabs a hold of my arm, steadying me before I can fall.

He doesn't let go.

For a moment we just stand there, our bodies pushed together, and I struggle to remember why I was so mad.

"Abby?"

I like it when he says my name. I like the way his lips move.

I wet my own as I stare at him, my breath coming out in sharp bursts of mist. Luke doesn't seem to be breathing at all.

God, I'm attracted to him. More so than when he was just some stranger on the road. More so than when he flirted with me over lunch. But before I can do anything about it the memory of him in the café flashes through my mind, the barely concealed distaste when he looked at me. Like I was something he scraped off the side of his shoe.

I shove him away, confused, but it's me who stumbles back, his body solid before me.

"Did you just push me?" he asks.

"No."

I try to go back to glaring, try to raise my gaze so I can look him in the eye and tell him all the ways he's wrong about me, but I can't seem to get past his mouth.

Just once. Just to see and maybe I'll stop feeling this way.

And then I can... then...

"Now what are you thinking about?" he asks warily, and this time there's no lying.

"You." And before either of us can stop me, I surge up on my toes and kiss him.

CHAPTER 8

It's over in an instant.

Luke freezes as soon as I touch him, his mouth unmoving against mine, and even through the fog in my brain I'm able to sense it. Embarrassment roils through me and I'm about to drop back down, horrified with myself, when he inhales sharply, his head tilting just enough that the kiss becomes a *kiss*. I sway in surprise, barely noticing when the grocery bag knocks off me once more as his hands rise to cup my face, holding me to him.

He's a good kisser. Though the way my blood feels like it's boiling beneath his touch, I think even if he were a bad one, I wouldn't really mind. I cling to his biceps as one of his hands curves around the back of my neck, tangling deliciously in my hair. A gentle tug sends nerves tingling down my spine and I press myself against him as my imagination runs riot, the way he's taking control sending a buzz of anticipation through me. And then his tongue slips into my mouth and I don't think about anything at all.

I make a noise, high and breathy and very not me, and when I do he breaks away, running his thumb along his bottom lip as he stares at me.

"You kissed me back," I say before he can deny it.

He doesn't, but he doesn't seem thrilled with himself either.

"With tongue," I add.

That seems to break the spell. The slightly dazed look on his face vanishes as he rolls his eyes. "I'll drive you home." He opens the car door, but I don't move, watching him with equal parts interest and confusion.

"You kissed me back," I repeat. It comes out like a question. You can't be mad at someone if you kiss them back.

"Please get in the car."

"No."

"Abby."

"Luke." I slap my hand against the wall, ignoring the vague stinging in my palm as I stake my claim. Plant my stake? Whatever. I'm not going to let him just ignore this, ignore *me*.

There's a few seconds of standoff as we watch each other. And then I win.

"Fine." He closes the door and I feel a wave of victory as he locks it. The grocery bag slips down his wrist as he takes out a set of keys with one hand and his phone with the other.

"What are you doing?"

"Texting Louise so she doesn't think you're dead."

"I think you should kiss me again."

He ignores me, crouching to reach the steel padlock at the bottom of the café door. I use the opportunity to run my hand through his hair, reveling in the short strands.

"You like me," I insist as he rises.

I can feel him looking at me, but I'm focused on his shirt now, specifically the top buttons. He lets me get two undone before his hands capture mine, prying them easily away. Only this time he doesn't let go. Instead, he turns, shouldering open the café door and tugging me inside.

I stand in the dark, breathing in the smell of coffee beans as he locks up behind us.

"Where are we going?" I ask when he takes my hand again.

"Upstairs."

I stumble in surprise. "Okay."

"Okay," he mutters, leading me to the painted wooden steps by the counter. Upstairs. *Upstairs to have sex?*

My nerves kick in as I try to remember if I shaved my legs or not and I shiver as he palms the back of my head, dipping me so I don't bump into the low ceiling.

He brings me quickly up the steps and I somehow don't trip as we reach the top and encounter another door. Luke positions my back against the wall as if afraid I'm going to topple back down before he opens that one too.

We enter a small apartment with peeling wallpaper and sloping ceilings and that's about as much as I take in before I catch sight of a bed shoved against the far wall.

Luke steers me toward it, tossing the grocery bag somewhere to the side before he flips the cover back and sits me down. The movement is a little abrupt for my liking but, hey, whatever floats his boat.

I scoot up to make room as he takes off his coat but instead of joining me on the bed, he kneels at my feet.

Turns out I like that a lot.

My heart beats out a staccato rhythm as he pulls off my boots, setting them to the side. He goes for my jacket next and I help him impatiently with the sleeves when they get tangled at my wrists. My phone and a few coins rattle to the ground as I tug myself free but I barely notice them as his fingers brush mine.

"Lie down," he orders.

Again, not the most romantic of beginnings but I comply, shifting my hips to get to the button of my jeans. I don't get very far when he moves again.

"What are you doing?" I ask as he pulls the heavy duvet over me.

"I'll be back in a minute."

I struggle to sit up. "I'll—"

"No," he says, pushing me back down. "You wait there. I'll be right back."

"But—"

"I have to go lock up," he says, and I still as his gaze meets mine. He has the most beautiful eyes.

"I'll be right back," he says slowly. He waits until I nod and then, not taking his eyes off me, he walks to the other side of the room and slips out the door, leaving me alone.

I settle back against the pillow, unexpectedly nervous.

Luke Bailey. I'm going to have sex with Luke Bailey.

I snort at the thought, immediately happy he isn't around to hear it.

This is good. This is a good if unplanned development.

Maybe this will be a disappointing experience and I can get him out of my system.

Or maybe it will be the opposite of that.

Going by that kiss, I think it's going to be the opposite.

Above me a pipe creaks and I stifle a yawn, pulling my tank top over my head before arranging my hair so it sits just right. I keep my bra on. It's a nice bra. Hot pink. Lacy straps. I rearrange my boobs in it and lace my fingers on my stomach.

I can't hear anything from below.

Lock up.

I frown at the ceiling as my eyes grow heavy.

Didn't he already lock up?

*

The next thing I know, it's morning.

Early morning, judging by the weak light creeping through the window. My nose is cold, my throat is dry, and it feels like my eyelashes are glued together.

Something's wrong.

It's not that I'm confused. The night before comes back to me with humiliating clarity but there's something else. Something...

And that's when I feel it. A sharp cramping sensation low in my abdomen. As if someone grabbed a hold of my insides and twisted. Hard.

Oh *shit*.

I scramble into a sitting position, the cold air hitting me as I whip the duvet off and look for any incriminating evidence. The last thing I need after throwing myself at him is to bleed all over his bed. But there's nothing. The sheets remain spotless beneath me.

Just debilitating pain then. Thank God for that.

Calmer now, I look around properly for the first time. The apartment is small enough that all it takes is one glance to know I'm alone. There's no sign of Luke.

But there is a glass of water on the nightstand, next to a granola bar and packet of painkillers. I partake of all three, examining the stack of serious-looking textbooks behind them. On top of them lies what must have fallen from my pockets last night. My phone, one euro thirty in change... and my engagement ring.

Crap.

When I've drained the water, I step out of the bed, wincing as my feet meet the floorboards. I'm still wearing my jeans and my bra. The other clothes are where Luke left them and I quickly pull them on. It's chilly in here. The windows are small and single glazed, the paint on the windowsills chipped with mold creeping through. Exposed pipework runs along the wall, *not* the fancy kind, and there's a poster of some sunny continental city above the dresser, slightly faded from age.

Other than the "bedroom," there's a door near me that must lead to the bathroom and a makeshift living area comprised of a couch and a small kitchen galley. Everything is very clean.

I sleep there. That's about it.

That's what Luke had told me in the car and that's what it looks like. There are no touches of personality here, nothing to tell me who he is.

I don't know why that disappoints me so much.

My phone is out of battery, so I plug it in and head to the bathroom, keeping an ear out in case Luke comes back. I need a shower. A long shower. And while his one certainly looks like it would do the job, I know better than to try.

Too shy to go check if he's downstairs, I perch on the arm of the couch, guiltily eyeing the blanket folded beneath a spare pillow.

There's a sturdy coffee table beside the couch that seems to double up as a desk and a place to eat. As well as an empty beer bottle and a dinner plate pushed to the side, there's more textbooks and a crumpled class schedule. Luke's old-school. Despite the laptop, there's reams of paper and notebooks, half-finished lecture notes, and sketches of muscles and limbs, and, I see with a smile, a self-portrait of him falling asleep in class. I pull that one toward me only to hear footsteps sound on the stairs and I barely have time to compose myself when a moment later the door opens.

Despite everything that happened last night, I still feel an unexpected flutter when Luke steps inside. He's dressed in jeans and a navy sweatshirt and looks very, very good for someone who slept on the couch.

He doesn't see me at first. His eyes go straight to the bed, pausing when he sees it empty. For a moment I simply watch him before I realize I'm lurking.

"Good morning."

His head whips toward me, his confused expression vanishing in an instant, schooled into neutrality.

"How's the head?" he asks after a second.

"Not too bad. But the few times I've had a hangover, it's taken a while to kick in. Ask me in an hour and I might not have the same answer." I wait but he doesn't smile. "Is the café open?"

"Not until ten."

I nod. My hands feel clammy. "I'm sorry about last night. I can't believe you slept on your couch. You should have just sent me on my way."

"I tried that."

"Right. I was with Beth," I add when he doesn't continue.

"Yeah, she messaged. Apparently you're her new best friend."

"She's been really nice. We made up about what happened the other day."

"Good for you."

"Mm-hm." I smile, trying to gauge his mood. "Look, Luke, I'm sorry about what happened."

"You said that already."

"And I'm saying it again. I wasn't telling the truth before. I'm not—"

"I just want to make one thing very clear," he interrupts. "And that's whatever midlife crisis you're having—"

"Midlife? I'm thirty years old."

"Whatever breakdown this is then, I don't want to be part of it."

I stare at him, stung. "Well... you're not."

"Good."

"Great." I cross my arms and uncross them. Neither of us moves. "If you're mad about last night—"

He cuts me off with a laugh. It's not a nice one. "I'm mad you didn't tell me about your fiancé."

"But that's what I wanted to—" I break off with a hiss as another cramp strikes.

Luke frowns. "What is it?"

"Nothing." I glance toward the bed sheets in case I missed a spot. "I was wrong, the hangover's starting."

He watches me for a moment and I struggle not to sit back down or, more realistically, curl up into the fetal position and ask him to bring me a pastry.

"You know," he says eventually. "Just because your job went sour doesn't mean you can get away with stuff like this. You can't just disappear for years and then waltz back into people's lives like it's nothing. Like it doesn't affect things."

"I know that."

"Do you?"

"*Yes.*" Now it's my turn to be mad. "Believe what you want to believe about me, Luke, but I didn't come back to mess with you. And I certainly didn't waltz. I came back because I didn't have a choice."

"No. God forbid it would be for any other reason."

"Well, it certainly wasn't for the warm welcome," I snap. "And you know what? It's none of your business what I do or why I do it. All I know is I was very drunk last night and *clearly* not thinking."

I pluck my phone from the charger as he stalks over to the bed, redoing my attempt at making it. He's ignoring me now. Like a child.

Fine.

Freaking fine.

Let him think what he wants. I don't owe him an explanation. I don't owe him anything.

"Thanks again," I call, a little louder than necessary, and slam the door as I go.

I meet no one on my way home. Or maybe I do and I don't see them, just storm past them muttering to myself.

Stupid period. Stupid period and stupid period emotions. I would have been able to keep my cool and set him straight if it weren't for my ridiculous hormones.

Tears prick my eyes as I turn onto my street but at least the painkillers have started to kick in, my cramps now a dull throb as I hurry up the driveway.

"Abby?" Louise calls from the kitchen as I run up the stairs. "Is that you?"

"It's me," I yell. "Do you have any tampons?"

"In my room. Second drawer in the dresser."

I almost go into her old bedroom, now converted into an office, before I spin around and head to the master bedroom at the front of the house.

She's repainted it since Mam and Dad left and moved the bed around so it faces the window. My parent's ancient closet that used to take up so much space has been thrown out along with the wobbly bureau. Now an IKEA dresser sits in the corner next to a floor-length mirror and Tomasz's dumbbells.

I crack open the drawer, feeling a headache forming as I reach inside.

Breakdown. I'm not having a breakdown. I have *lists*. Lists and a *plan*. This is my plan! I didn't say anything about it being a good one, I just...

I lose track of my rant as I stare down at the slim cardboard box in my hands.

Confused, I pull the drawer open fully, peering inside to see a dozen more just like it, rattling about with spare batteries and a pair of sunglasses.

Not tampons.

Pregnancy tests.

"What do you think you're doing?" I jump as Louise marches into the room, her face pale. "That's private."

"Sorry," I say as she snatches the box from me. "I didn't mean to snoop."

"Then don't. I said the second drawer."

"I'm sorry," I repeat, baffled by her attitude. It's not exactly shocking news; she and Tomasz have been married for years. "I didn't know you two were trying."

"Well, we are." She drops the box back inside, something almost like doubt flickering across her face. "We've been trying for a while."

Oh.

Oh.

She waits for me to say something and I wait too, because even as I feel a rush of understanding, of concern for her, nothing comes out.

I don't know what to say.

And she knows it.

With a final scowl, she opens the second drawer and takes out a box of tampons, shoving it into my hands.

"You smell like an alleyway," she says, and storms out of the room.

CHAPTER 9

"It's not good, Abby. Mike says they've got him on contract work."

Jess's glistening face bobs in and out of the screen as she walks on the treadmill, her breathing loud but controlled. "You made a good move turning down that Marshall's role."

"I didn't turn it down. I wasn't offered anything."

"I know, I was being nice."

I roll my eyes, lying back against my pillow. Another week has passed, another week when I haven't booked a ticket home, when I've avoided Louise's questions when I haven't managed to avoid her entirely. Dad keeps sending me companies he thinks I should work for ("Why don't you just knock on the door and start a conversation," he said, like I was applying to work in a grocery store in 1956) whereas Mam is texting me daily stories about her friends' children and their various difficulties, convinced all I needed to do was to compare myself to people she thought had it worse than me. (Shauna's daughter is divorced. *Twice*. And her not even thirty-two.)

"Did you hear a Reuters reporter was parked outside Emma Wallace's house last week?" Jess continues. "Some 'where are they now' article."

"Are you serious? It's been two months."

"They're desperate for it. You'd think by now some B-lister would have tweeted something questionable but there's been nothing. It's never a slow news day when you need it." Her eyes flick to the phone. "Any luck yet?"

"Tons. Why else do you think I look so happy?"

"Sarcasm will get you nowhere, Reynolds."

"What about the others?" I ask. Even though Jess left the company years ago, I've never known anyone with such a gift for keeping in touch with people. "Did you hear from Kenny?"

"Private equity. And Arnold's already got a book deal about his experience, so he's a douche. Chrissy's gone to work for her father."

"Didn't you guys have a thing once?"

"Are you saying because she has a crush on me I can get you a foot in the door?"

"Kind of."

"I already tried." Jess sighs. "You need to be here, Abby."

"I've only been gone a few weeks."

"And you're already going out of your mind. I can see it in your eyes."

"If I'm going nuts here, I'll be even more nuts over there. At least I'm not maxing out credit cards trying to pretend everything's fine."

She doesn't answer, her gaze somewhere to the left as she stares straight ahead of her. It's seven a.m. in New York and, though I can only see the upper half of her torso from where she's positioned me on the treadmill, I can picture the sleek lines of the gym in her office skyscraper, the sun rising over Manhattan as she looks out. I feel a pang of longing just thinking about it. But I know I'm right. *My* New York was only mine on my terms. Homeless, jobless, and skiving off my friends is not how I want to live.

"Then how about a change?" she asks. "Something different. Communications."

"*Communications?*"

"Joey moved into communications and she gets to travel all the time."

"I don't want to travel. And I don't want to go into communications. I don't want to do anything else."

"That's because you don't know anything else," she insists. "I mean look at me. I got out. I'm still alive."

"What an endorsement."

"I'm just saying."

I know she is. And it's not like I haven't considered it these last few weeks. But I meant what I said. I don't want to do anything else. I don't know how to do anything else. I could go back to college and retrain, sure, but as what? And where would I get the money? Or would I put myself in even more debt to do it?

"Okay," Jess says as her smartwatch flashes. "I've got to go do some deadlifts next to a bunch of men with bad form and veiny foreheads."

"Thanks for squeezing me in."

She comes to a stop as the treadmill stills beneath her. "It's not just for you, you know. You should come back for me as well."

"Is that your way of saying you miss me?"

"I miss stress-smoking outside a bar while you stress-watched me. Just don't disappear. I've decided I'm too old to meet new people."

"I'll do my best."

"Au revoir, Abby Reynolds. Try not to fall into a bog."

She disappears as the call disconnects and I roll onto my back, half squishing my carefully wrapped parcel. Two more packages sit on the desk, ready to be mailed. Yesterday morning I finally did what I knew I had to and put my last few designer pieces up for sale. I'd been keeping them for interviews, indulging in fantasies of looking the part during my first few days in a new job, but with neither a job nor an interview on the horizon, it was time to bite the bullet. I don't know why I waited so long. They were sold in a few hours for more or less what I was hoping for and this morning I raided Mam's old craft box for envelopes and tape to mail them out.

The world outside is nothing but gray drizzly mist, so I spend a few more minutes stalking old co-workers' Instagrams before finally bringing myself to pull on my sneakers and leave my room. The house is quiet. Tomasz is fast asleep after a night shift but as I tiptoe past Louise's home office I can hear her talking on the phone.

We haven't spoken much since the whole tampon debacle last week. We'll have to eventually. We'll be adults and hug it out or make up or whatever the nearest thing to that we can do, which knowing Louise and I might not be that much. But for now, I embrace the coward's way out as I hurry down the stairs and out the front door.

The post office is located on the edge of town, housed in an old cottage that makes the inside cramped and cold. The owner is the same one as when I was younger and seems starved for a chat, so I spend fifteen minutes longer than I need to talking about her hip surgery and her new neighbors and how you just never know what the weather's going to do these days. Global warming, we agree. Finally another customer comes in and she presses three cubes of butterscotch into my hands, sending me on my way.

I pop one into my mouth as I step outside, almost bumping into a man walking past. It takes me only a second before I realize who he is.

"Rory?"

Rory O'Meara, my first ex-boyfriend and teenage partner in crime, glances over his shoulder, polite expectation turning to confusion and then to shock.

"Abby?"

"Yeah." I hesitate, suddenly a little unsure. We'd been close before, but we haven't spoken in years. "I heard you might come—"

He hugs me, a quick squeeze that cuts off my words and for one bizarre moment, I'm transported back to being fifteen again. Rory always gave the best hugs. And it's no different now as he envelops me, his beard tickling the side of my face, his tan jacket cold and slightly damp from the wind.

He pulls back to look at me, still smiling, and I find I'm smiling too, his enthusiasm infectious.

"You smell like my nan's place."

"That's the butterscotch," I say, nodding to the post office.

"Sure it is."

"Shut up. What's this?" I grab his hand, spotting the gold band. "You're married?"

"I am. The poor girl."

"Someone local?"

"No." He smirks. "Her name's Sinead. She's from Cork and she's a civil servant. Mam loves her. *Great* pension."

"Well, that's all that matters."

He cocks his head, taking me in. "So did I miss something?" he asks. "Are you back now? Your folks okay?"

"They're grand. Everyone's fine. I'm just visiting."

"Liar. You think I don't know when you're lying? You do this." He smiles pleasantly at me, blinking once. "Didn't you work for the devil? Lost a lot of people a lot of money?"

"I personally didn't, no."

"And now you've come crawling back to us." He pauses to nod hello at an older man passing us by. "Where are you staying?" he asks. "With your sister? I bet that's fun."

"Let's just say we're both trying very hard."

He grins but it vanishes as quickly it came. "Seriously though. Are you okay? It was on the news."

"So everyone keeps telling me." I sigh, seeing no point in lying any more than I need to. "I'm not great," I say. "Though you've probably guessed that by me wandering around here."

"The Abby Reynolds I knew never wandered. She strode. A little bit heavy on her instep but—"

"I get it. Thank you."

"It's good to see you," he says gently. "Even if it's under shitty circumstances." He eyes me carefully, seeming to decide something. "You sticking around?" he asks. "I need to get back to my parents now, but I'll be back up in a few weeks to see people. Maybe a little something on the beach? Pretend it's not raining? You can meet Sinead."

"I'd love that," I say, surprised by how much I mean it. "And I'd love to meet her."

We make tentative plans and I head back to the house in a significantly better mood than I'd left it. Losing touch with people wasn't exactly a choice I made when I left Clonard. It happened naturally. College was intense and when we did message in those first few months, I found I had little in common with people like Rory, who stayed behind. His world had suddenly seemed very small to me, whereas mine felt big and exciting. New. I guess a part of me felt it would always be that way. That I would always feel one step removed from this place and the life I worked so hard not to have. And yet, while it's been years since I've stayed so long here, years since I've been back at all, I'm a little shocked at how quickly I've grown used to it again, how easy people are to talk to over here. How Rory just shrugged off a decade apart like it had been only a few weeks.

It bugs me all the way home and I almost miss when someone calls my name, stopping only when Pat Bailey pops up from the flowerbed he'd been weeding.

"I was hoping I'd run into you," he says as I tug out my earbuds. "I gave my cousin a ring."

"Your cousin?"

"The one in Dublin."

"Oh. Right." I vaguely remember Pat talking about him at the lunch the first weekend.

"Now," he continues, pointing with his trowel. "He spoke to his neighbor who spoke to his son and he said they had something called rolling openings, so I told him I'd pass along your details. Now where did he say they worked?"

"That's so kind of you," I say, distracted as he limps around the hedge. I didn't notice it when he came for lunch but now we're outside it's more prominent, a pull of his right leg, almost like he's dragging it along. I frown. "Are you o—"

"Steven's?"

I stare at him, the limp instantly forgotten. "Stewarts?"

"That's the one," he says, brightening. "You know it?"

"Your cousin works at Stewarts?"

"His neighbor's son," Pat corrects.

Stewarts.

MacFarlane's competitor. Or they would be if they didn't keep losing business left, right and center. Not willing to get as down and dirty as the larger banks, their scrupulous business practice now mean they call themselves *boutique*. But hey, even if they're small, at least they're still standing.

"Can't say I've heard of them myself," Pat continues as my mind races trying to remember everything I've ever heard of them. "But then what would I know about these things? Anyway, I told him all about you and how you were looking to get back into the swing of things, so to speak, and he said he'd be happy to pass on your details, so if you like, I can do just that."

"Yes," I say. "Yes, yes, please. That would be great."

"Ah, good." He looks delighted with himself. "I'm glad I could help. Susan wasn't too sure but I get a feeling about these things. I've always had very good instincts."

I stay a few more minutes, listening without really listening as he talks me through a particularly risky bet he made on a horse when he was a young man. But my mind is on Stewarts. Stewarts, where I didn't even try to apply to, knowing I wouldn't get near the place. But a personal connection? That's different in my world, no matter how tenuous it might be.

This is something. It has to be.

CHAPTER 10

Dear Ms. Reynolds, many thanks for your recent application. Unfortunately...

Have you ever thought about teaching? Your cousin Alice teaches.

Dear Applicant, we regret to inform you...

She's in one of those alternative education schools though.

We will keep your details on file.

"Unstructured play," she calls it. It wouldn't be for me.

We wish you all the best.

Did you talk to your sister?

I slouch back on the cold metal chair, ignoring my mother's texts as I skim through the latest batch of rejections. They all read exactly the same. But at least these are the ones who got back to me.

"Donate now to help our fight against ocean pollution!"

Nothing yet from Stewarts. Obviously I wouldn't expect anything so soon but I still had a little bit of hope that everything might magically fall into place.

"Industrial fishing is destroying our waters!"

Maybe I could get a book deal. If Arnold could get a book deal, I could get a book deal. I just need an angle. Some kind of sexy commercial angle.

"Marine debris is killing our cetaceans!"

"What's a cetacean?" I call, sorting my rejections into my rejection folder.

Louise doesn't even turn around. "A whale."

"So just say that."

"Abby—"

"No one knows what a cetacean is."

She shoots me a harassed look before turning back to the muddy field.

"Donate now to save a whale!" she calls, shouting to no one in particular. "For as little as fifteen euro a month you can help us raise enough money to buy a new boat to monitor our waters for sightings and strandings of these endangered creatures."

An elderly woman covers her ears, glaring at us as she hurries past. I dump my phone back onto the table. I'm supposed to be keeping track of donations. Which I would happily do if there were any. "Louise?"

She ignores me, trying to get the attention of a young couple pushing a stroller. They smile politely at her with friendly "no thanks!" energy.

"Louise!"

"What!" she snaps.

"It's not working. You need to be more emotive."

"I didn't ask for your help."

"You literally asked for my help this morning."

"With setting up the stall. I know what I'm doing."

"We've been here for two hours and you haven't signed up a single person. And fifteen euros is not a little amount. Make it three and you'll get ten times as many people."

"I said I didn't ask for your—"

"Who wants juice?" Tomasz ducks under the flap with a tray of wheatgrass shots in his hands. "I took as many samples as I could without it being weird." He glances between the two of us as Louise turns stiffly away. "What happened?"

"I talked to her," I sigh as he hands me a shot.

"I told you not to do that."

"I can hear you," Louise says.

Tomasz grins at me and settles into the other chair.

We're at the Easter Fun Day. Or to use its proper title, the Clonard Easter Family Fun Day.

Whatever you want to call it, it's... not as fun as I remember. The games are still here. As are the activities and the chocolate and the man dressed up in a surprisingly decent bunny suit. But it's not as exciting when you're older than nine and I'm beginning to understand why my parents sat in the adult corner for the three hours it took for Louise and me to tire ourselves out. It doesn't help that I haven't been able to leave our stall and check out anything else. According to Louise, we're here to work, which again would be fine if she stopped scaring away anyone who came within five feet of us.

"What's on the list today?" Tomasz asks, nodding at my planner.

I hold it up, pointing to where I've written SAVE THE WHALES in large block capitals.

"Wow. You really are ambitious."

"She needs to change her fundraising tactic," I say as he knocks back his wheatgrass and immediately starts coughing. "You only have three seconds to get someone's attention. Her message is too confusing."

He wipes his mouth with the back of his hand. "You could help her," he says.

"I offered. You heard me offering."

"No, I heard you telling her what you thought she was doing wrong. That's not helping."

"It's my kind of helping." I glance at my phone as it buzzes with a text from Jess.

Can I get a train from London?

Crap. I'd really hoped she'd forgotten about the "I'm coming to see you" thing.

No, I reply. *There's a whole sea in between.*

Don't you have that sea train?

It's called the Eurotunnel and it's between England and France. Don't visit. The water's hard here and it will wreck your hair.

I send the text, knowing it won't be enough. Once Jess gets something into her head like this there's no going back.

"But we don't have any here." A stranger's voice drags my attention away and I look up to see Louise cornering a frowning woman in a bulky anorak.

"Just last week a bottlenose dolphin was spotted off Nimmo's Pier in Galway," Louise says. "All Irish waters within the Irish Exclusive Economic Zone are a whale and dolphin sanctuary and—"

"If it's already sanctuary then why do they need our help?" the woman interrupts.

"Maybe you could go on some expeditions with her," Tomasz says as they start to argue. "Or to the speeches she gives at the schools. Spend some quality time together."

"I know what you're doing," I say. "And it's a kind thought. But the last time we went a day without wanting to kill each other I was five years old. We're not going to be friends."

"You don't have to be friends," he says. "Friendlier maybe."

"You try talking some sense into her. She's not going to listen to me." I shove my phone into my pocket and pick up a stack of leaflets from the table. "Tell her she needs some stuffed animals. And a poster of *Free Willy*."

"Where are you going?"

"To drop these off at other stalls. I'm no use sitting here."

I sneak out the back of the tent before Louise can notice. The atmosphere changes immediately when I do. Besides the force field around our little patch, the Easter Fun Day is packed with families and locals from the surrounding towns and villages. Only instead of a few folding tables with homemade brownies and cups of tea, there are dozens of professional stalls selling everything from local honey to bog stones to hand-painted pottery, all with signs telling you to follow them on Instagram. A few even accept Bitcoin.

But it's nice. Charming, even. And among the slicker setups I spy a few neighbors still selling brownies, though now they come with a list of allergies and a salted caramel option.

I take my time walking through them, dropping off leaflets and saying hello as I make my way to the edge of the forest, where, standing behind a picnic table, is Andrew O'Donoghue, the original organizer of the fair. Back then he'd been a middle-aged busybody. Now he looks like a slightly older middle-aged busybody, in his element as he directs a horde of children toward the petting zoo, which consists of one sheep, two guinea pigs, a very bored looking goat, and someone's Labrador puppy who's slipped from its lead. A large chalkboard timetables the day's activities behind him along with all the raffle prizes.

"Your sister told me you were back," he says when I reach the front of the line. I'm still feeling a little flush from my recent clothes sales, so go crazy and buy two tickets for fifty cents each.

"I'm just visiting," I say, examining the table. "Everything looks really impressive, Andrew."

He falters, thrown by the praise. "Well... yes, thank you. Just because we're a small community doesn't mean we don't know how to put on a show. Will you be entering the egg hunt this year? It's ten euro."

"To enter? Are you serious?"

"It helps us maintain a high standard of prizes," he says, gesturing grandly to the list of things to be won.

To my surprise, it's not just misshapen pottery and match tickets for the local team up for grabs, but cash prizes now too: 250, 500...

"One thousand euros?"

"We were gifted it in a will a few years ago," Andrew says, only a little smug.

"Who leaves something for the Easter Fun Day in their will?"

"Someone who got a lot of enjoyment out of family activities," he says sharply. "It's the grand prize. Shall I put your name down?"

I have vague memories of scrambling around a muddy forest with a hundred other children looking for the same supermarket chocolate Mam had at home.

"I think I'll pass," I say, buying an extra ticket for a titanium flatiron.

"Then kindly stop taking up space." He makes a shooing motion with his hands and I obey, dropping some leaflets on the desk when he's not looking.

With nothing else to do, I start to loop back to Louise when I spot Beth jumping up and down at a small, cheerfully decorated stall, trying to keep warm.

"Abby!" Her voice is so loud several heads turn her way.

"Hi." I smile as I head toward her. "I didn't know you were—"

"Thank God, you're here," she interrupts. "Could you hold the fort for me? I really have to pee."

"Oh." I hesitate, glancing at the miniature coffee shop she's set up behind her. "By myself?"

"Two minutes tops. You just need to keep any customers here until I come back. Or try to sell them some pastries."

I'm already shaking my head. "Beth—"

"Thank you thank you thank you." She whips off her Coffee-branded apron and throws it at me.

"But—"

"Two minutes!" she calls, ducking under the flap.

"*Beth!*"

She's gone. And not only has she gone but her sudden fleeing has drawn attention. I smile at the curious looks as I fumble with the straps of the apron, squeezing behind the makeshift counter.

Okay. This isn't a problem. How many times have I watched someone make me coffee? How many times have I—

"Can I get a cappuccino?"

The man in front of me is already opening his wallet. "I... no."

"What do you mean no?"

"We don't have any."

He looks confused. "Can you not make one?"

"I don't know how to make coffee."

"But you're working at a coffee stall."

"I'm minding a coffee stall."

"But—"

"Abby?" Luke appears to my left, carrying a crate of supplies and looking at me as though I've grown two heads. "Where's Beth?"

"Peeing," I say without thinking before I turn back to the man. "Hygienically peeing. And then washing her hands."

Luke makes an "oh God" face and puts the crate down.

"Sorry about that," Luke says in a cheerful voice he never uses with me. "What can I get you?"

I stand awkwardly to the side as he makes the man's drink. And then two more for the woman after him and then a hot chocolate for an already sugar-crazed child before finally there's a break in the line and we're alone again.

"Beth asked me to mind the place," I say when he turns to me. "Who's looking after the café?"

"Ollie."

"Right." I watch as he does something complicated-looking with the machine. He's dressed for the cold in a beanie and a fitted black fleece. Tightly fitted. Tightly fitted and— "I'm here with Louise," I add before I start staring.

"You don't have to hang around."

"I know. But this stall is much nicer than her one." Though just as frosty. I glance about, looking for something to do. "Do you need—"

"How are you keeping, Mike?"

I fight back a sigh as he calls out to a passerby.

"Luke," the man greets, stopping near the table. "Not bad. Busy this morning?"

"Busy enough. The usual is it?"

"Ah, sure I've already had my cup today."

"Only one?" Luke begins to make the drink before Mike can say anything further. "Brenda here too?" he asks.

"Yeah, go on. Make hers a decaf though," Mike adds with a frown. "And I better get her one of those scones as well. She'll say she doesn't want it but then guess who'll be in trouble for not getting one."

"Always the way. I'll just—"

He breaks off when I step up beside him, using the tongs to slip one of the large raspberry scones into a paper bag like the little helper I am.

"You're good at that," I say when the man goes.

Luke shrugs, rifling through a box for more cups. "It's just talking to people."

"That can be harder than it sounds. Did you ever think about going into sales?"

"Nope."

Nope. I twirl the tongs in my hand, losing my patience. "So you're not going to look at me now, is that it?"

"I'm tired, Abby. Okay? I don't have the energy for this right now."

"This?"

"You."

Our eyes meet briefly but before I can snap back, I realize with some surprise that he does look tired. And not in the dark circles, bloodshot eyes, always yawning kind of way. His movements are a little slow, his frown lines more pronounced. He sounds tired too. His words not mean, more just brutally honest. When I don't respond he turns back to the crate, unloading stacks of branded paper cups and I know I should just leave him to it but I don't want to.

"Up studying?" I try again. "You're doing a physiotherapy course, right?"

"Year two of two. It's an accelerated MSc one so..."

"A lot," I finish. "Did you do it for your undergrad as well? I'm being polite," I add before he can ignore me again. "I'm making an effort and I'm being polite."

His lips twitch in the barest hint of a smile but I'll take it.

"I did science," he says. "I didn't know what I wanted to do with it until a few years ago." He knocks back an espresso shot and starts making another. "We don't all have it figured out at seventeen, I guess."

"Do you want to open your own practice?"

"Maybe." He hesitates, as if trying to decide how much to tell me. Luckily for me, with a mother like Susan, the man was trained to be polite. "I've been looking at sports medicine as well."

"Really? That's cool. I don't remember you playing sports when we were younger."

"That's because I didn't. It wasn't until I got to college."

"I'm a runner. Not competitively or anything but Tyler and I used to—"

Ah, crap.

Luke's jaw tightens at Tyler's name but before I can rescue the situation, Beth dips back under the tent. "Sorry! Line for the toilets was *manic*. That juice they're giving out must be going through everyone. I think I saw your sister," she adds to me. "She was yelling at an old woman?"

"That sounds like Louise." I shrug out of my apron, handing it back to her.

Luke passes her the tongs as she bounds up next to him and I watch as he pulls playfully on her apron strap. They fall instantly into easy movements around each other, used to working closely, and I realize once again I've become the third wheel.

"Do you want something?" Beth asks, gesturing to the machine.

I shake my head. "I should get back to my sister. Before all the cetaceans die out."

"The what?"

"Thanks for stepping in," Luke says shortly as a customer approaches.

Beth glances between us, starting to frown, but I squeeze back around the counter before she can say anything more.

"Have a busy day," I call, my voice unnaturally bright even to my ears.

In a determinedly worse mood, I drop off the remaining leaflets at some stalls near the front, procrastinating before I make my way back to my sister.

I find her sitting alone in the tent, not even bothering to try and win over visitors as she scrolls dejectedly through her phone. Tomasz isn't there, probably off to get more juice shots and I pause beside a stall selling pasta sauce and sock puppets as I watch her. She looks as tense as she always does, as if furious at everyone else for not seeing how the world is collapsing around them. Or for just not caring when she cares so much.

You could help her.

Tomasz's words come back to me and with it the familiar guilt I've felt over the past few weeks. Maybe we're just too alike. Too stubborn for our own good.

But I also know I never tried with her, using the excuse that she never tried with me. If anything, I enjoyed riling her up. Going in the opposite direction just to annoy her. Which is fine when you're six years old and fighting over the television, but not so much when you're both adults and you're all each other has.

And that's it, isn't it? She's my sister. My only sister. And if I didn't have her to turn to right now, I don't know where I'd be.

She puts her phone down, standing with an expectant look as she grabs her clipboard. Break over. But I turn on my heel before she can see me, almost tripping into the pasta sauce display as I head back to the forest where Andrew still stands, overseeing his kingdom.

"I've changed my mind," I say, depositing ten euro in coins on the table. "I'd like to enter the Easter egg hunt."

"We've closed entrants."

Oh.

"Closed at three," he continues, checking the sign up forms.

"But that was five minutes ago."

"Which doesn't make it any less true."

"But I want to—"

"Closed."

"Andrew, this is a family emergency." My hands go to my hips as a short line forms behind me. "And this is a *family* event. Are you seriously going to stop me, a paying attendee of the Clonard Easter Family Fun Day, from entering the Clonard Easter Family Fun Day Easter Egg Hunt just because—"

"Why is it that at every village celebration there is a Reynolds sister around to ruin my day?"

"Andrew!"

"Fine," he snaps. "Join the hunt, just keep your voice down." He smiles cheerfully at some wide-eyed children in the petting zoo beside us and shoves a signup page toward me. "Who's your partner?"

"My what?"

He sighs loudly. "You can only enter in a pair."

"Since when?"

He drops his voice. "We had a child go missing one year, only for a few minutes, mind you. She was found safe and sound but her parents threatened to sue and now I have to print out waiver forms. Also I'll need you to sign a waiver form."

"I'm an adult. I don't need a partner. I'm not going to wander off and get lost."

"I don't make the rules, Abby."

"Yes, you do!"

"I'm sure there's some introverted child who doesn't have a friend you can pair with."

"But—"

"I'll do it with you."

I freeze at the familiar voice and glance over my shoulder to see Luke standing right behind me.

"There now," Andrew says as I stare at him. "Thank you, Luke. It's nice to see you taking part for once."

"I don't need a partner," I repeat, turning back to him.

Andrew glares at me. "No partner. No egg. No money."

"Not that pairing with me will give you much luck there," Luke says, stepping past me to sign the form. "This will be the fifth year in a row without anyone winning the grand prize." He frowns thoughtfully. "Almost like it's impossible to find."

"Yes, well. It wouldn't be any fun if it were easy now, would it?" Andrew doesn't meet his gaze, fumbling with the microphone. "Don't forget to take a basket."

"You don't have to do this with me," I say to Luke as Andrew starts calling people to the edge of the woods.

"I could really use the money."

"So could I." And the last thing I need is to be distracted by him. "Unemployed and broke, remember?"

"Graduate student living in a studio apartment with no heating."

I ignore him and take a map from the table, examining the cartoon drawing of the forest and the winding paths interlocking inside it. A dozen clues are listed on the side for spot prizes. The last one is for a golden egg, which doesn't have any clue at all. You just have to find it, simple as that.

I can already picture it, emerging from the tree in a blaze of triumph. I'll give the money to Louise and then I'll be the good sister and when she's drowning in gratitude I'll simply tell her that the wedding is canceled and, oh, by the way, I might be staying here a little while longer while I— "Hey!"

Luke plucks the map from my hand as Andrew blares a novelty horn that makes a child near me start to cry.

"Shouldn't you be at the stall?" I ask as the rest of the participants run into the forest.

"Beth kicked me out," he says, examining the clues. He looks a little more awake now, probably from the five shots of coffee he just had. "I'm not supposed to come back until I apologize to you. Apparently I'm in a mood again."

"Well, apology accepted. You're free to— That's my map!"

Luke walks off without waiting for me and I'm forced to run after him, grabbing one of the small wicker baskets as I go, following him into the woods.

CHAPTER 11

We walk in silence, surrounded by shrieking children as we follow the trail. The sun shines weakly through the trees but it rained heavily this morning and the ground is soft and muddy beneath my feet, coating the sides of my sneakers. Every few steps, I get sprinkled from droplets still lingering on the leaves and eventually I pull my hood up, as one fat one catches me on the back of my neck.

"For someone who doesn't like me very much you're sure doing your best to spend a lot of time with me," I say as I dodge a chocolate-fingered toddler running away from her father.

Luke doesn't even turn around. "I'd spend a whole day with you if I got a thousand euros at the end of it."

"Five hundred euros."

"Half a day then."

I scowl as I halfheartedly pluck a few of the prizes "hidden" around us. I leave most for the kids, even though they quickly get bored and start heading back to the clearing so they can eat what they found. It's not the worst idea. No one else seems focused on finding the grand prize, which makes me think what Luke said to Andrew about no one winning it is true and I'm about to tell him to drop the whole thing when he suddenly veers left, heading deeper into the trees.

"Where are you going?" I ask, stopping on the edge of the path. "Do you know how to read a map?"

"Yes."

"Then you know that this part of the forest is *not on it*."

He keeps walking and because he has all the clues, so do I. It's not exactly Blair Witch territory. The forest isn't that big and even from here I can hear the noise from the clearing easily. But it's still a waste of my time.

"There are no eggs here."

"They're hidden," he says. "That's the whole point of the event."

"You know what I mean."

"You're not going to find it on the trail," he says. "No one has ever found it. I'm not even sure Andrew puts the egg in here. He just uses it to get people to take part so they can get money for next year."

"You think he cheats?"

"I think he chooses his words carefully. But you want to find it, so we'll try and find it. Someone came this way recently." He points to the ground. "There's footprints in the mud."

"Uh, okay, Mr. Hunter Man." I glare at his back as he keeps walking. "You better not get us lost."

"I know what I'm doing."

That's what people always say before they get lost. I unwrap a miniature chocolate egg, chewing it mournfully as Luke keeps five steps ahead of me, like I'm not even there.

I'm surprised by how much it bugs me. This acting like I'm nothing to him. Like we weren't halfway to the bedroom before he heard about Tyler. You don't just turn off a person that easily.

Another drop of water falls, this time square on my head, and I stop beside a swollen tree trunk, done. "This is dumb. Let's go back."

"Abby—"

"I'm serious."

"So am I. Would you just—" He breaks off as he turns, the annoyed look on his face vanishing in an instant.

"Would I just what?"

"You..."

My confidences slips a little. It's almost like he's fighting back a laugh.

"You used to do that all the time," he says finally. "I'd forgotten."

"Do what?"

He shifts his weight, sliding one foot out as his hands go to his hips. I realize with a start he's mirroring my stance and quickly drop my arms.

"When we were kids," he continues. "Whenever you wanted to pick a fight."

"I didn't pick fights."

"What TV shows we watched, what game we played—"

"I was a confident child."

"You were a brat," he snorts. "But I was a pushover, so I didn't help the situation. Come on. We'll hit the trail in about five minutes and then we can head back."

"And you can tell Beth that you did your duty?"

He tips his head back, glancing to the sky as if he's praying for patience. Maybe he is.

My irritation fades, leaving a hollow kind of hurt in its place.

I've never really cared what people think of me. It never bothered me if I came off as too cold or too pushy or too ambitious. I didn't have time to care. But with Luke...

"I didn't waltz, you know."

He looks at me in bewilderment. "What?"

"You said before that I waltzed back here, like it meant nothing. But it was really hard. Coming back here was hard. It's still hard."

"And you want points for that, is that it?"

"*No*. But I want you to..."

He raises a brow when I don't continue. "To what?"

I frown, distracted, as something glimmers in the corner of my eye. "To understand that I'm..." There it is again.

"Abby?"

I don't answer, walking past him to a large oak tree up ahead. It could just be a piece of trash but it's very...

"There." I point at the golden egg nestled high in the branches.

Luke stands next to me, following my finger. "Holy shit."

"That can't be following health and safety regulations," I say, staring up at it.

"I'll find a stick."

"You won't be able to reach that high."

He ignores me, kicking away leaves on the ground as he looks for a fallen branch.

"It's too far up," I insist. I eye the rest of the tree. It's high. But Andrew had to get someone to put it there in the first place. Unless he just threw it.

"You could help, you know," Luke calls from somewhere behind me.

I don't answer, shaking a low branch. It doesn't move and, as Luke shuffles around behind me, I circle the trunk, marking out my path. Or at least trying to. I'm not sure if I'm doing it right or what I should be looking for. But if I can make it to that bough I should be able to...

"What are you doing?" he asks as I grab hold of the first branch again and pull myself up.

"MacFarlane had a wall-climbing room."

"Was that beside the room where they kept all their stolen money?"

"I'm choosing not to respond to that." My arm muscles burn after weeks of no training but I manage to last a few seconds before falling back down.

"Let me—"

I try again, cutting Luke off as this time I successfully hoist myself onto the branch. "I'm good at climbing," I explain, eyeing the next one.

"That's great. Now get down."

"Just let me try."

"You're going to fall and break something."

"I'm not twelve years old."

"Then stop acting like it."

The next one isn't as sturdy, so I eye another a little farther away. Thank God I wore leggings instead of jeans this morning.

"Abby? Could you just— Christ!"

I swing out my leg, my foot making contact with the branch as I cling to the bark of the trunk.

"I'm *Free Solo*-ing," I call as I swing myself forward. "This is my Yosemite."

"Would you stop?" He's angry now, but I've never felt surer of myself. With each branch I pass the egg gets closer. That money gets closer. And the look on Louise's face when I show up with the stupid prize gets so clear it's like she's right in front of me. "What are you trying to prove right now?"

"I'm not trying to prove anything! I'm trying to get the stupid egg to give to my stupid sister!"

"Your sister?"

He sounds confused. Of course he does. As if he'd ever think I had a heart. "I'm going to give the money to her," I explain. "Not that you'd ever assume that. You'd much rather think the worst of me." I bring myself level with the egg. "You and Louise always act like I have the worst possible motivations. Like I'm only here to mess with you."

"Aren't you?"

"No!" I take a swipe at the egg and risk a glance down to see Luke staring up at me. From this angle, the ground looks very far away, even though it can't be more than a couple of feet. "I wasn't trying to lead you on, Luke. I don't do things like that."

"Fine. Come down."

"I mean it," I say, trying to reach the egg again. "I thought you were cute so I flirted with you. I don't cheat. I've never cheated in my life."

"Then why didn't you tell me you were engaged?"

"Because I'm not!" I exclaim. "I lied, okay? I don't have a fiancé."

"What?"

"I said I don't—" I yelp as my left hand slips from the branch. Something hard whacks against my shoulder and suddenly I'm falling, the wind whistling past my ears for approximately two seconds before I land flat on my ass in the mud.

Ow.

"Abby?" Luke's concerned face floats above me. "Are you okay?"

"No," I moan. "I fell like twelve feet."

"It was four feet. Don't move," he adds when I try to sit up. "You could have a concussion."

"The chivalrous thing would have been to break my fall," I mutter as he glances over me.

"Then I would be the one on the ground."

I blink up at the foliage above. "Did you just make a joke? A joke when I'm dying? *Ow*."

"Sorry," he mutters, pressing lightly on my shoulder. He leans back, seemingly satisfied that I didn't break every bone in my body.

"Did I get the egg?"

"No," he says. "But you did do some damage."

I ease myself into a sitting position as Luke picks up a sturdy branch near the trunk of the tree. No doubt I have that to thank for the pain in my shoulder.

I watch as he hoists himself onto the first branch before swinging it deftly above his head. Leaves rustle frantically and a moment later there's a light thump on the ground.

The egg is ours.

"How's that for teamwork?" I ask.

"I said don't move," he says, exasperated. "You might have broken something."

"Besides my pride?" I wince as I shift into a better position. It hurts a little but I'm not too bad. The mud must have helped.

He crouches beside me, still looking worried as somewhere in the distance a horn blares, telling people to come back to the clearing.

"We should get back," I say. "Tell everyone how heroic I am and then get our money."

But Luke doesn't budge. "What do you mean you lied about having a fiancé?"

I sigh, wiggling my toes to see if they still work. "Exactly that. Tyler broke it off a few weeks ago."

"But Louise said—"

"She thinks we're still engaged. I didn't tell anyone except a few friends. That's why I wasn't wearing the ring and then I was wearing the ring and then I wasn't again. It's because I dug a big liar's hole for myself and I couldn't get out of it."

Luke Bailey does not have a poker face. Not like Tyler, with whom I was constantly trying to guess what he was thinking. With Luke, I can see every emotion clear on his face and so I don't watch as he processes what I just said to him. Mostly because I'm scared of what I'll see.

"I just didn't want you to think I was cheating on him," I say. "I'm not that kind of person. But I guess you don't know what kind of person I am because you don't know me. And that's because—" I break off when he touches me, brushing a hand by my temple.

"Leaf," he explains, holding it up as proof.

Leaf.

He drops it to the ground, his brow creased. "I had a girlfriend in college," he says after a beat. "She broke up with me the day before she was supposed to meet my parents, and instead of telling them, I went alone and pretended she had the flu. Mam did a surprise visit a few weeks later and I told her she moved to Lithuania."

"Lithuania?"

"It was the first place that came into my head. To this day, I have no idea why. I came clean then, obviously, but my first instinct was to lie. I didn't want to have to deal with their reaction, not when I didn't know my own yet."

"You get it," I say, relieved. It's not until then that I realize how much I needed him to.

"I think so, yeah." He sits fully on the ground beside me, not seeming to care about the mud. "I wish you hadn't lied to me. But I can see why you did."

He flinches then, wiping his forehead as a breeze shakes more raindrops from the trees. The brief pause allows me to take him in, the day's worth of stubble on his jaw, the green of his eyes startlingly bright as he peers mistrustfully upward. I swallow as the memory of what happened the last time we were this close flashes through my mind, and his gaze snaps back to me as though knowing exactly where my thoughts went.

"Can we start over?" I ask to distract him.

"What do you mean?"

"Just pretend like the last few weeks didn't happen? We can be friends. Or friendly at least."

He doesn't answer for a long moment and I begin to wonder if I've seriously misjudged this whole conversation when he sighs. "Beth didn't send me after you today," he says. "I told you she sent me to apologize? She didn't. I followed you because I felt bad. I've been feeling bad for the last few days. I just didn't know how to make up for it."

"So you lied to me too."

"A much smaller one," he says, giving me a look. "But yes. And yes, we can be friends."

"Friends with five hundred euro each."

"You can keep the money, Abby. I was only trying to annoy you."

"No, it was teamwork. Plus you need it just as much as I do."

He starts to argue when he frowns. "I guess I do."

"Then we'll split it," I say before he can change his mind. "It's still four hundred and ninety-five more than Louise was expecting today anyway."

He smiles but it fades quickly, his expression turning serious as he helps me up. "I'm sorry about Tyler."

"Thanks. Me too. But I'm okay. I'm actually starting to think..." I hesitate, embarrassed, but he just waits patiently, no judgement on his face. "I think he made the right call breaking it off," I say. "And honestly? In the weeks after it happened I was more upset about having to tell everyone we were done rather than *being* done. Like I missed the life he gave me more than I missed him." I push my hair back, finding a small twig. "I know how that sounds," I add, flicking it to the ground.

"It sounds like you're moving on. Would you prefer to be heartbroken?"

"No," I admit.

"If you were sad, people would tell you to cheer up. You can't win. So don't overthink it."

I sigh. "You're a nice guy, you know that?"

"So my mother tells me."

"I'm sorry I didn't tell you the truth. And I'm sorry I accosted you on the street and made you sleep on your couch."

He laughs at that, a surprised huff that makes his eyes crinkle. "It wasn't the best night's sleep I've had."

"You should try my bed," I say without thinking. "I mean, because the mattress is like thirty years old and—"

"Abby."

I clamp my mouth shut. "Maybe I do have a concussion."

"We'll get Tomasz to take a look. Can you walk?"

"I can try," I say gravely, and he smiles to himself, tossing the egg into the air as we make our way back to the clearing.

CHAPTER 12

It barely takes us a few minutes to reach the edge of the forest, even though I'm limping slightly from my fall. The prize-giving ceremony is already underway and dozens of people gather around Andrew, despite the heavy gray clouds overhead, threatening to burst.

"Maybe we should wait until everyone's finished," I suggest, and Luke starts to nod when Andrew catches sight of us.

"And it looks like *some* people got a little too caught up in all the excitement." He gestures toward us and our muddied clothes, throwing a knowing look at the adults in the crowd. "Took a little trip off the trail, did we?"

I turn to Luke. "Or maybe—"

"On it."

He holds up the golden egg and a child in front of us gasps like it's the holy grail. Silence falls over the crowd as everyone stares at us.

"This is weird," I mutter.

Luke starts toward Andrew, who's now openly glaring at us. "Yep."

"You found the egg," he says. He does not sound pleased.

"We did." Luke holds it up again for effect and I grin as a man nearby starts to clap. It's not even that impressive up close. Made of cheap plastic and painted gold for effect. Still, I guess it's the symbol that counts.

"We'll take that prize now," Luke says as Andrew's face goes white. "In cash."

"Abby!"

I leave Andrew to his disappointed grumbling as Louise winds her way through the crowd.

"What did you do to yourself? You're filthy."

My smile drops at her disapproving tone. "Well done on winning the grand prize, Abby."

"I only meant—"

"The victors!" Tomasz swoops in to hug me only to immediately let go when his hands come away covered in dirt.

Louise stands back, still eyeing my clothes as though calculating how many laundry pods it will take to get them clean.

"It was all Abby," Luke says, joining us. "I just tagged along for the ride." He hands me an envelope. "That's your share. I better get back to Beth." He pauses, momentarily awkward. "I'll see you around?"

"Definitely," I say, a little too quickly, and he smiles at me.

"Your share of what?" Louise asks as he leaves.

"Of my winnings. I entered on your behalf." I hold out the prize but she's already shaking her head.

"I can't take that. It's yours."

"I won it for you."

"I don't—"

"I'll take it." Tomasz grabs the envelope and forces it into Louise's hands. "Thank you for your kind donation, Abby."

"No problem," I mutter as Louise's frown deepens.

Well, that didn't go as planned.

With the main event of the day over, the crowd around us starts to disperse and we head back to pack up. Louise keeps fiddling with the edge of the envelope but says nothing to me. She says nothing to anyone, pretending to be busy counting signups and soon even Tomasz gives up trying to deal with her, disappearing off to get the car.

"Can we talk?" I ask when we're alone.

She doesn't look up from the calculator on her phone, even when I sit beside her. "I guess."

"Can we actually talk?"

Her eyes flick to mine, the distracted look on her face replaced by instant wariness. "Okay."

Okay.

"I—"

"Are you sick?"

I pause, confused as Louise brings one hand to her heart.

"Is that why you came back? You're sick, aren't you? I knew you—"

"I'm not sick," I interrupt. "At least not that I'm aware of."

"You're not?"

"No."

"Then why do you look so serious?"

"That's just my face!"

"Abby!" We're back to angry now. "Don't scare me like that. Why do you have to be so dramatic about everything?"

"I'm *sorry*." I resist the urge to bang my head against the table as she turns back to her work. "Look, I wanted to talk about me staying longer than we originally discussed."

"Oh yeah?" She smooths out another donation form, almost tearing it. "How long are we talking?"

"Another week maybe. Or two. Five. I don't know," I say when she looks up again. "I don't really have anywhere else to go."

"No shit."

"What?"

"*I haven't booked my flight yet*," she says in a perfect imitation of me. "A child could come up with a better excuse."

I blink at her. "You knew?"

It's the wrong thing to say.

The phone goes down with a bang as she turns to me, her jaw set. "I know I'm not as smart as you, Abby, but just how stupid do you think I am?"

"You *knew*?"

"You call me out of the blue asking if you can visit and then you arrive with a very large suitcase filled with random crap that no one needs for a two-week trip to Clonard. Who brings summer dresses to the west of Ireland in March? You seriously think I didn't know something was up? When was the last time you even *called* me?"

"But you—"

"I kept waiting for you to tell me. I gave you multiple openings and each time you lied, and you've been acting so *weird* about the engagement and about Tyler and I just..." She slumps back in her chair, crossing her arms, and for one moment she looks so much like our dad that I'm a little freaked out. "So what happened?" she asks. "You broke up with him, right? You broke up with Tyler and you moved out and then you lost your job and now you have nowhere else to go? I mean, I'm glad to see you finally came to your senses, but—"

"He broke up with *me*."

There's a loud bleating to our left as Andrew herds the petting zoo animals past our stall. I barely risk them a glance as Louise, in a feat I didn't know was possible, gets even more irate.

"He *what*?"

"Louise—"

"That dick!" She's furious. "He proposed to you!"

"Yes."

"And then he just what? Changed his mind?"

"Apparently so."

"When?" she asks sharply. "When did it happen? Because if it was after MacFarlane, I swear to God I'll—"

"It was before," I interrupt. "A few weeks before. He's actually tried to get in touch with me since but I'm not really talking to him. Or I'm trying not to or..." I trail off, suddenly tired. "It had nothing to do with that," I finish lamely. "He didn't want to marry me, so he didn't. It was just me."

I must sound as pathetic as I feel because she swallows her next words.

"Why didn't you tell me?" she asks.

"I was going to as soon as I came home but I was late and you made pancakes and you were annoyed at me and—"

"I wasn't annoyed at you."

"You're always annoyed with me."

"Because you're annoying," she snaps. "And apparently a liar now too."

"I was embarrassed, okay? It's humiliating getting dumped at the best of times, but getting dumped by your fiancé a few weeks before your company goes under sucks even more. I didn't want everyone to know how I messed everything up."

"Oh, this is so you. Acting like you're in control of everything. Sometimes bad things happen, Abby. No matter what you do." She eyes me moodily. "Who else knows? Mam and Dad?"

I nod. "And I just told Luke."

"Of course you did. You can't flirt with him if he thinks you're cheating on someone. Don't," she adds when I go to object. "Every tourist who comes here tries their luck with him. Ever since he hit late puberty."

My mouth drops open. "You said you didn't notice!"

"I'm not blind."

"Then how come at the restaurant you said—"

"Because I thought you were engaged!" she exclaims. "And that was after you two made heart eyes at each other over lunch. I didn't want you messing around with him. Especially when he used to have that silly little crush on you."

When he what? I stare at her, wide-eyed but she's not looking at me, her gaze on the emptying field outside the stall.

"I can't believe you didn't think you could talk to me," she says. "You can stay as long as you need to. You don't ever have to worry about something like that. You know that, right?"

I nod even though I didn't. I now realize I didn't know that at all and maybe that was just one of the reasons I was so worried about telling her in the first place.

"Thank you."

She shrugs, still not meeting my eye.

"What did you mean when you said you thought I'd come to my senses?"

"Nothing," she says. If I didn't know any better, I'd say she looked a little embarrassed. "I guess I wasn't Tyler's biggest fan."

"You never met him."

"Yeah, and who's fault is that? Three years together and I never met the man who was going to be your husband. You were in New York, Abby, not on the moon."

I don't point out that she wouldn't have come even if I'd invited her. But she's right. There's no reason why Tyler and I couldn't have come here. But Tyler had never really shown an interest in Ireland. Besides a few questions when we first met, he never once asked about my childhood. And I never talked about it.

"Dad said he never liked him."

"Dad was half in love with the man," Louise huffs. "But he loves you more so, of course, he'd say that. What did Mam say?"

"She was more concerned about the wedding plans."

"You know she was worried about you right? As soon as the news of MacFarlane broke. She lost her mind with it."

I sigh, feeling bad. "I should have spoken to them more at the time."

"You had to look after yourself first. They get that. Plus they've always been a little bit in awe of you. Their genius child with too much confidence for her own good."

"And you?" I ask, trying to lighten the mood. "Were you in awe of me?"

"I seem to be the only one who remembers you thinking that it only rained when you personally did something bad."

"Because that's what Dad *told* me."

"Or that time you were convinced that cow was following you home from—"

"Okay," I interrupt. "I get it."

She smirks as it becomes my turn to scowl.

"Of course I was in awe of you," she says, surprising me. "I still am. You decided what you wanted to do and you did it. Everyone thought you would drop out of MacFarlane. Everyone thought you would drop out of college. Hell, everyone thought you would drop out of honors maths at school but you did it. Every time. You proved everyone wrong. And you'll do it again."

"Careful," I say, trying not to show how touched I am by her words. "That almost sounds like a compliment."

"Yeah, well..." She looks away, clearing her throat. "Is that it? Any more bombshells to tell me about?"

"Not today."

"Then do you want to help triple-count our signups?"

Her finger traces random shapes on the table as she waits for my answer. It's probably the closest we'll get to a hug.

"I'd love to," I say.

And when Tomasz returns five minutes later he finds us side by side, doing just that.

CHAPTER 13

It gets a little easier after that. A week passes and with it my initial leaving date and suddenly there's no more pretending that I'm here for a visit but for as long as it takes. And while a job doesn't magically fall into my lap, it's nice not to lie to people anymore. Nice not to have to pretend that everything's okay when it's not.

Louise gives me the old laptop to work from and I throw myself back into the job hunt, reaching out to every contact I have from New York, from London, from friends of friends Jess sends my way. Some respond to my emails, some even lead to first-round phone calls but the answer is always the same. There are simply too many of us looking for the same jobs and no matter my experience or my skill, the door remained closed.

I don't see Luke. He must have meant it when he said he was barely around. Beth tells me that with the schools off for Easter he's wrapped up in the sports camps for a bit of extra cash on top of studying. We ended things well at the fair, but I can never think of an excuse to stay late enough to see him again. Instead, I take to sitting on the bench in the café, working away while Beth chats to me and the slowly increasing number of customers who come in as the season changes.

The good weather and the Easter break draw families to the village and, as if on cue, a handful of pop-up stores and restaurants join them, meaning the vacant streets aren't so vacant. Beth's slushie machine gets dusted off and I convince her to move the bench back and display it in the window in order to compete with the new gelato place across the road.

One day, toward the end of the week, Rory comes back for the promised beach trip and this time is accompanied by his wife.

Sinead is a petite redheaded woman with a fake tan line up to her neck, who looks at me skeptically as soon as I get into the back seat of his car.

"Rory says you were his first girlfriend," she says by way of introduction. "I didn't believe him."

"It's true," I say. "For a very angsty four months."

"Told you," he mutters, and she turns to him with an impressed look.

"Look at you," she says. "Punching above your weight. Do you like the beach, Abby? I hate the beach and yet this is where my husband takes me on my precious time off."

"I like tropical beaches."

"You'll both love it," Rory dismisses. "Chilly wind, warm beer."

"Stop," Sinead says. "This is so much better than the romantic B&B I wanted to book. It's our anniversary," she tells me, twisting around again.

"It is not," Rory says.

"It's one of our anniversaries."

"Which one?" I ask, liking her more by the minute.

"The first time he saw me naked."

I grin. "You have an anniversary for the first time you had sex?"

"No one said anything about sex," Rory mutters. "And we're not telling the story."

"He was sleeping with my roommate," she explains as he groans. "That's all he was to me for months. The man who was always in my kitchen when I wanted to cook. And then one morning my roommate's gone to work, I'm getting out of the shower and he walks in without even knocking."

"I didn't know you were in there and your shitty student apartment didn't have a lock."

"He sees me. *Freaks* out. Slips on the floor and whacks his head off the toilet. I spent six hours waiting with him in the emergency room. Turns out I would have spent six days with him if I had to. I thought he was the funniest, most interesting person I'd ever met."

"Some couples spot each other across a crowded dance floor," Rory says. "We have that."

"What happened to the roommate?" I ask.

"She's doing okay," Sinead says. "She has a three-legged dog with sixty thousand followers on Instagram."

"She's also has her own dental practice," Rory says. "As well as the dog thing. Remember we talked about putting normal achievements first?"

"And to think," Sinead sighs. "If I was someone who showered in the evenings, none of this would ever have happened."

"Please stop trying to make it romantic."

I smile to myself as we turn out of the village. "Is Beth not coming?" Rory had texted earlier to say that she was.

"The fridge at the café broke, so she's getting someone out to fix it," he says. "She'll catch a ride with Sean later. You remember my cousin?"

I nod. A year or two younger, he used to live up the road from Rory.

"I think his partner, Harry, is joining. Sounds like we'll have ourselves a little gang." He grins at me in the rearview mirror. "Hope you enjoy in-jokes you don't understand."

It takes an hour to get to the beach. Despite the sun shining overhead, there's a chill on the breeze and I'm relieved I brought an old school sweatshirt of Louise's. I also borrowed one of her swimsuits. And a T-shirt. She'd handed over all three items with pursed lips before suggesting we take a trip to the local superstore a few towns over to stock me up on the *essentials*.

Now I take a deep breath, tasting the tang of the ocean. The horizon seems impossibly far, a misty white line that looks like I can pinch it with my fingers and pull toward me. Several thousand miles straight ahead is the edge of Canada with plenty of storms and sea monsters and "I'm flying, Jack" icebergs in the way. But right here are green cliffs and yellow sand and three ice cream trucks competing for customers. It's a place I've been to dozens of times before, but I'm surprised by the sudden pull I feel for it and look longingly at the people in the water, all of them with big goofy grins on their faces.

"Luke's not done yet."

"What?" I glance sharply at Rory as he joins me.

"Luke." Rory nods to the water where I can just make him out teaching a bunch of children how to stand on a surfboard.

"You didn't tell me he was joining."

He gives me a long look. "Is that a problem?"

"No."

"Mm-hm." But he drops it. "We're going to drive to the village and get some supplies. Well, I say supplies. I mean beer."

I look back to the water. "I think I'll stay. I want to go in the ocean for a bit before it gets too cold."

Rory makes a face. "Children pee in there."

"You mean you pee in there. I'm going to rent a wetsuit and go paddleboarding. Come find me when you're back."

"You know they don't actually clean those things," he calls after me. "They just throw them into a vat of disinfectant and offer up a prayer."

I ignore him and head to the little hut where I pay ten euro for an hour with a board and a wetsuit. It's not exactly top-of-the-range material and I almost twist my arm trying to pull the zipper up. But eventually I manage it and make my way to the shore.

I used to love playing in the water. I spent my summers by the sea in the sun and the wind and the rain and whatever else the west coast of Ireland threw at us. It was always more fun in the rain. Rain meant bigger waves, more squealing, more frantic movements as I ran from the water to the car where my dad would hold out a towel to wrap me in and not even bother to rub me dry, just bundle me into the back seat before my hands turned blue. Swimming in the sea as an adult meant brief vacation days with Tyler or expensive weeks away with Jess. It meant fine white sand and crystal blue water and floating around in a bikini, not whatever survival gear it is Louise has given me.

Picking up my steps, I grab a spare bodyboard from a pile by the edge, catching Luke's eye as I pass. He holds up a hand in greeting before immediately getting distracted by two kids screaming at each other. It's the most interaction we've had in days.

I enter the water, keeping within eyesight of the lifeguards. Everyone knows the currents could whip you up strong over here and though there's thankfully been no accidents in my lifetime, Mam had plenty of horror stories of people swept away. I'm not sure any of them were true, probably just tales to scare off any intention of straying too far but they still stick with me, so I paddle out only a few meters and practice standing on the board as I wait for the waves to come in.

It's nothing compared to the surfing in America or even down the coast here, where the white foamy waves draw people from around the world. This is gentle kids' stuff but it's also all I can manage for a few minutes before my body gets predictably cold and my muscles grow tired. Barely fifteen minutes in I start to get winded and I soon give up, heading back to the beach as literal children move smoothly and skillfully around me.

I'm almost at the sand when it happens. I hop off the board, tugging it behind me as the water reaches my knees but two steps in and I feel it, a sharp pain in my foot, like someone poked me with a branding iron.

I stop where I stand as the stinging grows in intensity, gazing into the water for the offending piece of trash or rock beneath me. But I don't see either. Instead, to my left I spy a few slithering blobs floating away.

A jellyfish sting. A goddamn jellyfish sting.

The burning sensation doesn't fade, so I hobble back to the beach where I sit with a thud, stretching out my leg to see a small red rash already forming on the top of my foot.

"You need to pee on it."

"What?" I glance up to see a boy standing beside me, no more than six or seven.

"You need to pee on it," he says. "Mum told me."

"Great."

"Do you want me to pee—"

"*No,*" I say sharply.

The kid only shrugs and runs off. By now, the beach is starting to empty, cars leaving en masse as the summer camp winds up, but I see Rory walking along the shoreline, clearly looking for me.

I yell his name and he waves, jogging over to my deathbed.

"What happened to you?" he asks. "Shark bite?"

"Jellyfish."

The smile drops from his face. "Seriously? Are you okay?"

"I can handle it. It's just sore."

"Do you want me to—"

"If you suggest peeing on it, Rory, I swear to God I'll—"

"Seawater will help."

"I was just in the sea!" I exclaim. "That's how I got like this in the first place."

He ignores me, hoisting me up before helping me hobble down to the edge of the water.

"What if it's a dangerous one?" I mutter as I dip my foot back in. "The Portuguese ones."

"There are no Portuguese ones around here and Sinead has some painkillers in the car. Hold still," he adds. "You're squirming."

"Because I'm in *pain*." But I do as he says and after a while, the burning lessens a bit.

"Better?" he asks.

"A bit." I flex it in the water. "But I need to get out of this wetsuit."

He grins. "You want some help with that?"

"You wish."

"If Sinead's your problem, I'm telling you now she'd love to join in."

I laugh as he helps me limp back up the beach. My bag and clothes are where I left them on the towel and I shake them out as Rory aims for the parking lot.

"I have to get the stuff out of the car," he says. "The bonfire will be at the north beach. And hey," he calls as I head toward the stalls. "Just because you're injured doesn't mean you're getting out of carrying stuff."

I wave a hand to show I've heard him and lock myself in one of the changing cubicles by the toilets. They're cold and cramped inside with barely any room to move. I hang my towel on the rusting metal hook, wrinkling my nose against the stench of the sea, sweat, and bleach as I reach back to yank the zipper down. It doesn't budge.

I yank harder, my fingers fumbling now as they stiffen. Warm-blooded people will never understand the struggle. Taking a breath, I try again, my shoulder protesting as I try and angle my arms into positions they should not be in.

"Abby?" Luke's voice sounds on the other side of the door accompanied by a knock. "Rory said you got stung. Are you okay?"

"I'm fine," I call as I almost wrench my arm out of its socket. I mumble a curse word, which Luke must hear because he doesn't leave.

"Do you need some help?"

"No."

"I've got a first aid kit in my car."

"I'm fine," I say. "I just need to— Crap." I give the zipper another pull and lose my footing on the wet floor, banging my elbow painfully against the wall as I try to keep my balance.

"I'm coming in."

"No, don't!" I scramble for the door, shutting his progress.

There's a short pause. "Are you naked?"

"No."

Another pause. "Are you stuck in your wetsuit?"

Kill me now. "Yes."

"Then let me in the door."

I think about asking him to get someone else, but I doubt he'd do that. It's something I'm learning about Luke. He's not one to leave a damsel in distress. Even if that distress is due to something really fricking stupid.

I undo the latch and step back as far as I can. Which isn't that far at all. "Okay," I call when I make sure my underwear isn't just hanging around anywhere.

He slips inside, glancing over me as though looking for any obvious signs of injury. He's still in swimming trunks, his feet bare, his skin wet. There's sand in his hair.

"The zipper's stuck," I say as if that weren't obvious.

"So you were just going to stay in it for the rest of time?"

"Potentially."

Luke only shakes his head. "It's okay to ask for help, Abby."

He takes a step farther inside, closing the door so we can both fit, and I turn in an awkward shuffle, careful not to let my body touch his.

We stay like that for a microsecond, me with my back to him, and I hear him take one perfectly normal breath while meanwhile my entire body seems to hum, vibrating from the very presence of him.

He tugs my hair free and I flinch when his fingers meet my skin.

"Sorry," he mutters. "Cold hands."

"That's my line."

Luke doesn't respond, pulling gently on the zipper and then harder when it doesn't budge.

In an ideal world, my fantasy world, he would seductively bring the zipper down, marveling at the hint of my skin as he brushes my wet hair from my shoulders. He'd be overcome by the delicate curve of my neck, maybe even press a kiss to it, which I'd graciously allow before turning my head to face his and then—

"Hold still." He yanks on it a third time and I yelp as he catches a bit of my hair. "Sorry," he says. "These things are really old. I'm going to have to get a pair of scissors."

"No. Just pull it." I brace my hands against the concrete wall.

Luke hesitates. "I'm either going to rip it or hurt you."

"You're not going to hurt me and it doesn't matter if you rip it. You were going to cut it up anyway." I close my eyes, concentrating on the cold concrete under my palms. "Hurry up before I freeze to death."

He holds the fabric in place as he yanks it again, hard enough to make me lose my grip on the wall and we both slip backward, Luke into the door and me into Luke.

For one humiliating moment we're aligned, his chest hard against my back, his trunks leaving little to the imagination even through the rubber of my suit. I feel his breath on my hair. I feel everything.

"Abby?" Luke's voice is tight.

"Sorry!" I push myself off him, adopting my previous position as I start to babble. "You know what? It's fine. Get the scissors. Or I'll just live like this. I'll adapt. I'm very—"

I stop talking when his hand lands heavily on my shoulder, keeping me faced forward. His foot taps my left ankle, and I slide it out so I've got a steadier stance.

"Let's try again," he says, and I nod, not trusting myself to speak.

It takes two more goes, then another breath, another pull, and this time there's movement as something aligns and I sigh in relief as cold air hits the nape of my neck.

The zipper gets stuck halfway down my back but it's enough to free my arms, and Luke helps me as I clumsily peel it over my hips and down my legs while making sure my swimsuit stays in place. I'm covered more than a lot of people on the beach, but he's still standing far too close and I'm aware of every stretchmark, every pucker of skin and goosebump, as my blood works overtime to keep me warm.

Before I can stop him, Luke crouches to tug the suit free of my ankles. "Is your sting okay?"

"It's just itchy now. I'll get some cream."

He doesn't say anything and I look over my shoulder to see him examining the rash in a thoroughly unromantic way.

"All done," I say sharply, and he rises as I face him. "Here." I hand him the sodden mass of rubber that is the wetsuit. "We can burn it on the bonfire."

He accepts it wordlessly, his gaze sliding down my body, and this time I don't think he's concerned about the sting. As if realizing what he's doing, his eyes snap back to mine, his neck flushing a gentle pink.

"You should get dressed," he says. "We'll be on the other side of the dunes." And in the space of a second, he slips back out and disappears.

CHAPTER 14

My leg no longer stinging but definitely itchy, I dress quickly, grateful for my dry clothes as the late April evening grows cool. Rory's waiting for me beside the car and I help him carry a box of food and a few beers through the long grass of the dunes and into the hidden but not really hidden section of beach on the other side.

This stretch of sand is small and only accessible through the awkward trek we're making now. With no lifeguards and nothing obvious to tell you it's there, the tourists don't use it and it's avoided too by locals, too small and patchy compared to the bigger beach. But it's perfect for times like this with the tide slowly drifting out and the sun still lingering.

"Is this the beach they're selling off?" I ask.

Rory frowns. "I didn't hear that."

"That's Castlebay," a voice says behind me. I turn to see a short, stocky man carrying an armful of driftwood. "It's about a mile south of here. Thanks," he adds as I take some of the sticks. "Nice to see you again, Abby."

"You remember Sean," Rory says.

"I do. Hi."

"Luke told me you were back," Sean says.

"Just for a visit."

We reach the fire, dumping the wood in a small pile. "My boyfriend, Harry," he introduces, gesturing to the man sitting cross-legged beside Sinead in front of the fire. "Who's put himself in charge of the beer rather than doing something useful."

"The beer doesn't give you splinters," Harry says. "And it's nice to meet you."

"What's this about Castlebay?" Rory asks.

"Louise says they want to build a hotel there," I explain. "Privatize the beach."

"You're joking! I love that beach."

Sinead rolls her eyes. "When was the last time you were even there?"

"That's not the point. The point is I should be able to go back whenever I want. I pay my taxes."

I leave them to argue as Beth appears through the grass, carrying a picnic basket with one hand and dragging a gym bag with the other.

"Thank you," she says when I jog over to help. "That walk is harder than it looks."

I grab the spare handle, grunting at its weight. "What do you have in here?"

"Luke insisted we bring water," she says. "Ever the adult."

"One of us has to be," Luke says, coming up behind us. He trades me a stack of beach towels, taking the bag with ease and I try not to stare at him. Try not to stare and remember the feel of his hands, or the way he looked at me when he—

"You okay?" he asks.

"Uh-huh!"

We both pause at the overly enthusiastic noise that comes out of my mouth but Beth saves the day with a dramatic groan as she drops the bag.

"My fingers hurt," she says, taking the towels from me. "I'll let you have the first pick of sandwiches," she promises, and heads to the bonfire before I can stop her.

"I've got it," Luke sighs, hoisting it up again.

"It's okay." I take the other side before he can, balancing it awkwardly between us. "I'm secretly very strong."

"All that tree climbing?"

"That's me."

He smiles as we walk toward the others, our feet sinking into the soft sand.

"Dad told me he passed your name onto someone?" he asks.

"He did. It was really good of him."

"He has a soft spot for you. I think he was even prouder than your parents when you left. You hear from anywhere else yet?"

I shake my head. "I did get rejection number ten last night though."

"Ten's not that many."

"Those are just the people who got back to me."

He grimaces as we lower the bag onto the sand. The others are busy adding to the bonfire and besides a lone dog walker in the distance, we have the place to ourselves.

"When does your course finish?" I ask to change the subject. "It must be soon."

"Soon enough. I have my final exams in July. Another placement before that. Then that's it. I'm hoping it will all be worth it."

"It will be," I say automatically. "Hard work pays off."

"A bit of that American confidence shining through there."

"Sorry."

"No, it's good," he says with a laugh. "I need it. Sometimes it feels like I'm a step behind everyone. I'm the oldest person on the course by about six years."

"That doesn't matter."

"Ah, I know. But this is the time when I'm supposed to be settling down, right? Not catching up with everyone else. It's..." He trails off, almost like he remembers who he's talking to.

"What?" I ask, teasing. "Sad? Pathetic?"

"I didn't mean—"

"It's okay. We'll be pathetic together."

"You're not pathetic."

"Just you then."

He laughs as a cheer goes up around the bonfire and we turn to see flames spark in the air.

"You weren't bad," he says, as Sinead arranges Rory for a picture. "Out on the water today."

"For an amateur, you mean?"

"I've seen a lot worse."

"Because you teach seven-year-olds." I reach down to unzip the bag, grabbing a bottle of water. "I didn't know you were watching me."

"The currents were strong today."

"Is that the only reason?"

He meets my gaze, clearly surprised, but I don't wait for his answer, already walking away. It's not exactly the sexy move I envisioned, seeing as I have to lurch my way through the sand, but still, shot taken.

"Finally," Rory says as we join them at the bonfire. "And there I was thinking no one would bring warm, bottled water to the party."

I settle next to Beth as we start distributing the food and for the next hour we eat and drink as the sun sinks lower in the sky. Afterward, Harry and Sean go for a walk while it's still light and Rory entertains Luke and Sinead with some very dramatic story. Or at least it looks that way from his hand gestures.

I stay where I am, with a beach towel around my shoulders, as Beth unwraps the last sandwich, splitting it in half.

"We have to finish it," she says. "I hate food waste."

"As if I need a reason to eat bread," I say. "And these are great. Are they from the café?"

"Kind of. Luke made them."

"He did?"

She laughs. "You sound so surprised. He makes a lot of food for us. Even though I tell him he doesn't have the time. I think it relaxes him. Plus who can resist my company?"

I smile as she bats her eyelashes. "You guys are pretty close, huh?"

"He was one of the first people I met when I moved here," she says. "He's a good friend." The softness in her tone catches my attention and I follow her gaze across the fire to where Luke sits, shaking his head at something Rory said. My smile fades as I think back to all the times I saw them together, the playfulness and the back and forth that I thought was just who Beth is. But maybe it's not.

"Is that all he is?" I ask. "A friend?"

"How do you mean?"

I tear a piece from my sandwich, but my appetite shrinks by the second. I can't believe I hadn't put two and two together. "Do you like him?"

Her eyes go wide. "No! No, God, it's not like that at all."

"Oh. Shit. Sorry." I almost laugh as I sit back, more relieved than I have a right to be. "It just sounded like—"

"I mean, he's my landlord," she interrupts, her voice a little shrill. Sinead glances over at us and Beth's eyes drop to her legs as she pretends to roll up the cuffs of her sweatpants. "And he doesn't see me like that," she whispers.

But she does. I start to feel a little sick.

"Don't say anything to him," she says, my silence making her panic. "It would ruin our friendship. I know it would."

"Beth—"

"It's just a little crush," she continues. "It's a small place and he's a nice guy who's gone out of his way to help me without expecting anything in return, even though, yeah, sometimes I wish he would, but it's not like I'd ever—"

I squeeze her arm, cutting her off. "I won't say anything."

"Thanks." She takes a breath, visibly calming herself. "Look at me, I'm blushing."

"It's the beer."

"It's the embarrassment." She stuffs the final bit of her sandwich into her mouth, swallowing thickly. "I mean," she says, around the bread. "Can you blame me?"

No. I can't blame her at all. "So there's nothing going on between you two?"

"No," she says vehemently. "Nothing. I swear. Only in my fan fiction. That was a joke. I don't write fan fiction. Well, I used to but—"

"Ladies?"

We both look up to see Rory standing before us. "You're looking far too dressed for my liking."

I'm about to ask how much he's had to drink when Beth stands, whipping off her sweatshirt with unexpected enthusiasm. Behind Rory, Harry and Sean are doing the same.

"What the hell is going on?"

"It's tradition." Rory grins, pulling off his T-shirt. He nods to the ocean, where the sun is just beginning to disappear beneath the horizon, making the water look like it's been set ablaze. But looks can be deceiving. I have no doubt it's just as cold as before, if not more so.

"Come on," Beth says. "While there's still a bit of light."

"I've already been in the water."

"You went paddling," Rory says. "This is skinny dipping."

"It is *not* skinny dipping," Harry calls. "No one is flashing anyone."

"It's getting dark," I protest.

"We're not going far. And Luke's a trained lifeguard."

At his name, Luke glances up, already down to his briefs. "It's just in and out," he says.

Thankfully, Sinead doesn't look too impressed either. "I'll tend the fire."

"You will not," Rory scoffs, turning to her.

"I'm allergic to seawater."

"Get up."

"No, I'm divorcing you."

"Hey." Luke steps toward me as they start to argue. "You don't have to. Especially if your foot's still sore."

Behind him, the others start running into the ocean with a collective shriek. I *don't* want to. It's not the stripping down to the underwear bit, God knows Luke's already seen me up close today. But the water is cold and dark and I'm nice and warm here and, yeah, okay, maybe a swimsuit is a little different to parading around in your bra and maybe I don't want Luke to see me pink- and purple-tinged and covered in goosebumps.

I try not to stare as he lays his T-shirt by his other clothes, his skin glowing in the firelight. Not so much the chiseled chest I'd fantasied about before, but broad and toned, a swimmer's body. An active body. One that has me thinking of all kinds of activities even as he turns back to me, hesitating.

"It's fun though," he says with a small smile.

Crap.

Ugggh.

Fine.

I stand, pulling both my hoodie and my T-shirt off before dropping my sweatpants unceremoniously to my ankles. My underwear is blue cotton, my bra black and unpadded and doing little to protect me against the chill.

I don't look at Luke again—I refuse to—and before I can lose my nerve, I run straight into the water. Rory lets out a whoop as he follows and the others cheer me on as a shock of cold hits my toes, my thighs, and then my stomach as I wade in deeper.

Holy *shit*.

"You've got to go under," Harry calls as Luke splashes in after us.

"No way," I say, my teeth already chattering.

"It will make it easier." He dips down before shooting back up, shaking himself all over Sean, who scowls at him.

I can't bring myself to do the same. If I get my hair wet, I'm doomed.

"Don't you feel alive?" Rory asks, wading toward me.

"I feel like I have hypothermia."

"You need to get used to the elements. You've been coddled by city life."

"I'll coddle you," I mutter, bobbing up and down to try and get warm. It's working a little, my body growing slowly used to the temperature, and I sink to my shoulders as Luke and Harry take turns trying to dunk each other.

"Yes!" Beth shrieks to my left and I turn to see Sinead shivering in her tank top and underwear by the water's edge.

Rory breaks away from me with a grin, his arms outstretched. "Come on. You're making it worse by stalling."

"It's cold!" she shouts.

"We *know*."

I join in with the catcalls until Sinead gives an almighty yell and charges in, causing Beth and I to scream as we get out the way of her splashing.

Before she reaches Rory, she dips fully under the water, emerging with a string of curse words. I grin as the others start laughing and I realize Rory's right though, even if I refuse to admit it.

I do feel alive.

Rory and Sinead kiss before she quickly breaks away, heading back to the sand.

"That was not fun and you're all insane," she yells.

We stay there for another minute, the initial excitement dying down as people just begin to swim. Luke and Sean talk quietly together while Rory and Harry start swimming short laps back and forth.

I can hear Beth humming to herself nearby as she floats on her back and I stare down into the inky water, brushing my hands across the rippling surface.

Screw it.

If I die, I die.

I take a breath, squeeze my eyes shut, and go under. We didn't wade out too deep and I hug my knees as I go, trying to go weightless as the ocean envelops me.

It's uncomfortable. And cold. And I'm trying to see how long I can stay down when a hand brushes my shoulder. I bob up quickly, swallowing half a mouthful as I go.

I assumed it was Rory, but as the water dribbles down my chin, I wipe my eyes clear to see Luke standing in front of me.

"Sorry," he says. "You went under for a long time."

"I have excellent lung capacity."

He doesn't answer, brushing a piece of seaweed from my shoulder. Behind him the others start to wade back to shore but I don't move. I can't move. Not with him looking at me like that, with an intensity that makes my skin prickle. The water laps around my breasts as we watch each other and I stare, fascinated as a drop slips from his forehead, traveling down the bridge of his nose.

"Abby!" Rory calls from the beach. "Move your ass! We've got marshmallows."

"I'm coming," I yell directly into Luke's face. He blinks at me, startled, but before I can feel embarrassed I turn and make my way clumsily back to the others. Luke catches up quickly, staying close behind as I make it to the sand. I can feel him looking at me. He looks and looks and looks but it's Sinead who wraps me in a towel, who briskly rubs me like I'm a child getting out of the bathtub. It's Rory who hands me my clothes. It's Harry who high-fives me and offers me a sip of brandy from a flask before we eat our toasted marshmallows and the rest of our food. The temperature drops sharply as darkness sets in and it isn't long before we pack up and put out the fire, using our phones to light our way back through the dunes.

As I'm visibly shivering now, Rory makes me sit in the back of his car to get warm while he helps the others divvy up the trash. Luke disappears to the clubhouse to make sure everything is locked up, but everyone else stays in a little huddle, discussing something.

"What's the holdup?" I ask when Rory knocks on the window a minute later. I crack open the car door as he leans down.

"Harry's invited us back around to his," he says, but I'm already shaking my head.

"I'm frozen and I need a shower. I just want to go home."

"You can have a shower at Harry's."

"Can't you just drop me off first?"

"It's an hour in the other direction. Don't be a party pooper."

"I can bring her home."

We both look toward the clubhouse, where Luke stands a few feet away.

"I need to be up early," he continues.

Rory turns back to me, eyebrows raised, but I ignore him.

"That would be great," I say. "If you're heading that way."

Luke only nods and disappears back into the changing rooms. Rory lets out a low whistle.

"Luke Bailey, huh?"

"I do not appreciate your tone."

"My knowing tone?"

"You think you know."

"I know I know. Use protection."

My fingers skim the side of his arm as he dodges my hit and I step out after him as he jogs over to Sinead. Sean and Harry drive away, rock music blaring from the car with Beth chatting animatedly in the back seat. A moment later Rory follows them, waving as he speeds off with Sinead, leaving Luke and me alone.

The noise of a grate closing makes me jump and I turn to see him emerge from the clubhouse, dusting his hands and looking just as wary as I am.

The car lights flash behind me as he unlocks it.

"You ready?" he asks.

I'm not ready at all. But I only nod and open the passenger door, sliding inside.

CHAPTER 15

My body stays cold despite the heat of the car, and I don't so much shiver as I do shudder every few seconds. Chilled to the bone is what my mother would say, my toes tingling almost painfully as the warmth seeps back into them.

I tie my damp hair back as best I can and hold up my fingers, clenching and unclenching as the blood works its way through them.

"You okay?" Luke asks as I watch them turn a mottled red and purple.

"Cold hands, remember? I have terrible circulation."

"You should have said something."

"I didn't even realize," I say truthfully as he turns the heater up further. "Thanks."

He shrugs, concentrating on the road, which gives me plenty of time to watch him.

It's hard to believe the last time I was sitting here I thought he was a stranger. A sexy, godlike stranger. Now he's a sexy, godlike Luke. And it's so confusing I can't even begin to explain it to myself. It doesn't help that his car feels smaller, more cramped than last time. Probably because of all the picnic stuff in the back. Probably because we're both cold and wet. He's different too. More serious for one. There's no joking this time, no teasing or smiling. Maybe he's just full of angst. Maybe he's thinking about me in the water like I'm thinking about him. Maybe he can't stop thinking about me and he's two seconds away from pulling over and—

"So how often does Sean come back to visit?" I ask, before my fantasy can go any further.

"All the time." He responds immediately, like he'd been waiting for me to say something. "He and Harry have a place in Galway."

"Oh great."

"He designs video games."

"That's cool."

"Yeah. Do you play?"

"Me? No. I never had the time. Do you?"

He shakes his head.

Silence.

The heat is blaring in the car now and I shrug out of my coat, pressing my fingers against the vent until I can move them freely again.

Luke shifts in his seat, not saying anything, but something in his expression catches my attention.

"Are you okay?"

"I'm fine."

"Are you sure?"

"Yeah." He clears his throat. "Is there a service station around here?"

"You're asking me?" I frown, trying to remember the journey down. "Not for another twenty minutes."

"No problem."

I glance at the dashboard. We still have half a tank of gas. "Do you want some water? I've still got a bottle of—"

"No," Luke says quickly. "I'm grand, thanks."

And suddenly the pinched expression on his face makes sense.

I bite my lip, trying not to smile. "Luke Bailey, do you need to go to the bathroom?"

He doesn't answer for a long second. And then: "It's fine."

"Oh my God."

"I can hold it."

"Luke, it's another forty minutes back before we get back. Just pull over." A pained look crosses his face and this time I can't help but laugh. "I promise I won't look."

And it must be bad because, though his embarrassment is clear, he slows down, stopping by the side of a hedgerow.

"One second," he mutters before he disappears into the darkness of the bushes.

I get a burst of affection for him and I relax back into the seat, feeling better. Feeling a lot better in fact. This is the best day I've had in years. Out on the water, seeing Rory again, spending time with people who don't just talk about work and numbers and money. I turn down the heat as I keep my eyes on the spot where Luke vanished. It's barely a minute before he reappears, studiously avoiding my gaze.

"Better?" I ask when he gets back in.

He only nods as he shuts the door, rooting around the glove department.

"Wet wipes," he mutters, producing a small plastic packet.

"How romantic."

Luke hesitates for only a second but it's enough to make me wish I never said it as the expression on his face changes to careful indifference.

Romantic.

I turn to the road, annoyed with myself as he shoves the packet down the side of the seat. Outside it starts to rain, a light but steady patter on the windshield. Neither of us speak.

Is this what it's going to be like? Freaking out over every slip of the tongue? Constantly guarding what I say while we tiptoe around because neither of us knows where the other stands? What mood we're both in?

It's exhausting.

Luke turns the wipers on but otherwise doesn't move, leaving the car to idle.

"Abby—"

"Do you know what happened on my first day at MacFarlane?" I ask abruptly.

Luke shakes his head.

"I got on the wrong subway. Like an-hour-late-to-orientation wrong. My apartment was only a couple of blocks from the office, but I'd bought these cheap heels that I couldn't walk in and I didn't know if there would be a place to change into them once I got there, so I thought I'd get the subway and save my toes. An hour late."

"Not a good first day."

"Not a good *year*," I say. "I thought about quitting every week those first few months. It's not like they don't tell you what it's going to be like. All you ever hear about is the hours you'll need to work and the pressure you'll be under but experiencing it is next level. Just..." I twist in my seat to face him again, needing him to understand. "What you said about being a step behind? I get it. Everyone worth anything thinks they're too old or too young or too whatever at some point but they're not. *You're* not. You shouldn't doubt yourself like that."

"Yeah?"

"*Yes*. I mean, I couldn't do it. Starting something new now? Trying to figure out what else I want to do with my life? If you found what you want then you need to go for it. Both hands. Full throttle. Similar saying."

He grins at the last bit, tilting his head back against the seat. "An hour late?"

"I almost threw up in the ladies' room, I was so scared." I gesture at my face. "Sweat everywhere."

"If it helps, you looked very impressive whenever I pictured you in New York. No sweat. Just you walking around a skyscraper. Usually in a power suit."

"A power suit?"

"For some reason it was always the eighties in my head."

I laugh. "Thought about me a lot, did you?"

I mean it as a joke but he just nods. "I used to."

"You did?"

"Sure I did."

He used to have that silly little crush on you.

Louise's words from Easter echo through my mind as my heart gives an uncomfortable thump and it's at that moment the automatic light switches off overhead. The headlights are still on though, only heightening the darkness on either side. It's the kind of night you never get in the city, even with the expensive blackout blinds Tyler had. It should be spooky, a little scary. But I don't feel scared.

"Why weren't we friends?" I ask.

"What?"

"When we were younger. Not when we were kids but when we got older. We lived next door to each other but we weren't friends."

"We were very different," he says like it's nothing. "You were this scarily focused, confident cool kid—"

"There are no cool kids in Clonard," I interrupt.

"True. But you were as close as we were going to get."

"I'll accept that."

"That was you," he continues. "And me... I was quiet, *painfully* shy, a late bloomer—"

"Come on."

"Hey, you grew at a normal pace. You don't understand what it's like to look like you're twelve until your late teens. I took it very personally. Real sullen, 'life isn't fair' stuff. I kept a journal."

"You didn't."

"I did. A little black diary."

"I would pay good money to read that."

"Then I'm glad you don't have any. I think I burned it anyway. Or threw it into the ocean in some dramatic gesture." He glances at me, some of the humor fading from his face. "We were just different people."

"Well, I'm glad we're friends now."

"Me too."

We watch each other as the rain falls heavier around us. You'd think it would set a mood, but no, it's just loud, almost violent as it hits the metal of the car. It's so loud I can't hear my own thoughts. Which is fortunate seeing as I don't have any. Just Luke. Just now. He has a way of doing that. Of making me forget about everything else.

"There are different types of friends," he says finally.

I don't even dare to breathe.

"I know you just got out of a relationship," he continues. "And I know you're probably not looking for anything right now, but if you want to..."

"I mean if *you* want to," I say.

The corner of his mouth twitches into an almost smile. "I want to."

I don't move, uncharacteristically nervous. But Luke doesn't look nervous at all. He looks very sure of himself sitting there, as if he knows exactly how I feel, exactly the effect he has on me. And for some reason, that makes it so much easier. Knowing I have nothing to hide.

When I don't respond he starts to lean toward me, but I sit back, undoing my seat belt, and before he can stop me, I climb over the gear shift, straddling him.

If he's surprised by my boldness, he doesn't show it, only pushes the seat back to make room for me. It isn't exactly the most comfortable of positions but it does bring me closer to him, which is all I want really.

"I feel like you're going to set the horn off," he says.

"Is that a euphemism?"

He laughs and I like the sound of it so much that I almost feel bad when I stop it by kissing him.

It's innocent at first, gentle and slow. He tastes like marshmallows and he smells like the bonfire and his body is so warm, I melt into him. Our mouths move together, uncertain at first and then surer as we learn the other, both of us growing in confidence until my heart starts to pound.

It occurs to me only then how I must look, dressed in my sister's ill-fitting clothing, probably stinking of sweat and seawater. With Tyler I always made an effort with my appearance, but now I don't care. And Luke doesn't seem to either, matching my enthusiasm as he pulls me closer.

And I try to keep my cool, I swear I do, but the way his fingers trail up and down my arms is very disconcerting and when his tongue runs along my lips, coaxing them open, it's like sparks are shooting through my veins. My thighs tighten instinctively around him as a heavy, heady want pools low in my stomach. I start to move, I *need* to move, but his hands squeeze my hips, keeping me in place, even as he presses more firmly against me.

As he does, a needy desperation rises inside and I rock harder against him, hard enough that he groans and when he does, I do it again, showing him what I want.

He takes the hint.

I hum approvingly as he deepens the kiss, and slip my hands under his sweatshirt only for him to jolt at my touch. Cold hands. I start to withdraw, but he moves quickly, holding my palm to his chest as though to keep me there, and I wonder if maybe it's not the cold that made him react. If maybe he's just as affected by my touch as I am by his.

My thoughts scramble and I barely register his fingers traveling upward, not until he cups my breasts, brushing my nipples through my bra. He does it again, massaging me before a gentle pinch makes me gasp so loud that I have no choice but to break away, dropping my forehead to his shoulder. His lips move to my jaw and down my neck as I peer into the back seat for a more comfortable space before I actually do set off the horn. And that's when I see it.

Beth's picnic basket placed neatly on top of her towel.

Beth.

Her face flashes through my mind. Her kind words. Her earnest smile.

And I suddenly realize what I'm doing.

What I'm doing to *her* even if she denies it. Even if I...

"Luke."

He doesn't hear me, his hands moving around my back, reaching for the clasp of my bra. I sit up before he can get to it, breaking his hold as he blinks, trying to focus on me. "What's wrong?"

Nothing. Everything.

Just the sight of him makes me want to pull him closer again. His lips swollen, the expression on his face so adorably confused. But I don't. I can't. Not with Beth hung up on him. Not when she's been so nice to me. Even if there's nothing between them, I *can't*. And I open my mouth to explain just that when I remember what I promised.

That I wouldn't share her secret.

"Abby?"

"I can't do this."

"Are you okay?" His brow creases in concern and he drops his arms completely away from me, as though trying to give me space. "I'm sorry. We can just—"

"No," I interrupt. "I mean *we* can't do this. This is a mistake."

"I don't... a mistake?" His frown deepens as my words register. "Are you serious?"

I don't answer, desperately trying to think of the right thing to say.

"You're serious. You—" He breaks off, lips pressed into a thin line. "Could you move?"

I hadn't realized I was still clutching him to me. I immediately let go and start climbing off, only for Luke to grunt when my knee lands somewhere it really, really shouldn't have.

"I'm sorry," I gasp. "I'm sorry. Are you okay?"

"No," he chokes out.

"Oh my God. Let me—"

"Could you just get off me?"

"Right. Right. I'm sorry." I scramble over to my side of the car and think briefly about continuing straight through the door and disappearing into the fields never to be seen again but settle for keeping as far away from him as I can. I'm pretty sure it's what he wants anyway going by how he is resolutely not looking at me at all, but instead, turned toward the opposite window as he covers himself with one hand.

My body feels cold without him against me, my breath erratic no matter how much I try to steady it.

Eventually, he turns back around. "You're the one who started—"

"I know."

His jaw is tight. "Could you just tell me... are you..."

He thinks I'm a tease. Worse. He thinks I'm playing with him, deliberately. He thinks I'm a liar. First Tyler and now this.

"It was a mistake," I say, the words a whisper as I think of Beth. "I'm sorry. I shouldn't have done that."

"The kiss or the injury?"

"Both."

Something almost like hurt flashes flickers in his eyes and for a second I see it, the boy I once knew. The little kid on the playground. But it's blink and you'll miss it, vanishing as quickly as it came.

He doesn't say anything for a long moment and then he nods, turning the ignition, and I know I need to say something, to make this right but I don't know how to without betraying Beth.

He doesn't speak to me again. He doesn't even look at me and the next thirty minutes are driven in utter, miserable silence as he brings me home.

CHAPTER 16

The whole thing is a mess and over the next few weeks all the progress I made with Luke goes right back to zero as he starts avoiding me again. It's like our happy day at the beach never happened, and as Rory goes and another round of job rejections come in, April turns to May and it's like nothing's changed at all.

The only thing that *has* gotten a little better is my relationship with Louise. While we still can't go a day without snapping at each other, it's easier now there are no more lies between us. I no longer have to skirt around her questions and she drops some of her act as well, our dinner eaten in front of the television rather than at the table and I'm finally allowed to help around the house, so I feel less like a guest with each passing day.

One Sunday morning she even grants me the greatest olive branch of all, a chance to accompany her on the weekly "big" shop since Tomasz is sleeping off a late shift. This involves us driving to the nearest superstore, where I trail her around the aisles as she uses a little self-scanner to keep track of everything she puts in the cart. It's the most excitement I've had in weeks. After that is the pharmacy, where she buys pain killers, hay fever tablets and six more pregnancy tests, which I pretend aren't a big deal and instead act very interested in their two-for-one body cream display. We don't argue once. Not when I make a bad parking space suggestion.

Not even when I forget to remind her to pick up some parmesan. It should have been a nice morning out, a little sisterly bonding session, except on the way back to Clonard she gets a phone call that wipes out our fragile peace in a matter of seconds.

"It's insulting is what it is," she tells me now as we speed home.

I brace a hand against the dashboard as the car almost flies over the bridge.

"They seriously think we're just going to lie down and let them take it."

"I think the reason they're pushing so hard is because they know you won't," I tell her. "It's really a compliment if you ask me."

"I didn't."

Noted.

The auction of Castlebay beach is not going well. Or rather the problem is it's going well for the developers of Ireland's newest five-star hotel. For Louise, it's a nightmare. A nightmare come true since the formal complaint she lodged was officially thrown out this morning.

"Can't the council just buy it off them?" I ask.

"The *council* is *useless*," she fumes as we turn onto our street. "They should never have let it go to auction in the first place. Do you know how much wildlife is on that stretch of coast?"

"Lots?"

"Abby."

"It was a serious guess!"

"They're just going to bulldoze over it," she mutters. "Like they do everything in this country and it's not like the politicians are doing anything about it. Once again it's up to us to— Who the hell is that?"

"Huh?"

I follow her gaze toward the house, where a sleek black BMW is parked outside. It might not look so odd anywhere else, but considering the last time someone got a new car in Clonard it was 1997, it does seem a little suspicious.

"Maybe it's the developers," I say. "With an offer you can't refuse."

"Abby, I swear I'll—"

"Sorry. Is Tomasz friends with any rich doctors?"

"Not that I know of. Unless… oh my God." Louise slows to a stop a few doors down, turning to me in horror. "Is this to do with MacFarlane?"

"What?"

"Is it the FBI?"

"Louise! No!"

"If you were in deeper than you said you were, I need you to tell me right now."

"It's not the FBI," I snap even as I start to panic. What if it *is* the FBI? "I was an associate. There were hundreds of us."

"But you fled the country."

"I didn't *flee* the— Oh no." I still as someone leans out of the driver's window.

Oh *no*.

"What?" Louise looks back toward the car. "Who is that?"

Jess peers down the street, one hand to her forehead as she blocks out the sun.

"A friend," I say, clearing my throat. "I think she might be coming to stay for a few days."

"She's doing *what*?"

"Guess who!" The shout is accompanied by a very loud honk of the horn and I immediately think of poor Tomasz in the house, trying to sleep. Jess steps out, waving enthusiastically, as Louise pulls into the drive.

"She's staying here?" Louise asks.

"Probably."

"We don't have any clean sheets."

"I'll clean them."

"Or spare towels."

"I'll spare them."

"Abby!"

"Yell at me later," I hiss, unbuckling my seat belt. "And this is not my fault. I told her not to come." I get out as Jess runs toward me, moving like she's in a pair of Nikes rather than her heeled boots.

"Jessica?"

Her arms fly out. "*Surpriiise!*"

"Yes, it is," I sing through clenched teeth. "What are you doing here?"

She wraps an arm around my shoulders, both of us still smiling as we talk in low voices. "I knew if I told you I was coming, you'd think of an excuse. It's much better to put people on the spot when you want things to go your way."

"Hilarious. I'm going to kill you."

"Like I haven't heard that before. You must be Louise!"

Jess pushes me to the side as Louise joins us, pulling my sister in for a hug.

"We talked on the phone, remember? Your hair is even prettier in person. Hi! Tomasz, right?"

The three of us turn toward the porch where a bewildered, and still a little sleepy, Tomasz gapes at her. It's not that I don't understand. Even in jeans and a T-shirt, Jess looks like a movie star who's just stepped off set. In Clonard she sticks out like a sore thumb. And while other people might feel self-conscious about that, I know Jess would only thrive.

"I brought gifts!" she announces with a luminous smile, staring at me until I sigh.

We head into the house as Jess doles out the expensive wine and boxes of chocolate, barely letting us get a word in as she chats endlessly about "what a lovely home" Louise has and how she "hoped she wouldn't be too much trouble."

There's an obligatory cup of coffee in the kitchen, where she tells us about her flight and her drive down and then, like a child bringing home a friend after school, I shepherd her up the stairs and into my bedroom so I can yell at her for not giving me a heads-up.

As soon as she stepped out of the car, I knew why I was so against her coming. I don't want Jess here. I want her in a cocktail bar overlooking the Manhattan skyline. I want her in some bougie thrift store looking for vintage dresses. I *need* her there. I need something in my life to remain unchanged. Her presence only makes everything here seem duller. Grayer. And that includes me.

And I'm furious that she still doesn't get that.

"I know," she says as soon I shut the door. "And I'm sorry but I'm also not sorry."

"You couldn't have at least given me an *hour's* notice? Louise's patience with me is thin enough as it is."

"She'll get over it."

"That's not the point," I snap. "What the hell are you doing here?"

"To see you! Shit, Abby, sorry for wanting to see my friend. And lest we forget, I'm not the one who ran away without saying goodbye. If anyone, I'm the person who should be mad in this situation."

"But you didn't think I might—"

"Oh, save the tantrum, okay? You're talking to the queen of them."

She dumps her purse on the bed and stalks the two steps to the window, sliding it open.

"It's stuffy in here," she mutters. She stays like that, her back to me in her "I'm upset now" pose and my initial anger starts to fade.

She's right. I did run away. And I suppose it's not the best welcome for someone who flew across an ocean to see you.

"I'm sorry," I say when she doesn't move. "Jess? I mean it."

She turns back around, crossing her arms as she rests against the windowsill. "I'm sorry too. I should have told you I was coming."

"You shouldn't have come at all."

"Why not?"

"Because it's weird," I say, gathering up the clothes strewn over the back of the chair.

"You know, from the way you spoke about this place I thought a horse and cart was going to pick me up. Some red-faced farmer in a tweed jacket who I couldn't understand a word of."

"I'll make sure you get the authentic experience for your flight out." I drop to the floor, sitting cross-legged in front of the mirror. Makeup will help. I haven't been wearing any the last few weeks, a little fearful that if I ran out I couldn't afford replacements, but now I'm determined to feel a little more normal.

Abandoning the window, Jess joins me on the carpet, her long legs stretched before her, crossed at the ankles.

"Bring your brush up," she says when I start on my bronzer. "You're lucky enough to have cheekbones, Abby. You might as well highlight them."

"I can't do it if you watch me."

"Then I'll do it." She snatches the brush from me, her fingers warm and dry as they pinch my chin, turning my face toward her. There's a burning behind my eyes that won't go away and I try not to blink as she examines me. "Are you still mad?" she asks.

"No."

"Good. Because I got you some foundation." Her attention is on my temples as she blends. "It's your present but we might need to check the shade. You've gotten paler."

"Oh, thanks."

"I didn't say it was a bad thing." She abandons the brush, reaching for some highlighter. "Remember when we first met and I used to do this?"

"You said it relaxed you."

"It does. And you were the only person who let me do it. No one else trusted me not to make them look bad. But you used to do whatever I told you to." Her thumb wipes away a tear I didn't even know had fallen. "When did you stop doing that?"

"I don't know," I say, my voice breaking. "I feel like I don't know anything anymore."

"Yes, you do. Hey. *Hey.*" She shushes me, drawing me in for a hug, and despite my half-finished face, she doesn't stop me as I bury my head in her shoulder and do what I haven't done since the day I lost my job. I cry.

They're awkward, breathy sobs that once I start I can't stop, and when I finally do it's another while before I sit up, my nose snotty and my head pounding and my eyes puffy and red.

Jess says nothing, passing me a tissue and plucking a makeup wipe from the packet. "At least we know your mascara is waterproof," she mutters, blinking away her own tears as she rubs my face clean.

"I'm sorry."

"You should be. Making me chase you like this. I had to make Amber my bad-date excuse. The first time I texted her like, "Oh, is there an emergency?" she was like, "What are you talking about?" That girl is dumb."

My laughs sounds like a hiccup. "I just feel like I'm the only one still struggling."

"That's my fault." She sighs. "I was trying to make you jealous so you'd come back. Yes, some people are doing okay but the last I heard Peter's gone to work on an alpaca farm in Peru and Jasmine freaked out one day and tried to open a bakery in Newark."

"I didn't know she baked."

"She doesn't. She said she just likes the smell. She's also growing bangs. It's a journey I'm trying to support as a friend but it's not one I would choose for her." She tosses the wipe to the side and starts rummaging through my makeup bag. "Tyler got in touch last week."

"He did?"

"He wanted to know if you'd mentioned his offer to me. That's about as far as he got because he sounded annoyed, so then I got annoyed because he sounded annoyed, and then I hung up. Should I not have hung up?"

I frown as she covers my face in a lemony smelling SPF. "What do you mean?"

"As in, are you two talking?"

"*No.*"

"Okay."

"We're not!"

"*Okay,*" she says, and I flinch as she tweezes a stray hair from my eyebrow.

"He wanted me to stay in his apartment," I explain. "While he's out of town."

"And you said no."

"Of course I said no."

"It's a really nice apartment."

"Jessica!"

"It's just that if it were me, I'd be taking what I could get."

"He dumped me," I remind her. "Four months after he proposed he broke up with me like I was a bad business deal. I don't care if he feels guilty. I don't need his pity."

"What about his water pressure? Okay, okay!" She rubs her forehead where I flicked her.

"Are you done?"

"Nowhere close," she says flatly. "You're an ugly crier." She sits back, stretching her arms above her head. "What's there to do around here? I need some nonrecycled air."

I shrug, pressing my fingers to my still puffy eyes. "It's a Sunday."

"So?"

"So nothing's open."

"Something has to be open."

There's only one place I can think of.

I feel Jess's enthusiasm diminish the farther we walk from the house. It's a gray, chilly day and the main street is almost deserted except for an old man smoking on the corner. Even the art gallery is closed and I know Jess is taking it all in, storing it away to use against me later, so I'm relieved when I see Beth's door propped open and the woman herself watering the hanging baskets outside, dressed in a bright pink dress despite the weather.

"Beth!"

Her eyes go wide when she sees me, and for a panicked moment I wonder if Luke told her about what happened between us, but then I realize her gaze isn't fixed on me.

"This is Jess," I say as we approach. "A friend from New York."

"Hello," Beth chirps. One hand goes to her hair, which she tucks behind her ear while the watering can goes slack in the other, dribbling onto the sidewalk.

"Jess, this is my friend Beth and this is her café."

"Shut up," Jess says. "You own this?"

Beth nods, her eyes flicking to Jess's boots in a way that makes me think they're another one of her happy places.

"It's so cute!" Jess exclaims, and she sounds so unintentionally condescending that I wince. Beth hears it too, her smile dropping, but Jess doesn't notice, already strolling inside.

We follow.

"You've got books! And the décor! Shabby chic, I love it."

Beth looks at her doubtfully as if not sure if she's making fun of her or not.

"Are these cookies vegan?" Jess asks, peering into the counter display.

"Um... no. The strawberry slice is."

Jess makes a face. "I don't like strawberries."

And that's enough. "Beth, can you give us one second?"

"Sure," she mumbles as I drag Jess back outside.

"Stop it," I say.

"Stop what?"

"Being you," I hiss. I risk a glance inside to see Beth rearranging the cookie display.

"What are you talking about? I'm being nice."

"No, you're being intimidating. You might not realize it but you are. Beth's been really kind to me and her café is not doing well, so could you please try and—"

"Oh my God."

Jess's eyes latch onto something behind me and I turn to see Luke emerge from the staircase, talking to Beth.

"Who is th— Hey! Stop doing that," Jess protests as I pull her farther from the café.

I ignore her, explaining in a frantic whisper about Luke and Beth and me and slowly her stubborn expression turns thoughtful.

"You know," she says. "You pretend you're super boring but you've always got some little drama happening, don't you? It's like the time you told me you had a migraine all weekend but really you'd gone to Aspen with that Hollister model from reception."

"Please don't make this a thing."

"Obviously," she says, looking insulted. "But if he's your first hookup after Tyler, I'm going to need a full rundown of what the sex is like. A blow by blow, if you will."

"You're incorrigible."

"So many big words," she pouts, pinching my cheek. "I can barely keep up with it all. I'll be good. Stop being weird."

We head back in and I'm relieved to see Luke has already disappeared upstairs, the floorboards creaking overhead.

"He was just getting a coffee," Beth says. "He's studying but I'm sure he wouldn't mind if you—"

"Oh no," I say quickly. "I'm just here for Jess."

"She really wanted to show me this place," Jess says brightly. "Skinny latte," she adds to a confused Ollie, who emerges from the back. "Oat milk if you have it. It's super nice. How long have you guys been open?"

"A couple of... months." Beth trails off, wide-eyed as Jess subtly slides a twenty euro note into the tip jar.

As if being operated by a machine, Ollie immediately starts moving faster.

"And what are these?" Jess asks. "Lemon tarts? Do you bake them yourself?"

"No, there's a woman in—"

"We should bring some back to your sister," Jess says, tossing her hair as she glances over at me. "As a thank you."

"Sounds good," I say with a "tone it down" look.

"We'll take eight."

Beth stares at her. "Eight?"

"Eight."

Beth's grinning from ear to ear as we leave, laden with the tarts, two coffees each, and an éclair for the road.

"I'll tag you on Instagram," Jess calls. "You're welcome," she adds under her breath as the door falls shut behind us. "Why doesn't she have more customers? She's a doll."

"I don't know. Maybe because there's hardly anyone here to begin with. There's a reason everyone else only opens seasonally."

"Their loss." Jess groans around her first bite of éclair. "Oh my God, I missed calories."

We stop by the river on the way back to drink our coffees, and though a rain cloud hovers threateningly overhead, it remains dry as we sit, our activity for the day finished.

"So that's it?" Jess asks as she runs a finger around the pink cardboard box, finding the last of the cream.

I stare out at the empty field on the other side of the water. "That's it."

She leans back against the bench, draping one leg over the other. A lingering breeze whips the hood back from my head, ruffling through my hair, but Jess's doesn't move, weighed down with product and good genes.

"I know I cried," I say haltingly. "But I've also got everything under control."

"Your life's a mess, babe."

"To the untrained eye," I begin, and she sighs.

"Look, if you had an epiphany and realized you hated your life and everything in it and decided to move home to renovate a cottage and start an organic-honey business I would *support you*. You know I would. I would place you on a pedestal and point at you and say that's my friend and this is her choice. But this?" She gestures at the river, at me. "As pretty as it all is, it isn't a choice. This was something you were forced to do because of a series of shitty circumstances. And what I don't want to happen is for you to settle and think this is all you are worth and be miserable."

"I'm not miserable."

"You look miserable," she says flatly. "Your skin looks bad and your hair looks frizzy and you've got a hardened 'where did my life go?' look in your eye. You've given up."

"No."

"Yes. You've given up even if you haven't realized it yet. You're not stuck here, Abby. It's bad now but it will get better. So you need to stop thinking that this is your life now and remember that this is all just a break. You are here to see your sister and her very cute husband. You are here to catch up with old friends, to get back to your roots and connect with your homeland. Treat it like a vacation. A cold, windy vacation that you'll never have to do again. You're one of the smartest people I know and you didn't climb all the way to the top floor only to settle for the basement."

"I didn't make it to the top floor."

"The analogy works," she says. "Okay?"

"Okay," I mumble.

She settles back, calmer now she's said her piece. "So is Beth single or what's her deal? It's just a question!" she adds at my look. "She was checking me out."

"She was not. Don't go near her. She's my friend."

"You make it sound like I'm some heartless womanizer."

"You are a womanizer."

"But also a woman, so it's *fine*. And I'm only that way because I haven't found the *right* woman. Maybe it will help if I—"

"It will not help. Do not engage."

"Whatever." She sighs, long and loud, and makes a show of looking around. "So now what do we do? Day-drink?"

I wish. "The pubs aren't open yet."

"So then what? Come on, give me the tour. I'm just going to keep talking otherwise. I'm just going to sit and give you advice and yell at you and—"

"Alright," I groan, standing up. "I'll show you the heron."

"Oh, goody."

CHAPTER 17

Jess tells me she's staying four days. Four days sleeping in the tiny spare bed in Louise's converted office. Four days in my tiny village where the Wi-Fi signal is spotty at best. Four days of having my best friend back. Four days of having the most unpredictable person I know be in the most predictable place.

Jess's mind moves too fast for any kind of plan to order her world. If she makes a bad decision, she doesn't dwell because she'll have made another before you can even question it. Which is why I'm not completely shocked when I return from brushing my teeth the next morning to see her sitting on her unmade bed, unwrapping a parcel that just arrived.

"What are those?"

"Hiking boots."

"And are we going on a hike?" I ask when she doesn't explain further.

"Ding ding! Ten points to the girl with too much dry shampoo in her hair." She discards a wad of tissue paper onto the floor. "I ordered them before I got on the plane. I thought we could go up those mountains you told me about."

"Today?"

"Yes, Abby, today. Unless you have other plans you've forgotten to share?"

"Don't you need to wear those in a bit first?"

"I have the perfect size-seven feet. I've never had to break in a pair of shoes." She sticks her foot into one, pulling the laces tight. "And don't look at me like that. It's not like you have anything better to do. I'm only here for a few days and I want to see the sights." She looks up at me, her smile dropping at my reluctance. "I don't know why I'm even pretending you have a choice," she continues. "Because you don't. Suit up. Boot up. We're going on a hike."

I know better than to try and change her mind. Louise lends me a pair of her old walking shoes and I grab a pair of leggings and a light T-shirt. Jess, of course, looks like she just stepped out of a Patagonia catalog but I'm used to that by now.

"It will take us an hour to get there," I say to her as I fill up our water bottles in the kitchen. "We can stop for lunch after and you can eat overpriced Guinness stew or something."

"You're making fun of me but I am totally going to do that. Do you want to come?"

I glance over my shoulder to see Louise hovering in the doorway.

My sister looks surprised. "Me?"

"Sure. You busy?"

"She's working," I say.

"I'm not," Louise says pointedly. "It's a bank holiday."

Oh.

"Then what about a bit of girl time?" Jess asks. "I'd love a local guide. Abby doesn't count. She got lost coming back from the forest yesterday."

"I did not." I scowl. "They changed the shortcut."

Louise is unsure. "Tomasz has a shift later. He's taking the car."

"We're using my one," Jess says. "Come on. It will be fun!"

"Okay." Louise glances my way as if waiting for me to protest and, when I don't, backs out of the room. "Give me five minutes to change."

"Take your time," Jess calls after her, and, ignoring my look, grabs her water bottle and heads out the front door.

"What are you doing?" I whisper as I catch up with her.

"I'm bringing you and your sister closer together."

"We don't need—"

"Yes, you do. You're like children throwing a tantrum in the back seat."

"We are not!"

"It's done now," she says reasonably. "So there's no use arguing about it."

"You're unbelievable."

"I know." She grins and throws her backpack into the trunk.

It takes Louise far less time to get ready than Jess and I, and soon the three of us are in the car, with Louise in the passenger seat so she can give directions.

That leaves me in the back, while not exactly throwing a tantrum, definitely getting a little hint of childish jealously at my best friend and older sister chatting away. But even that's pushed momentarily from my mind as we approach the mountains in the distance.

I tried to hide my Irishness when I first moved abroad, desperate to fit in. I used to think it was lucky that my name didn't immediately give the game away and that all I needed to do was tone down my accent and learn the vernacular and no one would think to question where I was from and if I deserved to be there. It was only later in New York that I realized I could use it to my advantage. I became "the Irish girl" and was adept at feigning interest when superiors discussed their third cousins twice removed in parts of the country I'd never even set foot in.

My country became nothing but a tool for me to stand out from the crowd. I didn't join any diaspora groups. I didn't even wear green on St. Patrick's Day. Ireland and Clonard were where I grew up but it wasn't my home—it didn't define me—and yet just as I felt on the beach those few weeks ago, the distinctive sight of Benbulbin mountain in the distance, with the sun moving steadily over its broad flat head, is undeniably moving. Dramatic and beautiful and mine.

And it is mine.

Whether I try to ignore it or not, this place belongs to me and I feel unusually proud as we pull into the parking lot for the local trails and Jess starts taking a million pictures.

It's the perfect day for a hike. Blue sky, white clouds, and a light breeze to keep you cool. Unfortunately, a lot of other people think so too and the base of the trail is full with similar-minded people but they spread out along the different paths and after a few minutes of nodding at everyone who goes past and moving to the side to let the more serious climbers overtake us, the three of us are left alone.

Jess keeps up a polite conversation at the start, peppering Louise with questions about her charity and in turn answering Louise's equally polite questions about the glamorous world of luxury real estate. But about thirty minutes into the climb the conversation peters out as the path grows steeper and soon the only noise is the sound of our heavy breathing. Jess quickly takes the lead, navigating the terrain as if she climbs it every day.

"You're good at this," Louise says at one point, sounding vaguely suspicious.

"That's because she's a fitness freak," I explain as Jess grins over her shoulder at me. "She's good at everything."

"Not everything."

"You should have been a personal trainer."

"And have to deal with people like you? I tried to take her to a CrossFit class once," Jess says to Louise. "But she doesn't like people yelling at her. Except in the office."

Louise glances my way. "They yelled at you?"

"Not *at* me," I say, uncomfortable. "Around me maybe."

"Don't worry about your little sister," Jess says, ruffling my hair. "Abby also did a little yelling. She's a badass, don't you know? Gives as good as she gets. At least to the men."

"Jess—"

"One time when we were interns, she stood up to our boss and I thought for sure this girl is getting fired. Like for sure. I've seen people go for less. But of course with Abby, he thought it was the most wonderful thing."

"Probably because I was a girl," I say. "There were only five of us after all."

"Out of how many?" Louise asks.

"You don't want to know."

"Hey, man, discrimination works both ways." Jess smirks. "He moved her onto his client that day. I couldn't keep up with her."

"You did pretty well for yourself," I mutter.

"I've got luck and privilege. You've got the talent."

We eventually reach the peak, timing it just as another group is heading back down, meaning we have the place to ourselves, and we gather a little from the edge, gazing out at the countryside below. As if on cue the clouds part, allowing a sharp bolt of sunlight through before it gentles over the rolling hills, illuminating the green and yellow fields.

The three of us simply stare at it for a few seconds before Jess breaks first with a choice curse word. "That's not a bad view," she adds. "I can feel my skin clearing." She throws her arms wide and takes in a deep breath. "I see why you care so much," she says to

Louise. "Abby said you're very keen about saving the world. What did you say, Abs? That Louise was the only thing standing between us and the destruction of the ocean?"

I said no such thing and she knows it but she only winks at my glare.

Louise looks embarrassed. A pleased kind of embarrassed.

"We do what we can," she says.

"Well, it's more than I do," Jess quips. "You're going to have to send me some links. Abby says you're fundraising for a new boat."

That perks her up. "We are. We'd be thrilled to have someone like you on board."

"You mean me and my money?"

Louise nods. "Yes."

Jess laughs, draping an arm around her shoulder. "I like you."

I snort, shrugging off my backpack. Now that we've paused I realize how hungry I am and I think longingly about the trail mix at the bottom of my bag.

"This is a good spot for a break," Louise says as my stomach rumbles and I dump my bag down gratefully, rooting around for the snacks.

Jess wanders off to film a video but Louise stays put, handing me a tinfoil-wrapped package as she sits beside me.

"When did you have the time to make food?"

"I knew you'd get hungry. You're always hungry."

"No, I'm not," I say, unwrapping a plain ham sandwich. The bread is a little squashed from the climb but is soft and delicious. I finish it in three bites. "I am," I admit. "And you always feed me. Even as kids, you'd always give me half your lunch when we were on car trips."

"That's because you'd complain if I didn't."

"No, it's because you took care of me."

She looks surprised. Of course, she is. I'm surprised too but I don't take it back and she doesn't correct me.

"She's not how I imagined your friends," she says instead, glancing at Jess.

"How did you imagine them?"

She shrugs. "I don't know. Snooty. Maybe a bit mean."

My smile fades. *Mean like me?*

"She's lovely," Louise continues.

"Tell her that to her face and then up her monthly donation. She won't be able to resist."

"What was that?" Jess calls. "My ears are burning."

"Then put on a hat," I yell back. "Hey, do you have a Band-Aid?"

"Blister?"

I nod, reaching down to tug my shoe off. I guess we don't all have perfect feet. Jess moves farther away as Louise digs inside her backpack and for a moment we're completely alone, just the two of us on the side of the mountain.

"This reminds me," she says, pulling out the first aid kit. "If you're here for a few more weeks, you should register with a doctor."

"I'm taking zinc."

"What?"

"Nothing. But yeah, probably. I think I might get my IUD out."

"Fun," she mutters. "How long have you had it?"

"A year? But my periods have been a bitch." And it's not like I'm getting the most use of my long-term birth control. "You ever have one?"

"No. I was on the pill for a few years but it messed me up. I could never find the right one."

"The joys of menstruation." I flex my foot, choosing my next words carefully. "Must be nice to be off them."

She says nothing, sorting through the Band-Aids.

I try again. "Did you notice a difference when you stopped? Or did you—"

"You can just ask me, Abby."

"Right." I take the Band-Aid from her, growing flustered as I press it to my heel. "Are you... I mean, did they say why you haven't been able to—"

"Get pregnant?"

I nod.

"No."

"Oh."

There's an awkward beat as I straighten and I think that's it when she goes on.

"There's nothing wrong with me," she says. "At least nothing that they can tell. I've done all the tests. Tomasz too. And everything's fine. Inside and out. We are two healthy, reproductively functioning adults. Who somehow are unable to conceive."

"How long have you been trying?"

"Two years." Her voice is matter-of-fact but she doesn't look at me, pretending to reorganize the kit. "I'm eating all the right food, having sex at all the right times, taking all the right vitamins—and nothing. And no one can tell me why except that sometimes this happens and there's nothing I can do about it." She shakes her head, her expression grim. "I almost wish there *was* something. Does that sound awful? At least then I'd know for sure."

"There are other ways to have a child though, aren't there?"

"Like what? IVF would wipe out our savings with no guarantee of anything. Adoption is..." She blows out a breath. "A long road. To commit to something like that I'd need to know for sure."

Two years. I think about the few occasions I spoke with her during that time. The quick layovers, the polite video calls, and birthday emails. And all the while she was trying for a child she so desperately wants.

And I didn't have a clue.

"I'm so sorry, Louise."

"Sometimes when I see a family I just..." she trails off, and I remember back to Roman's when I first came home. The odd expression on her face when the toddler began to cry. I'd put it down to annoyance at the time but now I wonder if it was something entirely different. "And I can't tell anyone," she continues.

"Of course you can."

"I can't. It's not talked about. Even now. Mam is dying for a grandchild. I told her we're waiting, but I don't know how long I can keep using that excuse. And there are websites and forums and stuff but they're mostly for people with actual problems and I feel bad invading their space and—" She takes a breath, shutting herself up. "I know there are people with bigger issues. I know that we're lucky we're healthy and we have a house and jobs and each other but I just... I want..."

My heart breaks at the sudden yearning in her face, a vulnerability I've never seen on her before.

"Why am I telling you this?" she asks suddenly. "Did you drug my water?"

"Maybe it's the dramatic vista," I say. "Or maybe it's because you really do need to talk about it."

"But with you?"

I laugh at the doubt in her voice. "I'm a good sister."

"You're fine." But she's smiling now. "Don't tell Mam, okay? Thirty-three years old and I'm still worried about disappointing her."

"It's not your fault. You know she'd hate it if you thought that."

"Look who's talking."

"Fair." I tug my shoe back on, lacing it tight before reaching for my phone. "You could get a dog."

Louise snorts. "Don't. Tomasz would love one."

"And you wouldn't? You have the space."

"Yeah, and who's going to be the one to look after it? Plus it's expensive. What if it gets sick?"

"You need to stop thinking about money."

"That's all I think about. That's all anyone thinks about when you don't have enough of it. You should know that by now." She nudges my foot. "How's the blister?"

"Okay. Rubbing a bit but..." I lose my train of thought, staring at my screen and the notification staring up at me.

A missed call from a Dublin number.

A second later another notification appears as if I summoned it. A voicemail.

"What's wrong?"

"Nothing," I say faintly. "Missed call. I better ring them back."

"Sure," Louise says as Jess finally returns, drawing her in for a selfie.

I leave them to it and walk a few steps away as I click into the voice message, holding the phone tight to my ear.

Hi, Abby. This is Caroline, calling from Stewarts. I'm just ringing in relation to your recent application for our associate post. If you could give me a ring back on this number, that would be great. I'm going to send you an email now too. Speak soon.

I listen to it a second time, the words just audible over the noise of the wind. My heart starts to thump, suddenly nervous, and I don't even think as I call the number back.

It rings and rings without connecting.

"You won't get any signal up here," Louise calls from behind me. "Try down there."

I turn without answering and go down a few meters to a small rocky outcrop. Another try and this time it connects.

Less than three minutes later I walk back up.

Jess is sitting on my upturned backpack, scrolling through her photos while Louise breaks open our snacks for the day.

"Everything okay?" she asks, distracted.

I nod, turning the phone over in my hands. Jess looks up when I don't answer, her eyes instantly narrowing.

"What?"

"Pat got me an interview."

"You mean Pat from next door?" Louise asks at the same time as Jess asks, "Who's Pat?"

"His cousin's neighbor's son works at Stewarts," I begin as Jess jumps to her feet, understanding dawning.

"You sneaky bitch. I *knew* you had a plan. I can't believe you kept your plan from me."

Louise rises too, dusting dirt from her pants.

"It's a smaller company," I say, trying to keep her in my sight as Jess throws her arms around me. "But they're good. They have offices all over the world."

"They offered you a job?" Louise asks.

"Only an interview."

"Only an interview," Jess mimics. "This girl is the queen of interviews. You thrive on interviews. You know she used to do them for fun? Said it kept her on her toes, the weirdo."

"It's a foot in the door," I say diplomatically.

Jess squeals, spinning me around. "I brought you some clothes in case this would happen."

There's a strange expression on Louise's face but it vanishes as soon as I turn to her.

"Congratulations," she says with a smile.

"It's only an interview," I repeat as Jess starts dancing around me.

"Everything will go back to normal!" she exclaims. "We can go home and you can show all those bitches what's what."

"What bitches?" I ask.

"No one," she says quickly, twirling me. I fight back a scowl. I can only guess I've been the source of pitying gossip since I left.

"We need to celebrate," Jess adds.

"Maybe Roman's can squeeze us in for dinner," Louise says. "I'll see what time Tomasz gets off at." She walks away, taking out her phone as Jess twirls me again.

"You're not nervous, are you?"

"No. But would you stop? It's one interview. Out of... *several* I applied for."

She just shakes her head. "This is the one. I can feel it in my bones. I'm your good luck charm."

"You're something alright. Stop. I'm dizzy."

Jess drapes an arm around my shoulders, looking victorious as my head spins.

"I was right," she says, tilting her face toward the sun. "This hike was an excellent idea."

CHAPTER 18

Jess spends her last two days in the café, helping me with interview prep in between redesigning Beth's marketing plan and ordering a ridiculous amount of coffee and cake. Because the thing is, Jess can be serious when she wants to be, even if she does flirt with Beth when she thinks I'm not looking.

I don't see Luke, who I learn is on a clinical placement in Galway. Otherwise, the only people we see are the trickle of usual customers. But there are more the second day, all of them sending curious looks toward our corner, and I wonder if word of Jess has become the latest source of village gossip. Beth certainly seems to think so, asking a little too casually if we'd like to sit at the bench by the window where there's more natural light. Jess proclaims it a brilliant idea and then compliments her earrings.

I let her get away with it, needing the help. She's in a good mood, already planning our lives when I return, despite my frequent reminders that it's just an interview. She doesn't like that. But the self-confidence I'd adapted so eagerly when I first moved to New York now seems alien to me, even more so now among the realistic (or as Jess would say, pessimistic) Irish attitude of what will be will be. But her presence is calming, bolstering even, and I find that, even though she's sitting right in front of me, I'm already starting to miss her.

When it's time for her to go, I don't want her to leave. And maybe that's another reason I was so against her coming here in the first place. I didn't say goodbye the first time. But now I have to, and though she seems more than convinced it's only a temporary one, I'm still not sure. How can I be when each passing day it feels like the goalposts are moving farther and farther out?

She leaves for the airport at five a.m. on a gloomy June morning, the day before my interview.

And then she's gone. Just like that.

The house feels very quiet without her. If we had a grandfather clock in the hall, I would hear it ticking. If I were in the desert, I would see tumbleweed drifting. But it's only me alone, sitting on my childhood bed, in my childhood room, and wishing desperately I could follow her. I stay there nearly all day, reading over my notes, and I know when evening comes I should go for a run to clear my mind but the rain pours as if to officially welcome in the Irish summer, so instead I wander down to where Tomasz slouches in the front room, mindlessly watching two soccer players dive over each other.

"Your friend gone?" he asks when I curl up on the opposite end of the sofa.

"Yeah. Thanks for putting up with her."

"Of course. We put up with you."

"Funny."

"You and Louise seem better."

"We're just waiting for the right moment. Then we'll be at each other's throats, don't worry." I hesitate as he leans forward, muttering at the referee's decision. "You didn't say something to her, did you?"

"Me?" He sounds amused. "I say things all the time. Doesn't mean she listens to me. You think I asked her to be nicer to you?"

"Yes."

He shakes his head. "She likes that you're staying longer."

"You mean she likes that I'm going."

"Why would she want you to go?"

I almost laugh. "Because all we do is fight. Even when we're being nice."

"That's just because she doesn't know how to talk to you," he dismisses. "And then you were so keen to leave again when she hasn't seen you properly in years. She misses you, Abby. Isn't it obvious?"

"*Misses* me?"

He looks at me like I'm the confused one and turns back to the television. "You're her sister, of course she does. She likes having you here. She'd never admit it but..." He shrugs. "I'm glad you took her on that hike," he says. "You should do that more often."

I watch him watch the game. "Tomasz?"

"Hmm?"

"Would you like a beer?"

He smiles gratefully and I stand, going to the kitchen.

The noise from the television is faint here and through the window above the sink I can see into the Baileys' backyard and the light streaming out from their own house.

She misses you.

I won't pretend that one of the reasons I stayed away for so long was Louise. Every time I came home from college there would be some sort of fight and when I got the internship at MacFarlane she acted like I did it just to spite her. Things got a little easier when she met Tomasz, when, because of the money I gave to Mam and Dad, they got the house here. That's when the emails started—the polite, infrequent *I am well, how are you?* messages we used to send when we remembered to. I thought she felt she had to, like she might have owed me after what I did, even though I never wanted her to feel that way.

But maybe they weren't. Maybe they were her way of trying. Trying badly but still.

I take out two cans from the fridge, trying to imagine myself slotting in here. Try to picture what it would be like, maybe getting an apartment in one of those new blocks near the beach or one of the houses around here. I'd get my coffee at Beth's and go to Roman's on special occasions. The idea doesn't fill me with horror the way it had a few weeks ago but nor do I feel any particular pull either. Just confusion.

The front door opens and I hear Louise and Tomasz call to each other before she enters the kitchen, her shoes squeaking on the floor as she flicks on the overhead light. The rain is heavier now and even in the short walk from the car to the door, her hair is plastered to her head, her jacket sodden. She looks like a drowned rat and, because I'm her younger sister, I tell her just that.

"Thanks," she says, dumping her purse on the table as I take a seat. "It's really coming down out there." Tomasz, too impatient with my procrastination, comes in to take the can from my hand before kissing Louise on the forehead and going straight back to the football.

"Is there another one of those?" she asks, nodding at the fridge.

"Sure." I get up to get her one but she's already moving.

"Bad day?" I ask, because this could be a thing we do now. Chat.

"Terrible day. What do you want for dinner?"

"I can cook something."

Louise side eyes me as she opens the can. "You cook?"

"A little."

She doesn't look convinced. "We've got some lamb. I'll just do a roast."

"At least let me help. I can be the gravy tester."

"Meaning you'll just drink the gravy."

"I haven't done that in years," I protest but she just snorts, taking out pans and dishes and everything else she needs. "Let me help," I repeat.

She looks confused, which is understandable given how I'd usually have left the room by now, but she's too tired to argue.

"Fine. Do you know how to chop?"

"I know the general principle of it."

"Then you're in charge of the potatoes. Do know how to boil a potato?"

"*Yes.*" Kind of.

"Wash. Peel. Chop evenly. Start with that."

At least she lets me boil the kettle by myself.

"Did you have a chef in New York?" she asks when I've managed that feat.

"No," I say, not raising to the bait. "I either ate at the office or got takeout. And when Tyler was there, Tyler cooked."

There's silence as I root around the drawer for a peeler.

"I can't imagine him cooking," Louise says eventually.

"He was a good cook. He was nuts about nutrition, so he kind of had to be."

"Ah. One of those."

"One of what?"

"You know," she says. "NutriBullet smoothies, micro-balanced salads. Did you ever see him eat butter?"

"Have *you* eaten the butter over there?" I ask. "I had to pay through the nose for a stick of Kerrygold."

"Did he ever cook for fun?"

I pause, a lie on the tip of my tongue, but not a single memory springs to mind. Tyler spent a lot of time in the kitchen, but Louise is right. It was always because he was measuring out grains and proteins.

"He could have fun other times," I say. "We used to have a lot of fun." Parties, vacations... we did a lot at the beginning, like any relationship.

Louise opens her mouth to respond but a frustrated shout from the living room interrupts her and she turns to wash the vegetables instead. For a few minutes we're quiet, working side by side. I add the potatoes to the pot.

"This is a good knife," I announce, just for something to say. "Hefty and sharp."

"Are you making small talk or are you threatening me?"

"It's like a proper grown-up knife," I insist, examining the handle.

"Because I'm a proper grown-up. Except not really because it's Susan's. She let me borrow it months ago."

"So, you stole it."

"In a neighborly way, yes. But she still has Dad's old crutches, so really we're even."

"Why did she take his crutches?"

"For Pat," Louise says absently. "After the accident."

I slice neatly through the final potato, frowning at her. "What are you talking about?"

"Pat's thing."

"Stop being vague."

"I'm not." She glances over in surprise. "Didn't Mam tell you? He was in a car accident."

"*No.*"

"Calm down. It was years ago. He was driving back from a match and one of those boy racers came out of nowhere. Smashed right into him."

"And no one thought to mention this to me?"

"He's fine now."

"I meant when it happened."

"We were a bit more concerned about him when it happened," she says pointedly, and we glare at each other. This time, she's the first one to back down. "I thought you knew," she says, and turns back to the vegetables. "You've seen him. He's grand now but he was in hospital for a few weeks and when he left Susan couldn't look after him by herself. Luke had to come back from Dublin to help."

"Luke was in Dublin?"

"He worked there for a few years after he finished his degree. But then the accident happened and he decided to come home. It was really good of him. I don't think they would have managed without him. Anyway, you can ask Pat about it if you like. He doesn't mind. He's got a bit of a limp some days but he's fine. A few pints down and he'll tell you the whole very dramatized story."

I turn up the heat on the stove, mulling over this new piece of information. "Luke never told me he lived in Dublin."

"Best friends now, are you?"

"I just didn't know he'd left, that's all. He always seemed like someone who would stay here forever."

"Boring, you mean?"

"*No.*" I stab a potato, testing its firmness. "Did you ever want to leave Clonard?"

"I did leave."

"For college. That doesn't count."

"Then no."

"Not even to Poland? I bet Tomasz must miss home."

"He does. But he hasn't lived there in years. He says this is home now."

"Right."

"Starting to get homesick?" she asks casually.

"Not for here if that's what you're thinking. It's just... I used to think you were mad at me for leaving."

She snorts. "I was *mad* that you went to work for MacFarlane, not that you left. How could I be mad at you for that?"

She turns to me when I don't answer, something in her expression softening slightly. "Abby, you were eighteen. And you ran off into the world with your arms wide open. You didn't look back because you didn't need to. But not everyone is like that. For me..." She sighs. "I know Clonard isn't perfect. I know it's small and shabby but I can't imagine living anywhere else. It's home. I've never needed more and I've never been mad that you did. Turn the temperature down."

"What? Oh." I lunge for the stove as the water starts to spill over, hissing down the side of the pot.

"Great job."

"Shut up," I mutter, and she smiles as Tomasz lets out another wail in the next room.

It was the nicest evening we had in a while though Louise is right. I can't cook. But she lets me stir the gravy. Afterward, I go to bed early, scrolling through Stewarts' website before I awake a few hours later to an earth-shaking, heart bursting boom of thunder. It's like nothing I've heard before and for a few moments, I simply lie there, staring at the ceiling where the twisted shadows of the trees outside don't so much dance as they do contort above me.

When it sounds again, I reach blindly to flick on the light, but nothing happens. One look at my alarm clock confirms it. The electricity is gone.

I fling off the covers and go to the window to see the rain coming down in sheets, almost sideways with the force of the wind.

A noise from the hallway draws me outside and I peek my head out to see Tomasz standing by his bedroom, dressed in old flannel pajamas.

"I have to be up at five," he says when he sees me.

"I have to be up at seven."

"So I win."

I grab a cardigan from the end of my bed as I step out. "The electricity is gone."

"I'll check the fuse box. Do you want coffee? I don't think we're going to get any sleep tonight."

"Can you make coffee with no power?"

He pauses, face falling. "No."

I give him a sympathetic smile and head into their bedroom to see Louise in a mirror image of the position I was in, her hands on the windowsill as she stares out at the storm.

"What time is it?" she asks when I join her.

"No clue. Either very late or very early."

We both gasp as the room lights up as bright as a camera flash and we count in unison, waiting for the thunder.

"It's right above us," Louise murmurs when it sounds.

"Do you think the trains will be okay?"

Her slight hesitation speaks volumes, but she follows it up with a convincing yes. "They're used to this kind of stuff," she adds. "It will be gone by morning."

Another flash of lightning and we both jump.

"I hate storms," she mutters.

"I think they're romantic."

We turn to see Tomasz in the doorway, a packet of crackers in his hands.

"What?" he asks. "I do."

Louise rolls her eyes. "I think I have some earplugs downstairs," she says, leaving the room. "We'll try and get some sleep. Don't worry, Abby."

"I'm not," I lie, and turn back to the window to watch the apocalypse.

CHAPTER 19

Louise was right. The storm is gone by the morning. The only problem is so is everything else.

The electricity comes back sometime around five a.m. I know this because my bedside light suddenly blinks to life, waking me just when I begin to drift off. Then a neighbor's house alarm goes off before another one joins it and the dogs start barking. There's no going back to sleep after that.

A weak version of our Wi-Fi comes back around seven and that's when I see the news.

The train lines are down.

Still in my pajamas, I rush to the kitchen, where Louise stands barefoot in her jeans and one of Tomasz's T-shirts, rummaging through the fridge as the radio blares the morning headlines.

"I need to borrow your car," I announce from the doorway. "And I also need you to drive that car."

"I have to work today," she says. "And we don't have the car. Tomasz was called into the hospital hours ago. They have a staff shortage with the storm."

"But the train lines are down. And the buses are running a skeleton service because the drivers can't get in and they're fully booked anyway and I—"

"Can't you do it virtually?" she interrupts, sniffing the milk.

"Not here. You know how bad our signal is."

"Then can't you ask them to change it? I'm sure they'll understand if you—"

"Louise," I interrupt. "I can't reschedule and I can't risk cutting out halfway through because of a bad connection. I need to be there. This is the only shot I've had in months. I have to show them that I want it."

She flicks the fridge door closed, thinking. Thinking way too slowly but still thinking.

"Okay," she says finally. "No car but we cat-sit for Mary down the road. Her husband used to be a taxi driver. If we play nice, he might do us a favor. Can you cry on command?"

"I can for this."

"Then put on some shoes."

Five seconds later, I follow her out the door. The sky is mockingly clear, almost cheerful, but it's still windy after the storm and there are branches and leaves scattered along our driveway, evidence of the overnight destruction. I spy Luke halfway up a ladder next door, repairing tiles on the porch roof. Susan stands beneath him, holding it steady. Or pretending to anyway. She immediately lets it go when she sees us, turning with a wave.

"Damn things almost flew away last night," she calls. "Where are you two off in such a hurry?"

"We need to talk to Paudie," Louise explains. "Abby's got a big interview in Dublin today."

"Oh, Pat mentioned! That's great news. Luke, did you hear?"

"That's great," he echoes, concentrating on the gutter.

"Trains are down," Louise continues. "We're going to butter him up for a lift."

"I didn't even think of that," Susan says, her brow furrowing. "When is it?"

"This afternoon," I say, already walking away and gesturing not so subtly for Louise to do the same. "I'll need to get going now in case the roads are bad."

"Maybe Luke could drive you."

"That's okay," I say as Luke glances at me. I am suddenly very aware of my braless, tank top state. "I'm sure Paudie will help us out."

"But Luke's—"

"I can't, Mam," he interrupts.

"What do you mean you can't?"

I cast one wistful look toward Paudie's house as I rejoin Louise by the hedge.

Susan is not impressed. "You heard her just now. She's got an interview and you've got nothing else to do today but help me clean up. You said so yourself."

"I—"

"*And* you can pick up some things in the city for me while you're there. I've got a shirt I want to return. You can do that while you're waiting and save me the stamp."

Luke looks like he's having an aneurism. I can almost see the vein popping out of his forehead. And I have to concur. Right now, the last thing I need is to spend three hours in a car with him.

"Well?" Susan asks sharply. "Did I raise you to be helpful or did I raise you to be sullen?"

They have a stare-off for about five seconds before he starts to climb down the ladder.

Susan whirls back to us with a wide smile. Louise gives me a nudge like I'm six years old thanking someone for a birthday present.

"That would be great," I say stiffly. "I really appreciate it."

He nods, jumping the last two rungs.

"There now," Susan says, throwing her hands in the air. "Finally. Like drawing water from a stone. Abby, dear, you go back inside and get ready and don't think about it a second more. You'll want to get on the road straight away in case there's diversions. He'll have you in Dublin in no time."

"Great," I say. Great.

But with no other option, there's no choice but to rush back inside and grab what I need. I had envisioned waking up and taking my time with my makeup and my hair but it's fine. If this is my curveball for today, then I'll deal with it. I didn't make it this far in my life without being able to adapt.

Twenty minutes later I bound back down the stairs to find Louise waiting for me in the hall.

"Luke's outside," she says, handing me a thermal flask with her charity's logo on the side. "I made you coffee. Mind the lid. It's a little wonky. And I put a bit of milk in it, so if you don't like—"

"A little bit of milk is perfect," I say.

"Great. Good." She nods. "Good luck, Abby."

"Thanks."

We stare at each other and for a moment I think she's going to hug me but instead she just nods again and disappears into the kitchen.

Luke's lounging against the side of his car when I emerge, his hands shoved deep into his pockets.

"Best of luck, Abby," Susan calls from her porch, and I turn with a wave as I follow him inside, tossing my travel bag in the back and my purse by my feet.

"We've got to stop meeting like this," I joke as I pull the door shut.

Nothing.

Okay then.

I stare forward as he backs out of the drive. It's not just Luke who's uncomfortable. It's been a while since I've worn formal clothing and Jess's skirt is tight around my waist, stretching across my thighs. I pull subtly at the waistband, thinking about my notes folded neatly in my purse. I had planned to read through them one final time on the journey but the thought of taking them out now in front of Luke makes me feel self-conscious. And then I get mad at myself for feeling that way. And then I get mad at him for *making* me feel that way.

"Do you mind if I put some music on?" I ask about five minutes out of the village. Five minutes of utter silence that was driving me insane.

He shrugs.

Well, it's better than nothing.

I press a button and the local radio station turns on, playing a song I don't know.

"That's about as much as I know about cars," I say, glancing at his stony expression. "I've never even had a lesson. Well, that's not true. Dad started giving me lessons. But they lasted about three minutes before he'd stop. He wouldn't even let me into the village."

Silencio.

Fine.

No. You know what? Not fine.

I turn to him, tugging down my seat belt so I can face him fully.

"Or we can just spend the next two and a half hours not talking?" I ask. "Whatever you want."

"It's three hours."

"He speaks!" I sit back with a huff. "If you hate me that much, you didn't have to give me a ride."

"I don't hate you."

"Could have fooled me," I mutter. "Look, any other time I would give this moment to you. I'm the one in the wrong here, I know. But not now. Not this morning. Not today. So please yell at me or snap at me or just talk to me. Don't sulk. Don't give me one more thing to worry about."

He doesn't respond. In fact, he doesn't respond for so long I think I've provoked him into giving me the silent treatment when he takes a breath. "It's just..."

"What? Tell me."

"I don't understand you!" he exclaims, and he sounds so genuinely confused that I swallow the retort on my tongue. "I don't understand any of this. From the moment you got back here, you made it pretty obvious that you're into me. But every time I see you since it's like I have to figure you out all over again. You have a fiancé but then you don't. You flirt with me, you kiss me, and you..." He shakes his head, hands flexing against the steering wheel. "You say you want to be friends but then you want more. We start more but then you pull away and you won't say why. You want me to talk? Fine. I'm asking why. Am I just a game to you? Some rebound after Tyler? Because that's what it feels like. And okay if that's what you get off on, but I don't do hot and cold. That's not what I'm looking for and I'm not going to fall for it again."

"Luke—"

"I'm driving you to Dublin because my mother asked me to," he says. "That is why I'm doing you a favor but let me be clear. We are not friends. We haven't been friends since we were eleven and I think the sooner we stop pretending we are, the better. Okay?"

"It's not a game."

"Whatever."

"It's not, Luke. I'm sorry for lying to you about Tyler. I'm not sorry for flirting with you. I was newly single, I'd lost my job, and I found and still do find you attractive, so yeah, I came on to you."

"Just forget it."

"No," I say, holding a hand up. My coffee swirls dangerously in the cup but I save it just in time. "I told you the truth when I said I thought we could be friends, but I'll be honest, I found that very hard to do because every time I saw you I got all fizzy inside."

A strange expression crosses his face. "Fizzy?"

"I did want more," I continue, starting to babble. "I thought, hey, the truth is out and I really like this guy and he seems to really like me and maybe there's something here. Maybe I can make something good out of this whole mess, and then you're all I can think about and all I *want* to think about, to the point where I'm not even applying for jobs some days, but then Beth starts talking and Louise and I are finally getting somewhere and—"

"Beth?"

"I thought we—" I break off, distracted. "What?"

"You said Beth."

"No, I didn't."

Luke glances at me, his anger fading into confusion. "What did Beth say?"

"Nothing." Shit. *Shit.*

"Abby—"

"Nothing," I repeat. "I was mid-rant. I misspoke."

His brows pull together before he pulls over sharply to the side of the road, so sharply I have to grip to the dashboard to keep from spilling my coffee.

"What are you doing! We're going to be late."

"We're hours early," he says. "What does Beth have to do with us?"

"Oh my God. *Nothing*. Keep driving."

"Beth's my friend. And if she's said something to you, I need to know."

I just won't play coy at the interview. That's it. I'll just march in there and say I can start right away and I'll beg them to let me sleep on the office floor and I'll never have to see any of these people again.

"Abby?"

"What?" I snap.

He doesn't so much as blink at the venom in my voice. "Talk to me. I don't want to keep running around in circles with you when that's all we need to do."

Why does he have to sound so sensible?

Luke turns off the engine, waiting.

"You're holding my interview hostage."

"I'm not," he says calmly. "I'll have you there in plenty of time and we can go right now if you really want me to. But I'm asking you to tell me what's going on."

Why was my life never this dramatic in New York? Why only in Clonard? Is it because nothing ever happens here? So every emotion gets heightened? Because that's what it feels like.

"Abby?"

"Beth likes you," I say. "As in she *like* likes you. She told me. So I can't be with you because that will hurt her."

"She likes me?"

"She told me at the bonfire. I promised I wouldn't tell you but now I have so..." I raise my coffee in a mock toast and take a sip.

Luke just looks at me.

"Can you drive already?"

"Abby." His voice is gentle. "Beth is my friend. One of my best friends. And I care about her deeply. But not in that way. She's like a sister to me."

"Don't say that," I groan, dropping my head back against the seat.

"But it's the truth. I didn't know. If I had, I would have talked to her. Is that why you stopped that night?"

"You mean before I kneed you in the groin?"

"Please," he says. "I want to know." And then: "I need to know."

I don't respond, staring straight ahead, and after a moment he puts the car in gear, pulling back onto the road.

"She's been so nice to me since I got back," I say eventually. "The nicest anyone's been to me and I couldn't do that to her. I couldn't be with you when she... and I'm sorry I let you think I was playing hot and cold. I'm sorry I didn't think up a better excuse. But she asked me not to say anything to you and I told her I wouldn't. She'd be so embarrassed if she knew about this. I mean, if I were in her shoes, I'd..." I trail off at the expression on his face. "Are you smiling?"

"No," he says quickly.

"You are! I'm telling you I'm a terrible person and you're smiling."

"I'm sorry," he says, not sounding sorry at all. "I guess I'm relieved."

"You're relieved I'm someone who goes around kissing other people's crushes?"

"I'm relieved we're finally starting to get somewhere. I'm relieved that horrified look on your face was because of Beth and not because of me." He straightens, looking determined. "It's good that you told me.'

"No, it's not."

"It is. I can talk to her. Clear the air."

"No! No talking! Did you hear a word of what I just said? You can't say anything. She can't know I said anything."

"I can't keep secrets, Abby."

"But it's bad enough that I told you about it in the first place. Do you know how many friends I have? Like real ones? Two. Two and a half if you count Rory. One is Jess and the other is Beth and I am not going to hurt her any more than I already have."

"You've got to trust me on this. I know her and no matter how badly you think she's going to—"

"Cow."

"What?"

"Cow!" I yell, pointing out the windshield. Luke curses, braking hard to avoid the animal standing in the middle of the road, and we're both thrust forward, straining against our seat belts.

"*Shit.*" The coffee does what it's been threatening to do and spills over the lid of the cup, going all down the front of my blouse.

"Christ." Luke pulls over again, the bushes scraping against the side of the car. "Are you okay? Did it burn you?"

"I'm fine. It's warm."

Luke takes the cup from me and gets out, tipping the remains into the bushes before trying to herd the unimpressed cow back into a neighboring field. I stare down at my ruined outfit. My punishment.

Cow successfully diverted, Luke hurries back to the car. "There's a shopping center a few miles up ahead," he says, getting in. "We can be in and out in no time."

"We don't need to," I say, reaching for my bag. "I've got another dress."

"You brought a spare change of clothes with you?"

"Of course I did. I'm a professional."

"Well, that's great," he says, relieved. "We'll just... what are you doing?"

He leans out of the way as I wiggle into the back seat. "Changing."

"Now? We can stop at a petrol station."

"Gross. No. I'm not dumping my clothes in a public restroom. This is Calvin Klein." I start unbuttoning and he turns quickly back to the front.

"Jesus, Abby."

"You've seen me in my underwear before."

"That's not the same and you know it."

"You can look if you want to, Luke. I don't care."

"I don't want to look. You're naked."

I toss my blouse at the side of his head and he grabs it, throwing it back at me as I slip my skirt down my legs with a smirk. I'm not even naked under there, I'm wearing tights for God's sake.

"You saw me in less than this at the beach," I remind him but he doesn't respond. He might as well be a statue in the front seat, he's so still. But I can see the faint blush of pink at the back of his neck, spreading to his ears.

I meant what I said. I didn't intend for this to be a striptease. And honestly, there's nothing sexy about it. The car is small and it's a struggle to fit into the clothes. I blow a curl from my face as I finally get the dress on, catching his eye in the rearview mirror. He immediately looks away and I climb back to the front.

"Enjoy the show?" I ask.

He doesn't respond, waiting for me to put my seat belt on before he starts driving again.

"Look," he says, sounding significantly calmer. "About what I said before. About Beth—"

"The cow stopped that conversation."

"Abby—"

"I mean it," I say. "Not now. Please. I have too much to think about."

"Fine. But we're not done," he warns. "You've got your interview but then we're going to talk." His eyes flick between me and the road as I reach down to get my purse. "What are you doing?"

I take out my makeup bag. "What does it look like?"

"Do you need me to stop the car again?"

I snort as I unscrew my mascara. "You think I've made it this far in life without doing my eyeliner in the back seat of a taxi? Just let me know if we hit any speed bumps between now and Dublin."

"We're supposed to be going to Dublin?"

"Does making unfunny jokes mean you forgive me?"

"I've been heading to Belfast this entire time."

"Just keep driving," I say, turning up the radio, and I hide my smile as he does just that.

CHAPTER 20

Our journey slows as we near the city, the road filling with cars all heading in the same direction. Dublin itself emerges from fields into industrial parks before the streets narrow and the sidewalks become crowded as we reach its heart. My nerves increase as we crawl to a halt at some junctions, but Luke was right, we are early, and even with the traffic we're right on time.

We manage to find a parking spot a few streets from the office, next to a manicured private park. Luke mutters about the extortionate price as he feeds a handful of coins into the meter but he only gives me a look when I suggest I pay for it.

Ticket displayed and car locked, we linger for a few seconds, stretching subtly after the journey. With the air cleared once more between us, the last hour or so had been kind of nice as we talked about everything and anything except Beth and us and my looming interview. We went through our favorite albums and TV shows, his placement at the clinic. I told him about the time Jess and I worked overnight in the office and caught two people having sex in the employee shower and another time when we thought someone was having sex in the stationery closet but they were actually just using the acoustics to record their true crime podcast ("all we could hear was loud breathing," I say). The conversation had been easy, flowing from one topic to the next with no rhyme nor reason but now we're both silent, almost awkward, as though a spell had been broken as soon as we got out of the car.

"Well," I say, stepping to the side to let a woman with a stroller pass. "If you want to return that stuff for your mam, I probably won't be more than an hour or so. Maybe a bit more if they're running behind."

"I can walk you there," is all he says. "It's on the way."

So we walk. We're on the south side of the city, on an avenue lined with elegant Georgian buildings now converted into offices, their façades covered in lush green vines and flowerboxes. Despite the good weather, we share the sidewalk with raincoat-clad tourists and I watch as they stop to take pictures of brightly painted doorways and gray church spires.

We reach the office quicker than I expect to, a five-story glass-fronted building that would look minuscule in New York but in Dublin has that impressive new-build gleam. STEWARTS shines in neat, clear lettering above the main entrance, where a security guard with a practiced blank look tries not to look bored as he watches people walk in and out. Block out the rest of the street and it could be anywhere in the world.

"How much time do you have left?" Luke asks as we stand to the side.

"About fifteen minutes."

"Are you nervous?"

"No."

It's the truth. I remember my last interview for MacFarlane, the one that didn't exactly get me a job as it did let me keep the one I had while others were cut, shown the door without so much as a thank you. It was only a few months after Tyler and I started dating and he'd made a big deal out of it, prepping patiently with me the evening before. In the morning, I went for a run while he made me breakfast (egg-white omelette with spinach, grapefruit juice) and then we walked the short distance to the office.

"You've got this," he'd said to me, and he'd looked so sure and so proud and I remember how relieved I'd been to have found someone who understood me so thoroughly, who matched my ambition, my desires.

I'd worn more or less the same outfit I'm wearing now. I realize it with a start as I catch a glimpse of myself in the lobby window. Same clothes. Same hairstyle. Same me.

Three years later and both the man and the city have changed. But the girl? She looks the same. For the first time since I came home, I recognize the woman in my reflection.

"Good luck," Luke says as I drag my gaze from her.

I suddenly want to know what he sees when he looks at me now. Because standing there in dirty jeans and the same T-shirt he was wearing this morning, he looks like he belongs to a different world. To a different me.

"You alright?"

I nod, smiling at him. "I'll text you when I'm out."

"Grand." He gives the building one more uncertain glance and then heads off toward the city center, leaving me alone. And though I know a lot of things are still left unsaid between us, I force him from my mind for now and head through the doors.

At three p.m. the lobby is busy with guests going to and coming from meetings. I'm directed by the receptionist to a comfortable leather chair, where I pop a mint into my mouth and check my reflection properly on my phone. My makeup is subtle, my skin behaving. My curls are a little frizzy but there's nothing I can do about that so I leave them be, crossing my ankles as I wait.

I try to meet the eye of every person who comes through the doors without seeming too obvious. I spot my contact immediately, the one I'd been emailing the past few days to arrange this because, of course, I'd looked her up. Caroline Mahoney. Twenty-six. Master's degree in international relations. Executive assistant.

"Ms. Reynolds?" She strides toward me, her heels clacking against the floor as she swipes her way through the turnstiles. The little panel on the glass blinks from red to green and then her hand is out, her nails short and painted a non-offensive burgundy. She wears no jewelry.

We exchange pleasantries. She asks if I want to go to the bathroom and would I like a coffee, and tells me there's water in the room. All the while we're walking. Back through the turnstiles, where we skip the elevator for a carpeted staircase and up to the first floor. There, we go through a set of thick wooden doors and into a busy office with its hum of conversation and sleek overhead lighting and people with jobs and goals and purpose. A small conference room is next, its glass walls frosted for privacy.

On the table is the promised water. Only one glass because there is no person on the other side of the table to meet me, only a large television screen, which in a few minutes will beam the faces of my interviewers.

"I'm going to be just over here," Caroline says, pointing to a chair out of my eyeline. "Just in case the screen goes." She crosses her fingers. "Hasn't happened yet."

I sit, pressing my fingers to the arms of the chair and to the table, trying to orientate myself. The air inside the room is cool, the blinds drawn to keep out the sunshine. Caroline takes her seat and I pour myself a glass of water as the screen flashes.

Three men in dark blue suits appear before me.

I take a breath and smile.

*

"Have a good evening!" Caroline calls as she sees me out of the building. I wait until she vanishes back inside before I check the time on my phone.

I was in there for just over an hour.

It went okay, I think. My Ireland excuse was perfect on why I wasn't picked up somewhere else. I needed a break. Needed time to see my family and catch my breath so I'd be raring to go. I joked about it and, thank God, they were the joking kind of interviewers, less grilling more conversation. They laughed. They understood. We went through my experience, through my work and then the questions came.

Would I be open to travel? Yes, I could make it work. No, I have no family obligations, no big commitments outside of work. That's not to say work is all there is. Oh no. That would be unhealthy. I like to run and I'm thinking about getting into cooking. Really into cooking. A life outside work is important to me, so long as that life doesn't interfere *with* my work.

Adrenaline has my hands shaking with a fine tremor, a smile pulling at my lips.

I nailed it.

I know I did. I...

I want to call Tyler. The urge is not wholly irrational. Calling Tyler is what I did after my last interview. Calling Tyler is what I did at every big moment of my life for the last three years. Tyler who would understand what I feel. Tyler who would always understand.

Or at least I thought he did.

I stare down at my phone, actually contemplating it when I hear my name. Luke appears through the passers-by, carrying a small Brown Thomas bag in his hand. Judging by the shortness of his hair, he looks like he squeezed in a cut as well.

He breaks into a relieved smile as soon as I look up and I realize he'd been nervous for me. And I'm suddenly so glad he drove me up. I'm so glad he's with me. The feeling hits me with such force that for a moment I can only stand there. I was wrong. I don't want Tyler here. I don't want anyone here but him.

"It went okay then?" he asks when he reaches my side.

"I said everything I wanted to."

"That's the important thing. You mentioned me right?"

"First thing out my mouth. They were very impressed." I spy a few stray hairs clinging to the side of his neck and fight the urge to brush them away. "You get your mam's stuff sorted?"

"Yeah. It wasn't too busy." He waits. "Well? Are you going to tell me about it?"

"No. It's boring. Let's just go. Beat the traffic."

He doesn't buy it. "You're one of those people who likes to dissect the entire interview word by word, aren't you?"

"Not at all."

He just waits.

"I think the big boss blinked at me in a really positive way," I say, ignoring his grin. "Like in a Morse code 'I'm going to hire you' way. And the assistant who brought me in? Caroline? Loved me."

"Oh yeah?"

"We clicked. And Yuusuf, the second big boss? Do you know what he asked me? What I wanted. Me. MacFarlane *never* asked me what I wanted. They always had this 'you're so lucky to be here' vibe. Like they were doing me a favor by hiring me in the first place. But with Stewarts it's like they—"

"Luke?"

I'm cut off mid-gush by a woman standing by the lobby entrance. She's staring at us. Or rather, she's staring at Luke.

She's pretty. In a cute red dress with thick dark hair pulled back into a French braid. A designer bag hangs from her shoulder, a navy blazer draped over her arm.

"Oh my God!" She laughs. "It is! Hi!"

"Alison." The sound of her name on his lips seems to shake Luke from his stupor and he jerks forward, kissing her on the cheek. "How are you?"

"I'm good. I'm surprised to see you here." Her eyes flick to me as she smiles, welcoming me into the conversation. "I don't think we've met."

"No." An unfamiliar jealousy spikes through my previous glow. I don't know what to do with it. "I'm Abby."

"Abby had an interview," Luke says.

"You did? Here? That's great." She sounds like she means it. "I'm actually doing some consultant work with them. They're good people." She adjusts the strap of her bag, glancing back at Luke. "We used to live together," she explains when he doesn't say anything. "Years ago. In this crappy little house in Rathmines."

"You were roommates?" I ask. Romantic roommates? Roommates with benefits?

"Along with four other people and a stray cat that Jeremy insisted on feeding. It threw up on my bed once. No! Twice."

Luke clears his throat, more uncomfortable than I've ever seen him. "How is Jeremy?"

"He's good! Got a job at RTÉ as a radio producer. He's loving it. My partner," she says to me, and I almost wilt in relief. "You should have told me you were coming up. He would have loved to see you."

"It was kind of a last-minute decision," Luke says awkwardly. "Next time."

"There better be a next time. You disappeared on us! How's home? How's your dad?"

"It's good. He's good."

Alison hesitates, finally picking up on his weird energy. To her credit, her smile doesn't change. "That's great," she says. "Do you guys have time to grab a drink or—"

"We should head back," Luke interrupts. "Get ahead of the traffic."

"Sure." She's surprised. I know she is because I am too and while I have a feeling she wants to say something more to him, maybe she can't with me there. "Well, hey, anytime you want to invite us for a countryside getaway, that's fine by me."

"Definitely." Luke smiles like he just remembered how to. "It was great seeing you."

"Yeah. Crazy." They hug. Awkwardly. And then she turns to me. "Abby! Congratulations, well done, good luck. Maybe I'll see you in there someday."

"Hopefully. It was nice meeting you."

"You too!" She steps back, pressing the button for the crosswalk. "I guess I've got an oven to scrub and dry cleaning to pick up. Teenage me would be horrified."

And with that she's off, winding her way through the stationary traffic toward a bus stop across the street.

"She seems nice," I say after a beat.

Luke doesn't answer, only turns on his heel and walks in the opposite direction, glancing once over his shoulder to make sure I'm following.

It takes me a few seconds to catch up with him and when I do, I have to say, I'm a little annoyed.

"Is she an ex or something?"

"No," he says quickly. "Nothing like that. She was a friend. *Is* a friend." He pauses at another crosswalk, jabbing the button.

"You're acting like you owe her money."

"She looks different, that's all."

"What did she used to look like?"

"Nothing... it's not..."

I've never seen him look so agitated before. Like he can't get out of the city fast enough. He reminds me of me in those last few days in New York. When all I wanted to do was escape.

"It doesn't matter," I say as he struggles to find the words. "Don't worry. It's none of my business."

And strangely, it's those words that seem to break through to him.

"I just didn't expect to see her," he says. "A million people in this city and of course I bump into one of the few people I know."

"Louise said you used to live here."

"For a while." The light goes green and we walk across together. "I went to college with Jeremy," he explains. "Her partner. He got me a room in his house share. It was horrible. The back door didn't lock and the boiler only worked for an hour a day but we were all broke and didn't care. Especially Alison," he adds after a pause. "She did not have a job as... whatever it is she does now. When I first met her she was working as an independent tour guide and self-publishing experimental poetry pamphlets. And Jeremy once crawled under the neighbor's shed as a dare and got stuck. We had to call the fire department. Jeremy who's now a radio producer at the national broadcaster."

"People change," I remind him when we reach the other side. "They grow up."

"They do. I know they do. It's just I was supposed to grow up with them." He glances at me, looking almost embarrassed. "I know you think I'm moving forward, but you're not the only person who feels like they took a step backward coming home."

Luke came back from Dublin to help.

I still, remembering what Louise had said about Pat's accident. I knew he came back because of his dad but I thought he'd stayed because he wanted to. I'd assumed it was where he wanted to be. But what if it wasn't? What if he cut short a different life here? One I have no idea about.

"I was rude," he sighs now. "I'll email her when we get back. Arrange something."

"You should," I say. I think about Jess and how easily I almost let her go. How I definitely would have if she weren't so stubborn. "She seems nice."

"She is nice. She's..." He trails off with a frown. "You thought she was my ex?"

"I..." Crap. "She's very pretty. And the way she was smiling at you, I thought you might—"

"You're getting flustered."

"*No.* I am full of adrenaline from my interview."

"Were you jealous?" The idea appears to cheer him up, and while I'm glad he's in a better mood, I wish it wasn't because he could see right through me.

"Let's go back to you being upset," I say.

"I wasn't upset. I was thrown. It's completely different."

"You looked like you wanted to run back to Clonard if it meant getting out of there faster."

We pass a pub, already busy with people sitting outside, enjoying the summer sunshine.

"I can't imagine you living here," I say, squeezing around a group of construction workers. "You're basically Mr. Clonard."

"Do I get a tiara with that?"

"Did you like it?"

"Dublin? Sure. I liked being away from home. I liked being around people who didn't know who I was. Meant I could be someone new."

"And who were you?"

"Kind of slutty, if I'm honest."

I burst out laughing.

"It was the best coming here," Luke continues. "Not having to worry about what people thought of me or what would get back to my parents. The clubs, the bars—"

"The STDs."

"I was very safe, I'll have you know. That video they showed us in school scared the life out of me."

"Not all of it, apparently."

"Well, what about you?"

"Me?"

He starts walking backward down the empty street, facing me. "You. Before Tyler."

Before Tyler...

He grins when I don't say anything. "Uh-oh."

"Not uh-oh."

"I can see you choosing what you want to tell me."

I shake my head, which only makes him smile harder. "When you spend a lot of time with the same people in a charged atmosphere things get intense. Plus I was one of only a few women in my job, so it wasn't like I was starved of attention."

"Yeah, I'm sure that was the reason."

"Excuse me?"

"Come on," he says. "You're beautiful, Abby." He stops walking when I do, again with that stupid smile on his face. "Are you blushing?"

"No."

"You are. You're embarrassed."

"It's warm!" I say, pressing my hands to my cheeks, which okay, are a little heated.

"I didn't mean to make you blush."

"Yes, you did," I grumble, but he's still smiling at me and I like that he is so I don't push it. "The accent worked for me as well," I say. "Not so much of a novelty here though."

"No. Definitely one of the downsides of moving home."

I start walking again but he doesn't, so two steps bring me straight to him.

"Thank you for bringing me today," I say, peering up at him. "It could have been a disaster."

"I wanted to," he says. "Even if I pretended I didn't." His eyes widen then and he takes a step back. "I almost forgot."

My heart skips a beat as he opens the Brown Thomas bag but he sees the look on my face immediately. "It's Mam's birthday present," he says before I can get ahead of myself. "But you don't come away completely empty-handed."

He draws out a bar of chocolate and tosses it to me.

"First thing you need after an adrenaline rush like that," he says as my mouth waters at the sight of it.

"You're a lifesaver."

"You don't think I noticed you eating all those eggs at the Fun Day?" He smiles. "Well done on the interview."

I rip it open, not realizing how hungry I was. But I shouldn't be surprised, I've barely eaten anything all day. "Do you want some?" I ask, or at least I try to around the four squares I just bit off. It is with supreme effort that I don't moan at the taste of it.

He shakes his head, looking pleased. "It's for you."

We start walking again, slower now as we turn the corner toward the car. I've almost finished the whole bar when he speaks again, ruining my good mood.

"I'm going to talk to Beth."

"No. Luke—"

"Yes," he says calmly. "As soon as I get back. I'm going to tell her how I feel about you and we'll take it from there."

I don't say anything, folding the wrapper into a tiny square. How he feels about me. How's that for a vague statement? But I know nothing I say now will deter him. And I know that's right. That's what adults do. They talk.

"Just..." I sigh. "Be nice, okay?"

"What do you think I'm going to do?"

"Please."

He pauses, realizing how serious I am. "I will be."

"And gentle. Be gentle."

"Abby—"

"Maybe buy her some flowers."

"That's a bit of a mixed signal, don't you think?"

"I guess." I slump against the door. "I just don't want to hurt her."

"Neither do I."

"I also don't want her to be mad at me."

"So talk to her too."

We look at each other over the roof of his car. Again, he makes it sound so simple.

"You ready to go home?" he asks when I don't respond.

I nod and this time I don't correct him.

Home.

CHAPTER 21

It's late by the time I get back. The driveway is empty, meaning Tomasz must still be at work, and there's only one light on in the upstairs landing.

I let myself in as quietly as I can, leaving my shoes by the door as I hurry up the stairs but Louise calls my name as soon as I reach the top step.

"I'm back," I yell, slipping into my bedroom. "Traffic was a nightmare."

"Could you come in here?"

"Give me a sec!" I strip out of my clothes and pull on a pair of pajamas, tying my hair into a loose ponytail, but when I stick my head into her bedroom, the room is empty.

"Abby?"

Her voice calls from the back of the house and I turn, my fuzzy socks sliding along the floorboards. "Where are you?"

"Bathroom."

"Are you alright?"

No answer. The door is open but there's no light on. Starting to feel like I'm in the middle of a scary movie, I flick the switch to see Louise sitting fully dressed in the empty bathtub, her knees drawn to her chest.

We stare at each other.

"Why are you sitting in the dark?" I ask eventually.

"It kind of just got dark around me."

"...Okay." I do a quick scan for any obvious injury, thinking maybe she hit her head but there's nothing. "What's happening right now?"

A tiny frown appears on her face. "I think I'm pregnant."

I wait for the punchline. Maybe that *is* the punchline.

Maybe it's not.

"You *think* you're pregnant?" I ask carefully, and my next thought is that she could have had a miscarriage. Horror fills me as I glance around the room but there's nothing out of place. Except for my sister in the bathtub.

She holds up something in her hand. A pregnancy test. I move instantly toward her, arm outstretched, but she hesitates.

"I peed on it."

"I don't care." I take it from her, examining the little blue plus sign. "And this means yes?"

She nods. "The box is over there."

I read that too, not trusting her. "And you've tried—"

"I've done three different ones," she says, straightening her legs with a wince. She must have been in there for hours. "What do you think it means?"

"What do I... I think it means you're pregnant, Louise."

"That's what I thought."

"This is a good thing, right?" I'm confused by her reaction. "You said you were trying."

"We are. We were. I guess we don't need to try anymore."

"No."

"Because I'm pregnant."

"Yes."

Her frown deepens. "The stick says so."

"It does." I hand it back to her and she cradles it in her hands.

"Do you want to get out of the bath?" I ask. "Maybe come downstairs and we can talk about it?"

"Not really." She looks up at me. "Do you want to come in?"

I stare at her, waiting to see if she's joking. She's not.

With a sigh, I climb carefully over the side. She draws her legs back up to make room for me and we fold them over each other so we can both fit. It is, shockingly, not comfortable at all.

"I haven't taken a test in weeks," she says, looking almost guilty. "And I've been so busy I didn't realize I was late. It was only after we talked the other day that I even thought to check."

"How far along do you think you are?"

"I have no idea."

"And you're feeling okay?"

"I'm fine. I'm just..."

"Processing."

"Mm-hm."

"Because you're pregnant."

And finally, *finally* the first hint of a smile. "Yeah."

"You're going to have a baby," I insist because she still doesn't seem to be getting it. "Have you told Tomasz yet?"

She shakes her head. "I didn't want to. I wanted to be sure."

"I'd say three positive pregnancy tests is pretty sure. But you two should go to the doctor tomorrow."

She takes a ragged breath. "Yeah."

"You know what this means, don't you? No more coffee. Or soft cheese."

"I don't like soft cheese."

"Well, then you're grand."

She laughs a little hiccup and leans her head back. "Ow," she mutters, adjusting herself around the faucet.

I smile at her, at my big stupid sister. "I'm going to be an aunt. The cool aunt. The cool rich aunt who spoils her whenever I see her and feeds her too much sugar before handing her back to you without any of the consequences."

"Her?"

"I have a feeling it's a girl. What do you think?"

"I have no idea." She puts the stick carefully on the side of the bath before placing her hands on her stomach.

"It's down a bit."

"I know." She scowls, but slides her hands down to where her baby rests.

"Are you scared? It's okay if you are."

"I *know*," she says, sounding more normal now I'm annoying her. She shifts against the side of the tub. "My leg is cramping."

"Because you've been sitting in the bath all night. Are you sure you don't want to call Tomasz?"

She shakes her head. "Let him work. I want to tell him in person, and if I ask him to come home, he'll just worry and..." She trails off with a sharp gasp.

"What? What is it?"

"How did your interview go?"

I gape at her, my heart racing. "That is not important right now."

"It is," she insists. "I can't believe I forgot to ask. I got you some chocolate and everything."

I sit back, my turn to be annoyed as I realize every time she so much as stubs her toe I'm probably going to freak out. "It was fine."

"That's it? Tell me how it went."

"You're so weird."

"Please," she says. "I'm too nervous. I don't want to talk about it. Talk about you."

She's starting to panic, her hand rubbing tiny circles into her stomach as if her baby is already several months and not several days old.

"It went fine," I repeat, trying to sound as soothing as possible. "I said what I needed to say. I don't know who I'm up against, but if the odds are in my favor, then I've worked hard enough to meet a little luck." I pause. "We bumped into a friend of Luke's," I add. "She works with them."

"Oh yeah? What kind of friend?"

"An old roommate. I thought she might have been an ex but Luke said she wasn't."

"You asked him that?" She seems surprised. "You actually like him, don't you?"

There's no point in denying it so I just nod.

"Because he got hot?"

"*No*," I say. "Though, yes, that's what started the initial attraction. You think I'm that shallow?"

"Kind of."

"He's just Luke." I don't know how else to explain it. At least not in a way that doesn't make me sound like a complete stalker. I don't know how to tell her that running into him that first night feels more like fate whenever I think about it. How whenever I look at him, I feel safe and warm in a way I never have before, even when I was with Tyler.

I don't know how to tell her but she must hear it in my silence because she stares at me, her hands stilling on her stomach as she turns suddenly serious.

"What are you going to do?" she asks when I don't continue.

"I don't know. I'm not sticking around here. He knows that."

"Does he?"

"I haven't given him any indication otherwise."

"That's not the same as him knowing. You need to make that clear if you're going to pursue each other."

"No one's *pursuing* anyone. He's not the stable boy, Louise."

"Look, obviously a lot has changed since you left. Luke's a grown man and you're a grown woman and you can do what you like. But just be careful. Actions have consequences and you never know what someone's thinking. Don't get his hopes up and leave, okay?"

"I haven't even gotten the job yet."

"And if you did get it? Would you take it?"

"I don't know."

"Yes, you do."

I pick at my nails, not able to meet her eyes. "Well, what would you do?"

"Abby."

"If it were Tomasz," I push, "what would you do?"

She sighs. "I don't know. There's never been a choice between Tomasz and something else. Maybe I always chose him and it never occurred to me to do otherwise."

"It's only been a few weeks," I say. "When we were kids doesn't count. I've only known this version of Luke for a few weeks."

"I knew Tomasz was the one the first night I met him."

"You were drunk," I scoff.

"And I still knew. Do you know what he did when he introduced himself?"

"Made a speech about rising sea levels?"

"He kissed my hand."

"I can't believe you're a secret romantic."

"He kissed my hand," she repeats with a smile. "And we talked all night. And in the morning, even though it was raining he went out and bought me a coffee and a croissant."

"In the morning?" I stare at her. "You slept with him on the first night?"

"No need to sound so surprised."

"I'm not surprised. I'm impressed."

"What I'm saying is, if you feel you have to make a choice, then sometimes you already know. Sometimes you're not making a choice at all. You're just delaying the inevitable."

"When did you get so wise?"

She smiles serenely. "When you have kids you'll under—"

"Oh, shut *up*."

"A mother knows."

"I knew you'd turn into one of those people. Holier than thou because you have a kid." I lean back, sinking farther into the tub. "You're going to be so annoying."

"I'll try." She takes a breath, easing her neck from one side to the other. "I'm ready to get out of the bathtub now."

"Thank God."

But neither of us move.

"You have to go first," I say, holding on to her calf, which is atop of mine.

"Right." She stares at it for a moment. "It's just I'm going to get pins and needles and—"

I roll my eyes, carefully extracting myself from under her and then, more awkwardly than either of us would like, I climb out before helping my stupid, stiff-limbed, pregnant, beautiful big sister do the same.

CHAPTER 22

We're both asleep on the couch by the time Tomasz pulls into the driveway. It's the beam of his headlights that wake me, sweeping over the front of the house. Louise doesn't stir, so I drape a blanket over her, and creep upstairs to my bed, leaving them to talk. The next morning I wake early and go for a run. It's the best one I've had in weeks. Months maybe. And I barely notice the time pass as I do a second loop through the town, only stopping when Louise calls me home for some celebratory pancakes, and who am I to say no to that?

Both she and Tomasz are ecstatic, barely able to keep the smiles off their faces, even when they both swear me to secrecy until they know everything's okay with the baby. Their happiness distracts me from the whirlwind of the day before and it's not until that evening when I take advantage of the good weather to go for a stroll that I remember what Luke had said about talking to Beth.

The reason I remember is because I meet her outside the café just as she's closing up and at the sight of me she stops and she stares and I know he did it. And I actually feel a little scared. As in clammy-hands, stomach-twisting scared. All I want to do is turn and run away, which is ridiculous. I've faced scarier people than Beth.

Except I haven't, have I?

Because the people in the office were nameless, smirking men and part of my whole thing there was the element of surprise. No one expects the small Irish girl to stand up to them, to talk back.

But this is different. This is Beth. I know Beth. I like Beth. And instead of being a friend to her, I broke her heart and betrayed her confidence and now I don't even know how to say I'm sorry.

The moment I open my mouth to try she turns and walks away and my heart drops, disappointment and guilt flooding through me, but she barely takes two steps before she stops, whirling to face me again.

"You go," I say when neither of us says anything.

"I talked to Luke," she says. "About everything. I'm sorry I didn't come see you sooner. I'm just so embarrassed."

I stare at her. "You have nothing to be embarrassed about."

"But just the *thought* of you feeling guilty for liking him and that I might have been the reason that you two didn't try and be together is *horrible*."

"Beth—"

"I mean, that's what I get for not thinking before I speak. I just talk, talk, talk and I'm so sorry you didn't think you could—"

"Would you stop?" I snap. "Just for once in your life would you stop being you?"

She pauses. "I don't understand."

"Stop being nice and apologizing to me when I should be the one saying sorry."

"I'm sorry."

"Beth!"

She claps a hand over her mouth. "I can't help it," she says, her voice muffled.

"I'm the bad person here," I remind her. "I'm the one who should feel guilty and bad and awful. I'm the one saying sorry."

"And I forgive you."

"No," I groan. "You have to yell at me. You have to be mad."

"I'm not a very yelly person."

My hands go to my hips as I glare at her. Then I realize I'm glaring at her and I stop. "And I'm not a very good apologizing person."

"You're really not," she says gently.

"Well..." I glance around, at a loss. "Do you want to get a drink?"

She looks uncertainly toward the café. "I could open back up, I guess."

I shake my head. "A real drink," I say, and two minutes later we're sitting in one of the back booths of Pete's with two glasses of wine between us.

"I didn't mean to say anything to him," I say as soon as she'd taken her first sip. "I know that's probably hard to believe but we were arguing and I was so mad at him and it just came out."

"He told me how upset you were."

"I thought you'd be furious at me."

She wrinkles her nose. "Why?"

"Because I..." I gaze at her, flustered. "Because we kissed! I kissed him. You should know that. It wasn't Luke at first. *I* initiated it. Not him. I'm to blame."

"But honestly, Abby, it's not like we were together or I had some sort of claim over him. I knew he didn't feel the same way about me. I've always known. But I didn't care. There's not a lot of people to choose from around here and it's not like I have the time to put myself out there and meet someone who isn't in a one-mile radius. He was the perfect excuse for me. Here was a guy I could tell myself I had a crush on and then I wouldn't have to risk everything again for someone new."

"You mean like you did with Ross?"

"I tend to follow others," she says. "Everyone thinks I'm a free spirit but I'm not. I'm a barnacle. I latch onto people. If people were boats," she clarifies.

"I get it."

"I followed Ross. I followed him all the way out here and when he left I was stuck because no one came along and picked me up. So I latched onto Luke."

"But you still have feelings for—"

"I never said anything to him. Not once. And I don't know if you've met me, but I say a lot of things to a lot of people. I'm not shy when it comes to people I like but I didn't say anything to him because I knew that my feelings were... not that they weren't real but that they were a reaction to my surroundings. And I liked how it was between us. I liked having him as a friend. Saying something would ruin that and that terrified me."

"So I ruined it for you."

"*No*," she says with a small smile. "Would you stop beating yourself up? It was the first thing he said to me. That he didn't want anything to change between us. He was really sweet. As usual," she adds with a roll of her eyes. "I mean, yes, will I still look at his butt sometimes? Of course I will. But he listed all the ways we would be terrible together and I've got to say he makes a convincing argument."

"He didn't."

"I don't know if I should be insulted that he thought that much about it but I appreciate it nonetheless." She smiles. "His main point was that he's too structured for me. That between his course and the café and his parents he blocks out his day by the hour. That it's the only thing that can clear his mind. He even schedules in his downtime. Can you imagine that?"

"No," I say, taking a long, *long* sip of wine.

"He said I need someone who'll drop everything at a moment's notice and take me to Paris. Or go with me if I want to sell the café and move to Brazil."

"Because you live intuitively."

"I do. And my intuition tells me that he's right. And that the two of you would make a pretty good thing."

I say nothing, trying to ignore how happy her words make me.

"I was just so *obtuse*," she continues. "I mean it's obvious now that I think about it. You should have seen him the day you first came to the café. He was so rattled. I mean, as soon as you left you were all he could talk about."

"Really?"

"Well, he didn't say anything good. It's more that he wouldn't let it go. He wouldn't let *you* go. Eventually, Ollie had to tell him to shut up, which is not a very Ollie thing to do. I think that spooked him. And then later he always did one of two things when you showed up. He'd either magically appear or run up the stairs like a frightened rabbit. I should have put two and two together."

"So you're not mad at me for spilling your biggest secret?"

She raises a brow. "You think a crush on Luke was my biggest secret?" she asks, and I smile. "Can we stop talking about it now?" She pouts. "It can just be a thing we laugh about five years from now from the headquarters of my food empire."

"Is that your new plan?"

"It's what Jess seemed to think. She left me with some very detailed marketing plans."

"That sounds like her."

Beth sits back, the giant silver earrings she's wearing jingling with the movement. "And are you going to tell me how your interview went or are we going to do what I used to after mine, which is pretend they never happened?"

I laugh. "The interview went fine. They said someone would get back to me in a few weeks, but who knows."

"It's so weird to think that your life could change again so quickly. Just like that."

"I know."

"I wonder what it would be like if you stayed," she muses. "I'd probably have to convince you to be my business partner."

"I wouldn't know the first thing about owning a business."

"No, but you're confident."

"So are you."

"I have a different kind of confidence," she says ruefully. "Don't think I don't know that. I have optimism. You have drive. It's very different. But I don't think even you could save me."

"With the café?" I frown. "Are things going badly?"

"No," she says. "Yes. It's pretty simple to explain. Outgoings are high and incomings are low. I'm losing money every day now."

"There must be somewhere you could cut costs. Maybe Luke could—"

She shakes her head, cutting me off. "Luke's already given me a huge discount on the space, not to mention free labor. He makes a show of helping out as if I'm doing a favor to him but we both know it's because I can't afford to bring on anyone else. Do you think he gets up early on a Sunday morning out of the goodness of his heart? He says he gets free coffee but he's usually a one-cup-a-day guy and as you can see from his stomach he doesn't exactly pack away the carbs." She sighs. "Ollie's already doing too much. Plus she never asks for a raise and it's not like she gets any tips. I just thought the village would get behind it, you know? I thought they'd be excited about somewhere new. Everyone's always complaining that nothing opens."

"You sound like you're thinking about closing."

"That's because I am. I thought about a fundraiser but people only have fundraisers for places they actually like."

"Beth," I protest.

"It's true! And I'm sad about it. Of course, I am. And not just because it's my money. I mean," she grimaces. "It's mostly because it's my money. No one likes to be broke but if I pull the plug now it won't be too bad. At least I won't get into any more debt. And the more I think about it, the more I ask myself, would it be so bad to let it go? To see through the summer season and then close up shop? I read that a lot of big-time Wall Street guys won't even look at you until you've got a couple of failed businesses under your belt."

"That's true. It's experience."

"So that's what I'm going to chalk it up to. I tried my best and I failed. More importantly, I failed without dragging anyone down with me. Which is more than a lot of people can say."

"That's a very positive way of looking at it." But I have to admit I'm impressed by her words. By her resolve. "I don't think you're a barnacle, Beth."

"No?"

"No," I say. "I think you're the ship."

"And I think *that's* the nicest thing anyone's ever said to me." She peers slyly into her almost empty glass. "You still want to make amends?"

"All week if that's what it takes." And I slide out of the booth to get another round.

CHAPTER 23

"What are you doing?"

Louise spins around, clutching the mascara tube as if I just caught her doing drugs.

"Are you putting on makeup?" I ask.

"Just a little bit," she says, defensive as she turns back to the mirror. "I wear makeup."

"No, you don't." I take in her white blouse, the gold pendant at her neck. "You're not getting dressed up for Mam and Dad, are you?"

She doesn't answer. With the doctor confirming she's a little over eight weeks, she's decided to tell our parents about the pregnancy. It's still early but she said she doesn't want to wait any longer, reasoning that if they were in Clonard, they'd know. But judging by how she's acting right now, you might think she's about to tell them she burned the house down.

"I don't know why you're so nervous," I say. "They're going to be thrilled. And you want to tell them."

"I do. But you know what they're like," she says as I perch on the end of her bed. "They're going to want to come back."

"For the birth of the first grandchild? Yeah, I'd hope so."

"Not for the birth. Obviously, I want them there for that. I mean they'll want to come back *now*. As in tomorrow."

I start to laugh when I realize she's right. "Oh my God, they will."

"A few weeks when the baby's born would be great. I'm going to ask Mam to do just that but..."

"She'll want to be here full-time," I finish. "Immediately."

"Exactly," she says, applying a thick coat of mascara. "And I want to nip that idea in the bud so there's no miscommunication. Therefore I need to look like I have everything under control, which means I need to look in control."

"She says, poking herself in the eye."

Louise glares at me as she wipes a smudge away.

"When are you going to tell Tomasz's folks?"

"Not for a while. We might go over and tell them in person." She makes a face at her reflection. "Why are my lashes clumping?"

"Because your makeup is cheap. Why don't you use mine?"

"That's so unhygienic."

"We share a toilet."

"Yeah, well, I'm not putting the toilet in my eye."

"You're not supposed to put the mascara in your eye either, you idiot."

She lets out a quiet screech and dumps the wand back on the dressing table.

"Oh yeah," I say, as it bounces to the floor. "You're totally in control."

"I don't like attention."

"You love attention. You had a megaphone in your hand when you were twelve years old. They wanted you to run for county councilor when you were eighteen! You've never been scared of telling anyone anything."

"But that was never about *me*. It was about everything else. This is completely different."

Tomasz walks into the room, looking very uncomfortable in a blue button-down shirt Mam got him for Christmas last year. "I look like I work at a golf club," he complains.

"Let's just get this over with," Louise says. "Everyone downstairs. Let's go."

Tomasz takes me in with a frown as I brush past him. "Why doesn't Abby have to dress up?"

"Because *I'm* going for a run," I say.

"You're escaping," he mutters.

In the living room, they sit on the old love seat while Louise opens the laptop, still looking a little peaky even with the makeup.

Tomasz notices it too. "Your face is melting," he says affectionately, brushing the hair from her shoulder. I sit at the bottom of the stairs, lacing up my shoes.

"It's because I'm sweating," Louise says. "It's too hot."

"It's mild at best," I scoff.

"We should wait another few weeks before telling them. Just to be sure."

"Okay," Tomasz says.

"But they deserve to know."

He shrugs. "Whatever you want to do."

It's not what she wants to hear.

"Don't look at me," I say when she turns her indecisive gaze my way. "I'm not the one who let my husband knock me up."

"Why don't you stay for the start?" she asks me. "You can distract them."

"From what? Your clumpy eyelashes?"

"Abby!"

"I don't like you like this," I say, getting to my feet. "Pregnant you is weird."

"I don't think your eyelashes look clumpy," Tomasz tells her as a ring tone blares from the laptop.

Louise just looks at it.

"They're going to be happy," I remind her.

"I know!" she says. "I know. It's just... it's my first time telling someone."

I frown. "You told me."

"I was in shock."

"You told Tomasz."

"That doesn't count. He helped make it."

"I did." He nods.

I try to keep my voice gentle. "You don't need to tell anyone else for a few weeks but you *want* to tell Mam and Dad, remember? This means you win."

"What?"

"The first grandchild," I say solemnly. "That's a big deal. That's like a hundred sibling points."

She blinks at me as the ringing continues. "It beats buying them a house in Portugal?"

"It does. The emotional value is like..." I raise a hand to my head. "I can't compete with that. This is your moment."

She looks suddenly thoughtful but Tomasz has had enough.

"You two are strange," he mutters, and leans forward to tap the keyboard, accepting the call.

"Hello," he calls, cheerfully waving at the laptop.

"Tomasz!" Mam's voice sounds through the speakers. "You look very sharp."

"Thank you."

"Louise, you look flushed."

"It's warm today," she says.

"The weather report says it's mild."

"Why are you looking at the weather report for here?"

"Why wouldn't I?"

I hide my smirk, giving the two of them a small wave as I head to the door.

"Abby's here too," Louise says loudly.

Mother of... *why* I mouth as she makes a rapid *come here* motion with her hands. Tomasz just smiles, scooting to the side as Louise pulls me down between them.

"Hello," I say at the screen. My parents sit in the same spot they always do. It's a cloudy day in the Algarve. Mam's wearing a blue blouse and my dad is in a polo shirt. They look as bewildered as I am.

"Out for a run, Abby?" Mam asks after a moment.

I glance at Louise but she's not looking at me. "Just about to."

"Have you heard back about the interview yet?"

I shake my head. "I'll tell you when I do. Though I think I might—"

"I'm pregnant," Louise blurts out.

Okay then.

"Good job," I whisper, wincing as she pinches my thigh.

"I'm pregnant," she repeats. "I'm... *we're* pregnant. We're going to have a baby."

Tomasz holds up his hands in a ta-da motion.

Mam's hands move from her lap to her chest and back again. "A baby?"

"We just found out," Louise says. "I'm only at eight weeks but the doctor confirmed it."

Dad, who hasn't moved a muscle in the last few seconds, finally stirs. "Which doctor?"

"Dr. Gavin."

"Is he that new one?"

"It's a she and yes."

"You should go to Dr. Mehtar," Dad says. "He's very good."

"He is," Mam says, nodding. "He helped with your father's hip."

"He's also retired," Louise points out.

"I'll give him a call."

"*No.* We're with Dr. Gavin and she's already arranging all the necessary checks and appointments."

"Sure, Dr. Mehtar could do that," Dad huffs.

"It's all very exciting," I say pointedly. "Your first grandchild!"

Tomasz does the thing with his hands again.

Dad blinks very hard as Mam stands suddenly, disappearing off-screen "You're feeling okay?" he asks.

"I feel fine," Louise says.

"No morning sickness?"

"Not yet."

"Your mother had awful morning sickness."

Louise's smile falters. "Great."

"When's the best time to come?" Mam calls. "End of the month?"

Louise's eyes shoot to me as our mother sits back on the couch, flipping through her small red diary.

"Don't be silly, Mam," I say, my voice bright. "You don't need to come all the way back here. It's too far."

"It's a two-hour flight."

"It will be a little cramped, don't you think?" I continue. "With me here? Plus it's not like—"

"You'll need all the help you can get."

"I'd love to have you over when the baby comes," Louise says quickly. "*We* would," she adds, and Tomasz nods. "But there's nothing to do now."

"But what if something goes wr—"

"Mam," I interrupt sharply, and she immediately goes quiet.

Louise is very still beside me. "Dr. Gavin said everything is completely normal so far," she says.

"Of course, it is," Mam says quickly. "I'm sure she has everything under control."

"She's a good doctor," Tomasz says. "I know her from the hospital."

"So there's no need for you to come just yet," I continue. "Once there's a due date..."

"I'd love for you to be here, Mam," Louise says earnestly. "For as long as you can be."

"Of course, I will, my darling. Of course." She leans forward, peering into the camera. "Everything will be fine," she says gently, and Louise nods, wilting a little in relief as I look to our other parent.

"Dad?"

My father has been staring off-camera with his arms crossed for the last few minutes. "I'm fine," he says gruffly.

"It's not the 1950s," I remind him. "You're allowed to cry. Especially if you're happy."

But he only waves a dismissive hand, still refusing to look at us.

"I'm very proud of you both," he says. "You'll make wonderful parents."

Louise smiles. "And you'll make a wonderful grandfather."

"Too much," I mutter as he stands, mumbling something about making tea.

"He'll call you later," Mam says as he wanders off. "You know how your father gets when he..."

"Has feelings?" I finish.

"Just wait. He'll be all excited now. Spending all our money. When I was pregnant with you, it was the only thing that made him feel useful. He'd come back every day with toys and books and anything that caught his eye. He brought that dollhouse of yours back from the pub one evening," she adds to Louise.

"The pink one?"

"Do *not* ask how much it cost. I almost had a heart attack when he told me."

"We still have it," Louise says, perking up. "I saw it in the attic last month."

"Well, now you can give it to your child," she says. "It would make his year."

"Hang on," I say. "What do you mean he bought presents? I never got a present."

"Because he spent all our money on Louise," Mam says crisply. "You got to play with them when she was done. Now, tell me," she continues as my mouth drops open. "What exactly did Dr. Gavin say?"

Louise finally releases me from the couch to talk to Mam, looking significantly more relaxed than before.

I thought I would be relieved to escape and get some fresh air but I'm oddly reluctant as I leave, my mind back in the front room, with my family. It hits me then that if everything goes as I want it to, my parents will come home, Louise will have her baby, and I... won't be here. Who knows where I'll be. Who knows, if I go, when I'll be able to get back. I'll be one of those people who watches their nieces and nephews grow up on camera.

And while I don't know exactly how I feel about that, I know it's not good.

CHAPTER 24

It's another few days before I see Luke again.

That Saturday, Susan and Pat come over for lunch, and for the first time since I got here, he messages to say he's joining them. I'm waiting by the upstairs window when I see him leave the house and I rush so fast down the stairs I almost trip.

"If you fall and die, I'm not naming my child after you," Louise yells.

I open the door before he can ring the bell and he grins when he sees me, startled but pleased.

"Hey."

"Hi."

"Hello!" Tomasz says, appearing behind my shoulder. "Did you bring dessert?"

"I did," Luke says, handing over a cheesecake from Beth's. His attention turns back to me. "How are you—"

"Abby!"

Susan edges around Luke, beaming at me. "How did it go? Have you heard anything yet?"

"Leave the child be," Pat says, coming in after her. "It's too early to hear back from a place like that." He turns to me, his voice dropping. "You haven't, have you?"

"No."

"Far too early," he declares. "Louise! Do I smell garlic potatoes?"

"You do," she calls from the kitchen as Tomasz leads them inside, prying open the lid to the cake.

Luke and I are left alone.

He clears his throat. "Shall we—"

"Yep," I say, spinning on my heel toward the kitchen.

The hour *drags*. Even with Luke beside me. Even with Louise's cooking. Even with Pat and Susan keeping up a steady stream of conversation until the last slice is gone. I'm distracted, irritable even. Surrounded by good food and people who love me and all I want to do is ask them to leave.

The only thing that gets me through it is knowing Luke feels the same way. He fidgets, he barely eats, he smiles a beat too late when someone makes a joke. I know this because I'm so aware of his every movement I swear I know when he blinks.

Finally, all the food is gone but Pat and Susan are still chatting away, about what I don't even know anymore, and I'm two seconds away from doing something drastic when Luke's knee nudges mine under the table.

"Do you want to—"

"Okay." I stand so quickly the chair scrapes against the floor. Everyone's eyes snap to us.

"Leaving, Abby?" Louise asks as if I'm sneaking out of the house to meet a boy. Which, okay, I guess I'm doing but she doesn't need to sound so smug about it.

"I thought we might..." I look to Luke.

"Find the heron," he finishes after a beat.

"You're going to find the heron," Louise repeats flatly.

"Yep!" I squeeze around the table before anyone can question us further. "We'll see you later."

Susan watches us go, a wide smile on her face.

"I saw a cormorant down there myself the other day," I hear Pat say as I close the door. "Impressive creatures."

"The heron?" I ask.

"You put me on the spot," he mutters as we head down the drive. "And everyone was looking at me."

We hurry to the car, seat belts on and door closed, only then realizing we have no further plan.

"Where do you want to go?" he asks.

I have no idea. "Out of Clonard?"

"We can do that. The beach?"

"It's a Saturday in June. It will be packed."

"Yeah." He drums his fingers against the steering wheel before seeming to decide, starting the engine.

"Wait," I say. "Don't do the thing where you surprise me with the destination. This is not a movie and I might need to change my shoes and/or pee first."

He laughs. "I was thinking the lake."

The lake?

There are many lakes in this part of Ireland, but in Clonard only one was known as *the* lake. Lough Carra, a calm picturesque body of water northeast of the village. It isn't as popular as others in the area, with their salmon fishing and kayaking. It's more of a sit-and-contemplate kind of place, but with a forest on one side and marshy wetland on the other, there are plenty of places to disappear to.

Luke raises a brow. "Footwear acceptable?"

"Footwear acceptable," I confirm, glancing down at my sneaker-clad feet.

"And they have public facilities."

"Stop, you're making me swoon."

It's a thirty-minute drive. On a sunny day like this, the place is busy, but I was right in thinking most people would head to the coast, and the lake is big enough that the farther we walk along the edge of the forest, the fewer people we see. For someone who grew up in the countryside, I have never been much of a nature person. Maybe it's why I always gravitated toward big cities, more at home surrounded by orderly concrete and masses of people than fields and silence. Waking to birdsong is all well and good until they're outside your window at five a.m. and won't shut up.

But this? Yeah. I'm good with this.

The woods are different than the forest at Easter, when the ground had been wet mud beneath my feet, the world a muted gray and green. Now the air is warm and smelling of pine. The earth is soft and dry, with a slight crunch underfoot, and the lake shimmers between the trees, blue and placid. After about twenty minutes of walking, we find a small clearing by the water. A makeshift camping spot, there's nothing but a circle of parched earth where two logs have been pulled together to form a seating area. It's perfect.

I shrug off my cotton shirt, tying it around my waist as we settle on our separate logs, an appropriate space between us.

"This is nice," I declare because I feel it needs to be said.

"It is."

"Very romantic."

"Very." Luke smiles. "Not a bad place to spend my day off."

His day off. My good mood slips a little when I remember how busy he is and I watch from the corner of my eye as he brushes a few sticks and leaves from the log, getting more comfortable.

"Can I ask you something?"

"Anything." He sounds like he means it.

"How's your dad doing?"

"You mean in general or…" His confusion clears. "You heard about the accident."

"Louise mentioned it. I didn't know. I'm sorry."

"Don't be. He's fine. Or as fine as he can be, I guess. His leg still gets a little stiff some days."

"It sounded awful."

"Yeah, pretty scary."

I wait for him to continue. "And you came back for him," I nudge gently.

He leans forward, resting his arms on his thighs as he realizes what I'm getting it. "I did. I was in Dublin working in marketing for this pharma company. It was real bottom-of-the-rung, taking-notes-at-meetings, and getting-people's-lunches stuff. But I liked it just fine. I wasn't too worried about the future. But then Dad's crash happened and it became pretty clear that Mam couldn't handle it. He couldn't walk on his own for months, couldn't get up the stairs. He needed help getting in and out of the bath, that kind of thing. So I quit my job and came home. Did the heavy lifting, ran errands... I thought it would only be for a few months and then I'd leave again, pick up where I left off."

"But you stayed."

"I used to bring Dad into his physio sessions," he explains. "And then they had me joining in so I could help him at home. I fell in love with it."

"That's why you went back to college," I say, the pieces clicking together.

He nods. "You should have seen them, Abby. I mean, these people are miracle workers. There was this girl who used to be there at the same time as Dad. She had to get her leg amputated after an infection and could barely stand the first time I saw her. She'd have two guys holding her upright and she'd be screaming at them the entire time, just so angry and in pain, but they stayed calm and they stayed with her and by Dad's last few sessions she could walk by herself. Slowly but still."

"That's incredible."

"Yeah. I knew that's what I wanted to do. But I needed twenty-four K to get there and I didn't have anywhere near that. So I stayed home and started saving as much as I could. Dublin rent was no longer an option. Dad owned the coffee shop from years ago but never did anything with it. I renovated it one winter and leased it out. When Dad started moving around by himself, I moved into the apartment. Got a job with the council to earn cash and then two years ago took out a loan to make up the rest. I quit that job, got into the course, and now here I am."

Here he is. "You're scarily impressive, you know that?"

"There was a lot of dragging my feet between each of those steps."

"That doesn't matter," I say. "You're out in the world doing your own thing and you give it all up for your family. Then you find something you love and you decide to go for it instead of settling. Do you know how many people settle? A lot. But you worked hard, you made sacrifices, and you went for it. All the while still being there for your parents and helping Beth and *me* and..." I stare at him. "How are you not just constantly exhausted? Please. Tell me your secret."

"Pilates."

I laugh and he smiles as I do.

"Thank you," he says. "It's hard not to worry about whether you made the right choice or not. If I should have gone straight back to Dublin when I had the chance. That means a lot coming from you."

"Little Miss Had a Freak-out, Lied to Everyone, and Came Home?"

His gaze grows warm. "I think that's the first time I've heard you refer to Clonard as home."

"It is?"

He nods. "Do you think you'll come back more now?"

"I do," I say, careful not to mention the still unshared news of the baby. "I guess this place isn't as scary as I thought it was." I frown. "*Scary* is the wrong word."

"I know what you mean."

"Plus Louise and I are... well, not friends exactly but we're better. I no longer want to avoid her for the rest of my life."

"That's good."

I trace a circle in the dirt with my foot, squinting out at the lake. "There are other things too," I add.

"Oh yeah?" He plays innocent. "Like what?"

I shrug, slowly sliding down my log until I'm sitting right next to him.

"Smooth."

"I'm flirting with you."

"I know," he says, and this time he kisses me first.

It's a quick one. A soft, light "is this okay?" one that I quickly return, twisting my body to face his, giving permission for more. My hands go to the rough stubble of his cheeks, his to my jeans, hooking his fingers through the belt loops as he tugs me gently to him.

I wonder what it would have been like to kiss him at lunch, if I'd still be able to taste the dessert on his lips. I wonder what it would be like to kiss him whenever I wanted to.

Nerves bubble through me at the thought, but before I know what to do with them, Luke moves his head, the slant of his mouth changing against mine, and that's all it takes for me to forget everything.

He is warmer than the sun, the heat of him almost dangerous as his touch moves to the small of my back, and when his teeth nip my bottom lip, I decide I need more, intending to scoot over fully to his log but I slip off my own instead, landing with a soft thud on the ground. I don't have time to be embarrassed because Luke follows me down, propping his fists on either side of my head as he hovers over me.

Unhappy with this lack of contact, I lift my hips as our kiss deepens, pressing myself against him until we both groan.

There's a tearing sound as I lose my grip on his shirt, but I ignore it. I hear a happy shriek and a splash somewhere in the distance, but I ignore that too. I ignore everything but him, everything but how he makes me feel. And oh, how I feel.

I squirm as his hand slips under my tank top, caressing my stomach, and I'm trying to decide whether I want him to move up or down when he breaks away without warning, leaving a gust of cool air in his wake. I open my eyes as he pushes himself up, and I go to drag him back down when the hazy, horny fog in my brain clears and I realize what Luke already has.

Public place. Very public place. Very public family place on a Saturday afternoon.

And we're halfway to...

"Bad idea," he says, his voice hoarse.

Very bad.

I nod and he helps me sit up, brushing the pine needles from my clothes. My movements are clumsy, my limbs heavy as if I'm moving through water. I don't even want to think about what my hair looks like.

Luke pulls up the strap of my tank top, his breathing still disjointed.

"Did I seduce you with my brazen display of skin?" I ask, my voice a little shaky.

"You started it," he reminds me. "In fact..." He pulls the fabric of his T-shirt around, showing me a small tear. "You literally tried to rip my clothes off."

"That was the log," I lie. "The bark can be very sharp. You should be more careful."

"I'll remember that next time." He pulls a stick from my hair and then pushes himself off the ground, helping me up until we're back in our seats. Only this time with no space between us. This time with our arms pressed against each other and his hand holding mine.

CHAPTER 25

There should have been a natural ending to the day. An expected ending even. But it's so sunny we stay longer than we mean to, and by the time we get back to his apartment it's dark and I'm tired and hungry and a little sunburned. Luke picks up Chinese food for dinner, which we eat on his couch, and even though it's technically only eleven p.m. both of us are tired and at least one of us is bloated from said Chinese food, so we settle silently for making out on his bed until we fall asleep, fully clothed.

A routine begins.

It's a strange one.

I leave early on Sunday before Beth arrives because that feels rude and return that night for more kissing and talking and touching. Just no sex. Even though we've both made it clear that's where we want this, whatever it is, to go. And it's not that we don't get close. Various clothing items are removed, bodies moderately explored, but there always comes a moment when we both stop. As if taking the final step means either ending what we have or having another more serious conversation that neither of us is ready for.

It continues the Monday and Tuesday night and it's only on Wednesday when we're drinking coffee downstairs when Beth asks Luke how the studying is going that I realize he hasn't touched a book in days. Furious with myself, I stay away, ignoring his protests that he's basically done it all anyway.

"You're so close to the finishing line," I tell him as he drops me back to the house. "And I'm distracting you."

"It's a very nice distraction."

I agree. But a distraction nonetheless. I stay away that night and the two after that and by then it's the weekend and I haven't seen him in two days and I'm going out of my goddamn mind.

"You look skittish."

"What?" I glance at Rory who's watching me suspiciously.

"Like a cat," he says. "A skittish cat. Are you on drugs?"

"No."

"If you're on drugs, you've got to share with the whole class."

"I'm not on the drugs. It's the solstice. I'm reflecting on my Celtic ancestors."

"Who all definitely took drugs. And I thought you marked the sunset on the *winter* solstice," he adds grumpily. "Not the summer."

I gaze out at the hundred or so people gathered around the edge of the village. "I think you mark the sunset when the rest of the country marks the sunrise and you can't compete with them."

"But the tourists are confused."

They are. I watch Andrew try to herd a family of increasingly skeptical Americans over to the designated prime viewing spot (the back of Dessie's truck). But he's done his best. Fairy lights and ribbons hang from the trees bordering the western side of the village and the local trad band plays the old favorites as we wait for the ceremony to start. It's a perfect day for a solstice party, for any party, the sky clear and a hazy soft yellow as the sun begins to set.

We've never celebrated the solstice before. Another one of Andrew's grand plans for the village. But as money-grabbing schemes go, this one has a nice aesthetic at least.

"Guess what I got!" Sinead returns from her trip to the food stalls, balancing three mugs in her hands.

"If it's poitín, I can't drink it before eleven or I'll need a nap," Rory warns, taking one from her.

"It's *mead*," she says as if she's never heard of anything more wonderous. "They said they make it with local honey."

Rory gives his a sniff. "And who is they exactly?"

"The man in the car."

"The man in the... great." He turns to me. "She's going to make a wonderful mother one day."

Sinead whacks him in the arm.

"I'm good," I say as she offers me the third mug. "Thank you though."

"Don't worry," Rory says. "I'm sure it was a very clean car."

"He had a permit!" Sinead says loudly.

"You want to go to Pete's after this?" Rory asks me. "Sean and Harry are coming. We'll get the gang back together."

"The gang?"

"I made us jackets. I texted Luke but he didn't answer."

"I think he's studying," I say casually. "He's got those final exams coming up."

Rory shakes his head as Sinead takes a long sip from her mug. "I couldn't do it. I get tired just thinking about all the work he's doing."

"I think it's brilliant," Sinead says. "We should throw him a party when he's done. He needs a break."

"He does," Rory says, his attention elsewhere. "Abby, why is your sister berating that child?"

I follow his gaze to where Louise is indeed scolding what looks to be two teenagers over the plastic ring around their cans. "She's working."

"She better not let Andrew see her. He's making everyone... shite, we made eye contact." He turns abruptly to Sinead. "Pretend we're having a really interesting conversation."

"With you?"

I snort as Rory just blinks at her. "Mead makes you cruel. I want you to know that."

"Rory. Sinead." Louise stands before us. "Abby."

"Sister."

"Happy solstice. Would you like to buy a ticket to the Irish Oceans Charity Raffle?"

"What's the prize?" Sinead asks as Rory shakes his head.

"The continued protection of our marine life."

"And is there like a restaurant voucher with that or—"

"No," Rory says. "We're not entering. I am already somehow both a monthly and an annual donor. You're not getting me tonight."

"But I love raffles." Sinead pouts.

He ignores her. "Abby, please take your sister out of here and away from my impressionable wife."

"No problem." I tow Louise by the arm farther into the crowd, ignoring her scowl. "I really think you should hire someone else to do your fundraising," I tell her. "And shouldn't you be resting?" She started getting heartburn in the last few days, which according to our mother meant the baby would have a "thick head of hair."

"I'm pregnant, Abby. Not invalid. Are you in or out tonight?"

"Out, I think. Rory's invited me to Pete's."

"Good. Tomasz and I are having sex."

"But you're already—"

She turns to me, ready for a fight. "Are you actually about to say 'but you're already pregnant'?"

I hesitate. "No?"

Thankfully before I can get myself into even more trouble, Andrew strides past us, directing another group of tourists toward the front.

"Ladies," he greets, a wide, fake smile on his face. "Are we having a good time?"

"I think you've got a rogue mead operator," I tell him.

"What?" He looks, distracted, at Louise. "What are those?"

"Raffle tickets. It's for charity," she adds when he starts to protest.

"Anyone selling anything needs to have a permit. Charity or not. You need to give five euro to Maggie at the desk." He points a stern finger toward the back where Maggie sits, drinking her own cup of mead. "*Now*, young lady," he says when Louise doesn't move.

"Fine," she says. "But I'm increasing your monthly donation."

"And what are you up to?" he asks me when she's gone.

"Nothing! I'm with you, I hate charity."

"That's not what I—"

"Excuse me?"

We both turn as a man in brown slacks and a blue button-down shirt approaches, smiling pleasantly at us.

"Are you in charge?" he asks. "I'm looking for an Andrew O'Donoghue."

Andrew is instantly suspicious. "And you are?"

"Cormac Whelan." He smiles. "I'm performing the ceremony for today."

"*You're* the Druid?"

"We've got a Druid?" I ask, excited.

"To plant the oak tree," Andrew says.

"I didn't know that was a solstice thing."

He ignores me. "I thought you'd have a robe."

"We have no formal uniform," Cormac explains. "In fact, we encourage all our members to wear what they feel is—"

"Yes, yes, fine," he interrupts, clearly disappointed. "I'll need to sign you in. Health and safety. Do you have a... staff?"

"He's not a wizard, Andrew."

"It's fine," Cormac says. "We get that a lot. I'll just go get my things."

"Yes. Great, off you go." Andrew sighs, irritable, as Cormac the Druid heads to his car.

"You should have hired the guy you got to play the Easter bunny," I say.

He shoots me an exasperated look. "I thought you were just visiting."

"I'm staying a little longer."

"Well, if that's the case, I'd like to start seeing you at our Tidy Towns committee meeting. I need everyone in this village to pull their weight this year. Those good-for-nothings in Knockshannon think that just because—"

"Andrew?" I interrupt, nodding toward the street. "I think your Druid is parked illegally."

"What? Oh, for the love of— you can't park there!" he calls, hurrying after him. "The buses need to turn! They need to *turn*!"

I reach for my phone to take a picture of them only to yelp as familiar hands land heavy on my hips.

"There you are."

I twist around, Luke's arms sliding with me until he's almost embracing me. His hair is already growing back from his recent cut, but he shaved earlier, his face smooth and tanned from the summer sun.

"You look like you're in an advert for orange juice," I tell him.

"Excuse me?"

"Fresh white shirt, smiling healthy man. Orange juice."

"You say like it an accusation."

"Or laundry detergent."

He laughs, pulling me closer. "I think you look nice too."

"Yeah?" I glance down at my yellow sundress. I even wore my black strappy heels for the occasion. "I'm the sun."

"You're perfect."

"And you're supposed to be studying," I say.

"My brain is fried. I spent twenty minutes looking for a book before I found it in the fridge. Did I miss the party?"

"The Druid's just about to plant the tree."

"The Druid?"

"Andrew hired a Druid. He drives a Honda. He does *not* wear a cloak."

"See? Who needs big-city lights?"

"They don't know what they're missing." I hesitate as he smiles down at me. "Luke—"

"No," he says. "I can't. I've barely seen you in days and I need a break. At least let's watch a movie. Beth's in Connemara for her cousin's birthday. It's just us."

I waiver, looking back to the party, but the idea of spending more time with him is too strong. It's only been forty-eight hours but it might as well have been months with how much I miss him already.

"Okay," I say. "If you're sure you don't have to study."

"I'm sure."

"Then let's watch a movie."

He grins and I step back, suddenly a little shy.

"I better tell Rory," I say. "I was supposed to go to the pub with him. I'll meet you at the apartment?"

"Okay."

"And stop looking so smug."

"Never," he quips, and lopes off toward the café.

I find Rory with Sinead, standing where the tree is to be planted.

"Isn't nature amazing?" Sinead asks when I join them. "This is so exciting. I love the solstice."

"She's drunk," Rory says, patting her on the shoulder.

I give her a sympathetic smile. "I'm afraid I'm going to have to pass on tonight. Luke and I are going to hang out."

His brows rise. "Hang out?"

"We're going to watch a movie."

"Aha!" Sinead beams at me before turning to her husband. "I win! Gimme."

"We had a bet on whether you two were secretly hooking up," Rory explains, pulling his wallet from his pocket. "I didn't think he had the guts."

"And *I* am very good at this game," Sinead says triumphantly.

"Ten euro," Rory says, handing her a crumpled note. "From our *joint account*."

"The important thing is that you lost."

"It's just a movie," I protest.

Rory huffs. "Sure. And will your clothes be on or off while you watch it?"

My mouth drops open. "That's not... we're just... I don't have to explain myself to you."

Sinead takes another sip of mead. "When we first started dating, I went to Rory's place thinking we were going to have sex and instead we watched *Schindler's List*."

"I'd never seen it!" he exclaims.

"I'm going now," I say. "Enjoy the tree."

"I better not have lost ten quid for nothing," he calls, and I raise a finger to him as I head back into the crowd.

CHAPTER 26

I am going to have sex with Luke Bailey.

I decide this as I leave Rory and Sinead and the solstice behind me. I decide it as I turn down the empty street and head to the café, where Luke waits outside, lounging against the window. I wish I'd decided earlier. I wish I'd washed my hair and worn nicer underwear and brought a condom.

I wish I'd had a sip of that mead.

"Did you find Rory?" he asks, straightening when he sees me.

"He's crushed without my company but he'll survive. He's got front-row seats to the tree thing anyway." As if on cue a cheer rises from behind us. "The harvest is saved," I add.

Luke grins, shouldering open the door. "We must seem unbelievably corny to you," he says as I step past him. "Solstice parties. Family fun days."

"Andrew does seem more intense than I remember. He wants me to join the Tidy Towns committee."

"Well, be careful. He almost got us disqualified one year when they caught him tipping over flower boxes in Knockshannon."

"Shut up."

"I'm serious. Turns out he'd been going in once or twice a week to drop some gum on the pavement, leave the bins open for the foxes. That kind of thing."

"He's a criminal."

"Anything for the cause."

Luke locks up and I follow him up the stairs to his apartment. After a few days of spending far too much time up here, I know it pretty well, so instantly spot the changes. For one, the textbooks that usually pile high on the coffee table are gone, along with the stacks of essays, though God knows where he had space to put them. Instead, three fat white candles are arranged on a small metal coaster, waiting to be lit.

"What?" he asks at my look.

"Candles?"

"What's wrong with candles?"

"Nothing," I say, matching his innocent tone. "It's just that one time in college a guy lit a bunch for the one and only night we had sex and he forgot they were there and halfway through we rolled over and he burned his—"

"Okay," Luke interrupts. "I really need you to not finish that sentence."

"Got it," I say as my phone buzzes with a text. "Oh good, my mother wants to know if my iron levels are low."

"Are they?"

"I have no idea." I hold down the button to turn it off. "Rory knows about us."

"Yeah?" Luke's distracted as he turns on a light. "Did you tell him?"

"He guessed. I don't think we're being as discreet as we think we are."

Something in my voice makes him turn and he frowns when he sees me still lingering in the middle of the room.

"Does that bother you?" he asks. "That he knows?"

"No," I say truthfully. "It's just new. That's all."

"If you're uncomfortable about—"

"I'm not uncomfortable."

"Good." He pauses. "You're a little awkward now though."

"*No.*"

"*Yes.*" He looks amused. "You expecting something tonight, Reynolds?"

"I'm not the one who bought the candles."

"That's what I get for making an effort. Teasing."

"That's you making an effort?"

"Even more teasing." He steps forward, catching one of my hands in his. "We don't have to tell anyone if you don't want to," he says, and I'm distracted by how his fingers play with mine. "It can just be us for now. There's nothing wrong with that."

"I mean it. I don't mind." And I don't. Now that Beth has given us her blessing I don't mind who knows about us.

Luke's gaze grows warm as if he knows exactly what I'm thinking. "You want something to drink?"

"No."

"Something to eat?"

I shake my head and he reaches for my other hand. The light he turned on is not enough to counter the slow darkness as the sun begins to set and outside I can hear the muffled voices from the party, the soft sounds of a fiddle.

"You should really be studying," I say, my voice thick.

Luke ignores me, tucking a stray curl behind my ear. "I used to have a crush on you," he says. "When we were kids."

"Louise told me."

"She knew?" He smiles faintly. "Of course she did. I wouldn't be surprised if everyone knew."

Everyone but me. I'd been so focused on getting out of Clonard I hadn't even looked around to see what was here.

"When I realized it was you at that bus stop I couldn't believe it," he continues. "And Mam kept saying what a nice coincidence it was but it never felt like that. It felt like..."

Fate.

A small word for something that feels so big.

He stares down at me, suddenly serious. "I am really, really sorry for everything that happened to you, Abby. I mean that. I wish it hadn't. But a shitty, selfish part of me is also really glad that you came home. Even if you didn't have a choice."

"I think I did," I say. "I think it was my first choice. Deep down, I knew I would feel safe here. I just didn't want to admit it. I was used to being on my own." Because that's how I always was. In competition with everyone else whether they knew it or not. Even at school, I drew away from everyone. I put my head down to get through my exams, to leave them all behind. It was the same in college and then at MacFarlane, where we were pitted against each other, fighting for projects and clients. To rely on anyone but yourself was almost like a weakness. Even with Tyler, I was alone. I was just so used to it by then, I didn't think to question it.

I touch the side of Luke's face and he lets out a breath. "I'm glad you came home too," I say. I let my finger drift downward, my eyes following as I trace his jaw, his neck. When I reach his shoulder, Luke bends his head, his nose grazing mine briefly before he kisses me.

We stay like that for a while, gentle and unhurried, our hearts half open to each other. There is more to say, but for now, this is enough and I'm beginning to think that nothing will happen tonight, that we'll fall asleep as we usually do, one of us pulling away before it can go too far, but instead we continue to stand. Stand and kiss until every part of me grows loose and languid, until the music outside stops and the voices fade away and Luke sweeps a hand across my back, pulling me into him, and we're lined up so perfectly I gasp.

I blink my eyes open as Luke pulls back, his lips parted, his breathing heavy. My entire weight is pressed against him, leaving me slightly unstable in my heels. In the dim light of the apartment our eyes meet and I still at the sudden ache in my chest, a feeling that wasn't there before.

"What?" he murmurs.

But I'm too scared to voice it. I don't know how to. The sudden thought in my head, in my soul, that I won't even admit to myself.

So instead I do what I can to show him. I rise on my toes and kiss him for all he's worth. He's almost hesitant at first, as though waiting for me to stop, to slow down, but I don't. I kiss and I kiss until kissing isn't enough.

"Up," I mutter as my fingers find the hem of his T-shirt. He catches my eye for an instant before he complies, reaching behind his head to pull it off in one swift movement.

"Your turn," he says, and there's no time to be seductive as I bunch the material at my waist and bring it over my head. I can't help how I suck my stomach in, how I straighten my shoulders as I dump the dress on the floor, but Luke doesn't look, just continues to hold my gaze. His hands return to my hips, tracing patterns in the skin above my underwear and after a second I start to relax, my body loosening once more under his touch. Only then does his attention drift downward and I watch, fascinated as a muscle jumps in his jaw.

"Abby?"

"Yeah?"

"Keep the heels on."

He doesn't let me respond before he's all over me, crowding me until he's all I know. I'm not even aware of us moving until suddenly

I'm on the bed, the sheets cool and fresh beneath me. I scoot into the middle, not taking my eyes off him as he follows but when he reaches for me, I move so I'm on top, a position he seems more than happy with. For now.

"This is what I wanted to do to you before," I say, dragging my hands down his chest. "I wanted you so badly that night I saw you outside. More badly than I think I even realized."

I lean down to kiss him, tracing his muscles as I slip my tongue into his mouth. I stay there for only a second, ignoring his low noise of protest when I stop.

"I couldn't stop thinking about you after," I say, pressing my lips to his neck. "I think that's why I was so mad at you. I wanted you and I couldn't have you and I didn't know what to do."

His body moves under mine as he laughs. "You could have had me whenever you wanted,' he says hoarsely. "Believe me, Abby, my resolve was hanging by a thread."

"You didn't like me," I say, undoing the button of his jeans.

"I thought you were playing with me."

"I wasn't—"

"I know," he says quickly, his expression softening. "I know. And it doesn't matter anymore. None of that matters."

No. All that matters is the here. The now. I undo the zipper of his jeans, reaching inside, but he barely gives me a few seconds before he sits up, rolling me under him again.

"Okay," he pants. "You keep going like that and it's going to be a short night."

I stare up at him, feeling the first flicker of nerves. "It's been a while for me."

"We can go slow."

"No." I say the word so quickly he smirks.

"Just talk to me," he says as his hands move down the side of my breasts, my ribs. "Tell me what's good." He reaches my underwear and I lift my hips, helping him as he pulls them down my thighs and my calves, gently over my shoes.

I watch, barely able to breathe as he kneels between my legs, propping one on each of his shoulders. Holding my gaze, he presses a kiss to one ankle and then the other before undoing the straps of my heels, tugging them off. They join the pile on the floor and he sits there for a moment, just looking at me.

Is he going to—

Oh my God.

I squeeze my eyes shut, tilting my chin to the ceiling as he dips down, keeping my legs wrapped around his head as he kisses me, worships me until every muscle in my body tightens and releases in a glorious rush.

But even then it's not enough.

I scramble to sit up as he does, pulling him to me, impatient and needy and no longer caring that I am. I'm not as smooth as he is, so I yank at his jeans, helping him kick them off as I undo my bra. His briefs follow and a crinkle of foil and then there's no more slyness. No more grazes. No more brushes or sweetness or anything light as he pushes into me with my name on his lips, his lips on my skin. My legs fall apart as our bodies find their rhythm and I let him know that it feels good. That it feels very, very good.

The pressure builds again, surprising me, but I let myself go, giving into it as he soon follows, clutching me to him as he unravels. Afterward, we stay like that, the sweat cooling on our skin, murmuring to each other between kisses until eventually, almost unwillingly, Luke pulls away to lie by my loose-limbed side.

I turn my head to look at him and he smiles when I do. The ache in my chest doesn't go away and I wonder what I've done and how

I'm just supposed to leave him. How I'm supposed to do anything when I've been falling in love with him ever since he picked me up on that cold March night and did his best to make me smile.

CHAPTER 27

A morning in bed always seemed like a luxury to me. I used to try and squeeze as much as I could into the precious few hours before work, knowing I would be too tired at the end of the day to do much else. I ran. I cleaned. I booked early salon appointments and breakfasts with Jess. What I never did was sleep in. What I never did was wake next to a man and spend a lazy day doing nothing at all.

I was looking forward to my morning with Luke. My morning with nothing to do. So when I'm woken a little before seven by a loud hammering on the door downstairs, I am not impressed. I sit up as soon as it begins, my body used to the sound of an alarm, but only a sadist would have an alarm like this.

I glance at Luke, who blinks accusingly at me from where his head is buried in the pillow, as though I'm the one making the noise.

"I think someone's at the door," I say, and he groans.

"They'll stop in a minute."

"Does this happen a lot?"

"Sometimes people passing through think we're open."

"You should get a sign."

"We have a sign."

"A bigger sign."

He smiles into the pillow, closing his eyes again as the noise stops. "See?" he murmurs. "Gone."

"They've collapsed from a lack of caffeine."

"Coffee. Coffee sounds good."

I give him a look. "If only we knew a place that had some."

"Not it."

"Nuh-uh," I say. "This is your place and you're the host. I will take a double espresso and— Hey!"

His hand shoots out to tug me down and I land with a thump on the mattress as he moves over me.

"What are you doing?"

"Catering to my guests."

"I thought you wanted coffee."

"Now I want something else." He nips my shoulder before kissing it as his fingers find mine, drawing my hand down between us.

The knocking starts again.

I try not to laugh as Luke drops his forehead to mine before rolling off me, grabbing a pair of sweatpants as he slips out of bed. "Someone better be dying," he grumbles, stomping down the stairs.

I stretch languidly, burying myself in the covers as I hear him unlock the door below. I wonder if I have enough time to brush my teeth before he gets back.

"I've seen her naked before, Luke. Get out of my way."

I tense at the familiar voice. *Louise?*

My mind is not awake enough to process the fact that she's here, so I'm too slow to reach for my clothes when I hear footsteps on the stairs. Too slow to do anything but tuck the sheet around me as I scramble out of the bed. At least I manage to do that much as a moment later she bursts into the loft, wearing what looks like her pajamas with Luke hot on her heels.

"Louise!"

"Get dressed."

"Get out!" I scream.

Tomasz steps in behind Luke, his fingers over his eyes. "Hi," he calls into the room.

"Don't come in here," I snap.

"Okay." He turns immediately to face the staircase.

"Can I just say that for the majority of time I have been staying with you I have *respected your boundaries*," I hiss, tugging the sheet tighter around me.

"I got a call from the office," Louise says, her face pale. "The developers are starting on the Castlebay site today."

Oh.

Luke brushes past her to get a T-shirt.

"I thought that wasn't happening for months," I say.

"They lied. We need to get everyone down there before the diggers arrive. I need your help."

"I... yeah." I nod, trying to keep up. "Of course."

"We'll be there," Luke promises.

"Great. Thanks." She rubs her forehead, her eyes distant as she thinks. "And how do you feel about getting arrested?"

We both stare at her. "How many times have you been arrested?" I ask.

"Four."

"*Four?*"

"Five," Tomasz says. "That pipeline thing."

"Five," Louise amends.

Five.

Luke clears his throat. "Then I guess I'd prefer not to, but I'm still happy to help."

"I guess I'm the same?" I say.

Louise glances back at me. "Oh, no, you need to stay here, Abby. I need you to knock on doors and get the word out for people to come down. Everyone on the street, okay? As many as you can find."

"But I want to come with you. I want to be there."

No one says anything.

"What?" I ask.

Louise sighs. "It's just—"

"You're the bad guy," Tomasz calls, still with his back to the room.

"Because I worked for MacFarlane?" I turn to Louise for an explanation. "Do you bitch about me to your protestor friends?"

"Of course not," she says. "But it's not like MacFarlane were pioneers of climate change, Abby. Greenpeace targeted them all the time."

"But we had a climate committee," I protest. "We switched to bamboo cutlery in the break rooms and we got the CEO to give up his private jet."

Louise and Luke stare at me.

"Alright, I now realize how that sounds," I say. "But I don't care. Let me help. We can put a sign on the door. Ollie can tell them."

"Let her come," Luke says when Louise starts to argue. "Or you won't hear the end of it."

I scowl at him. "That was not kind of backup I was looking for."

"Okay." Louise sighs. "Just don't say anything. To anyone. Pretend you're my cousin."

"I'm not going to pretend I'm your—"

Tomasz clears his throat.

"Fine," I mutter. He flashes me a thumbs-up.

"Get dressed then," she says. "I have a spare pair of boots in the car."

"I'll stick around," Luke says. "Tell Ollie what's happening and meet you there."

"Thank you. Tell her it's important." She turns to me, exasperated. "Abby, did you hear me?"

"You need to leave first!" I exclaim, and she rolls her eyes, turning to the stairs.

"Five minutes," she calls as Luke shuts the door behind her. I drop the sheet, grabbing yesterday's underwear.

"She is not well," I say, clipping my bra into place. "And you need to be more protective of your property. Next time someone's hammering on the door, you threaten them until they leave. You do *not* let them inside."

Luke's still standing by the door, looking like he's trying not to smile.

"What?"

He puts his hand on his hips and I drop my arms, realizing I'm in my stance again.

"Whatever," I snap, and he laughs.

"I thought you were a morning person," he says as I locate my dress by the coffee table.

"No one is a morning person when their morning starts like that. Even if they—" I stop talking as he kisses me, catching me off guard. The back of my legs hit the couch and if it weren't for the iron rod of his arm welded to my back, I think I would have toppled right over it. It lasts only a few seconds but they're a few very good seconds and when he pulls away I struggle to remember what I was saying.

"Is that your way of telling me you're a morning person too?" I ask.

"That's my way of telling you that you're doing a good thing helping your sister. And that I'm sorry your morning is ruined. *And*," he says, pulling me into him, "that we'll just have to find some way to make it up to you."

"I can think of a few ways," I say seriously, and he grins before leaning down to kiss me again.

*

One hour and one very dangerous car ride later, we arrive at the dunes near Castlebay beach, where the builders are due to arrive. Despite the early hour, we're not the first ones there. A dozen or so people already mill about the makeshift parking lot, Louise's co-workers judging by the branded T-shirts and supplies they're unpacking. A small bearded man in a navy waterproof jacket and green rubber boots is waiting for us, waving a clipboard in his hands.

"It's a nightmare," he calls, blinking behind his glasses.

"My boss," Louise says as we get out of the car. "Ned."

"They're bringing the diggers and everything," he continues. "They lied to us. Complete lies."

"Have you contacted the *Leitrim Observer*?"

He nods. "And the *Connaught Telegraph* says they'll send someone today. We'll be on the morning radio too. I've called everyone I know. We're just waiting for the local council offices to open before we find out what the hell happened."

"We've prepared for this," Louise reassures him. "It's nothing we haven't been through before."

"I just wish we had a bit more time," he says. "But delighted to have you on board," he adds as Tomasz walks past, clapping him on the shoulder. His eyes flick to me with a distracted smile. "I don't believe we've met."

"No," I say as Louise stiffens beside me. I try not to roll my eyes. "I'm her—"

"Sister," Louise interrupts. "This is my sister, Abby."

Ned rears back in surprise. "*The* sister? Didn't you used to work for MacFarlane?"

I nod solemnly. "I brought them down from the inside."

"Oh, look," Louise says as Ned's eyes widen. She points to more arriving cars coming down the road. "Reinforcements."

"That will be the student union," Ned says, bristling with importance. "If you'll excuse me."

I turn to Louise as he hurries away from us. "I guess you love me after all. I think I might cry."

"The cousin thing was a stupid idea."

"It was your idea."

"Just distribute the T-shirts, okay?"

"Yes, ma'am."

The rest of the group isn't anywhere near as suspicious as Ned. In fact, they seem delighted to finally meet me, the mysterious sister they've never seen. There must be around two dozen people there. But by eight even more show including parents towing their children with homemade signs, tourists from the nearby rental cottages wanting to see what all the fuss is about, and, as Ned promised, a few reporters from the local radio stations, capturing soundbites for the morning headlines.

At eight-thirty, just as the developers are due to arrive, Louise starts her speech.

"This is a public beach," she says to the gathered crowd. She stands on a sea-beaten log with Ned beside her, looking like he's about to head into battle. "The oceans are for everyone; this *land* is for everyone. This beach has stood open to anyone who wants to visit it for hundreds of years and now they just want to seal it off? For some luxury hotel that'll take it from us? That'll continue to cordon off each bit of land until there's nothing left? Is that what we want?"

"No!" the crowd yells, and Tomasz laughs when I join in with them.

She doesn't need a megaphone, even with the wind and the roar of the ocean behind us. Her voice carries loud and clear, full of purpose. Full of promise. I've never seen her like this before. I didn't accompany her on her protests and marches when we were younger. I only saw her arguments around the family dinner table, which didn't have the same effect. Or at the Easter Fun Day, where her zeal had seemed misplaced among the petting zoo and painted eggs. But now she's in her element.

"She's really good at this," I say to Tomasz from where we linger at the back of the crowd.

"I know. It's how we first met."

"I thought you met on a night out?"

"We did," he says affectionately. "We were in the queue for Coppers," he explains, mentioning the famous nightclub in Dublin. "She was standing in front of me and someone had the misfortune to litter right beside her. I'd never seen anyone so fired up." He grins at the memory. "I thought she was drunk but then I learned that's just Louise. I fell a little bit in love with her right there."

"That's sweet. I think."

"She'll never be a diplomat," he says as a photographer snaps a picture of her. "But she cares. And she tries. I've never met anyone like her." His eyes drift over my shoulder. "Oh, look," he adds casually. "Your special friend."

"Abby!"

I turn to see Luke striding toward me, dressed inappropriately for the drizzly weather in shorts and an Oceans T-shirt.

"Did I miss anything?" he asks. Before I can respond he kisses me hello in front of everyone. Tomasz politely averts his gaze.

"They just started," I say when I find my voice again. "We're waiting for the developers."

As I speak, the crowd starts to break apart, taking up their positions along the entry points to the beach. Louise heads toward us.

"I brought some friends," he says when she nears, and gestures behind us to where even more cars are looking for a space to park.

"Is it press?" Louise asks.

"Even better," Luke says seriously. "It's Clonard's under-seventeen girl's football team. Division Three almost-champions."

"Almost?"

"You have to win it to be champions."

She stares at him. "You brought the whole team here?"

"Sure," he says. "I just sent a text around telling them to—" He breaks off as Louise grabs the front of his T-shirt, holding him steady as she kisses him firmly on the cheek. "Thank you," she says before she hurries over to them.

Tomasz takes a sip of tea from his flask. "She does that again and you're going on my list, my friend."

"Hi, Mr. Bailey," a few of the girls call in unison. Luke waves as they start to pull the T-shirts on over their clothes, but it's the mothers who are watching him, smiling broadly as their gazes linger. Suddenly Tomasz's list doesn't seem so ridiculous.

"What?" Luke asks at the look on my face.

"You really are oblivious, aren't you?"

"To what?"

He looks so confused that I laugh, kissing him on the other cheek for good measure.

"You better go say hello," I say, pushing him toward them as Ned corrals me into the water to get some pictures. I put a T-shirt on over my dress and wade into the ocean, holding up one end of a banner that says in large stern letters, OUR WATERS BELONG TO EVERYONE. They've just taken the first few pictures when the first trucks arrive.

The students start to boo as the builders get out, but they don't seem too bothered, probably not caring what happens so long as they're getting paid to be there. I rejoin Louise on the shore as a sleeker car pulls up to the dunes, the reporters gathering around us. To my surprise, only one suit man is there, and he's not even in a suit, but beige chinos and a blue-and-pink-striped shirt. His face is red, his hair is white, and he has the air of a middle-class man used to getting his way.

"Louise," he greets as she stomps over to him. "You want to tell me who tipped you off this time?"

"Not a chance."

"You can't stay here forever you know. This is a perfectly legal transaction and one that will hugely benefit our community."

"By restricting access to natural resources?"

"By bringing jobs to the surrounding area. By bringing tourists and visitors in to experience the beauty that you and I both love so much."

"And by kicking out locals to do so. I've been coming to this beach every year since I was a child, Mr. Agnew." Her voice rises to be heard by all. "And as an expectant *mother*, I intend to bring my own children here as well."

Agnew smiles at her, his voice dropping so no one could hear it but us. "You're pregnant?"

"And not afraid to use it."

His eyes flick to the side, taking in the crowd. "Is that a City FM reporter?"

"RTÉ have already come and gone," she says, matching his volume. "The *Irish Independent* will be out here this afternoon."

"A slow news day."

"Not anymore."

He hesitates, pursing his lips before his expression smooths once again. "Fine. No handcuffing this time, you hear me?"

"I'll make sure to run the list of demonstrations by your office."

He goes to retort when his eyes flick to her stomach and back again, frustration flashing across his face. "You can have today," he says, speaking louder again. "But we'll be back tomorrow."

"And we'll be here," Louise calls as he heads back to the car. The crowd behind us starts to cheer, the photographers snapping away.

"*That's* how you wanted to reveal your pregnancy?" I ask.

"It worked didn't it?"

"I guess," I say, as Agnew drives off. "Is that it?"

"Yes, Abby. They've given up and the beach is ours."

"I really can't tell if you're being sarcastic or—"

"No, that's not it."

"Oh." I watch as Tomasz offers a pack of biscuits to the builders. "So you're just going to do the same tomorrow."

"Yep."

"And you really think you'll be able to stop it?"

"No."

"*No?*" I stare at her. "Then what are we all doing here?"

"We rarely stop these things," she says. "It's David and Goliath. But that doesn't mean we shouldn't try. And maybe we'll get lucky. Maybe we'll get some interest, but at the end of the day, he's right. It's a legal transaction. It's not our land."

"But it *is* our land," I protest.

"Careful," she says with a smile. "You're starting to sound like me."

"I'm learning that's not really a bad thing."

Her gaze softens at the almost-compliment. "We try, Abby. And we keep trying. We keep standing up for what we know is right and sometimes it works. We won't go without a fight."

I gaze out over the assembled crowd, more relaxed now that the man in the nice car has gone. There's a buzz about the place, the younger kids starting to play in the water, the older ones sitting in the sand, making posters. A few photographers still linger, taking random shots of their beaming faces.

"You know," I say. "This is kind of fun. Why didn't you ask me to come to these things before?

"I asked you to come every weekend!" Louise exclaims.

"No, you didn't."

"Yes, I did! I..." She trails off when she sees my grin. "You're in a good mood."

"All this people power. Maybe I'll—" I break off as she wraps her arms around me, squeezing me so tight it almost hurts. "Ow."

"Shut up." A final squeeze and she lets me go. "I'm glad you're here, Abby."

And I don't know whether she means *here* as in the protest or *here* as in Ireland, but I like to think it's a bit of both. "Anytime, sis."

I clear my throat as my phone vibrates in my pocket. "That's probably the president for you," I say, and she smirks as I step away, clicking accept on the private number.

"Hello?"

"Is this Abby Reynolds?"

I still at the English accent in my ear. Cheerful and polite and what I've spent weeks wishing for.

"Speaking," I say.

Louise's smile fades at the formality of my tone.

"This is Yuusuf Davies. I'm calling from Stewarts. I'm sorry to catch you on the weekend."

I turn my back on my sister, facing the dunes as we speak, though she doesn't leave to give me privacy.

"We liked your ... impressed with... willing to relocate..."

I pick up the words faintly as if I'm listening to a conversation between two other people but manage to make all the appropriate noises in all the right places.

When I finish I don't move, standing there refreshing my phone for the email I asked for, so I would have written confirmation of what just happened.

It lands in my inbox as someone calls my name and I turn just in time to be swept into the arms of Luke. He lifts me until my boots leave the ground and I laugh as he instantly drops me back down, the front of my T-shirt covered in sand and seawater.

"Shit." He laughs. "Sorry."

"It's fine, I don't care."

"Are you okay? You've gone really pale."

"I'm cold."

"Of course you are," he mutters, leaning down to kiss me, once, twice, and a third lingering time.

"Ahem." Louise coughs beside us but she doesn't sound mad.

"I'm just off the phone with Mam and Dad," Luke says to her when he lifts his head. "They want you to come around for an early lunch. Said you'll be too tired to cook."

"Well, they're not wrong about that."

"You think you'll be ready in an hour? Or do you need to stay here longer?"

"I can go. Some of the students said they're going to camp out tonight. Let me just check in with them."

"Grand. I'll meet you back at the house?" he asks me, and I nod, smiling as he kisses me again. "I'm going to say goodbye to the team."

I watch him jog off toward the water, where the girls are taking selfies, and feel a longing so great it almost hurts.

"Be careful."

Louise's expression is grim as she gazes after him.

"He knows what this is," I say.

"Do you?"

She only looks at me when I don't respond, touching my arm briefly before she gets back to work.

*

It's a while before we're able to leave. Louise does a couple more interviews and then coordinates the plan for tomorrow before we're finally in the car. With nothing to bring to Pat and Susan's, Tomasz drops me a few minutes from the house so I can jump in the shower while they take a detour to pick up dessert from Beth's.

I've just turned onto our street when I remember I don't have any keys and I take out my phone to ask where they keep the spare set when I see a list of notifications peering up at me.

Three missed calls from Jess. One voicemail.

I pause in the driveway confused as I listen to it. It's nothing unusual. I used to get drunken voicemails from her all the time. But this one, a quick "Call me when you get the chance" one, is different. She sounds nervous and, even more worryingly, sober.

When I call back she answers immediately.

"Abby?" Her voice is quiet and I wonder what time it is in New York.

"What's wrong?"

"Have you heard from Tyler recently?"

I frown, shifting my phone to the other ear. "No."

"He texted me a few hours ago. I don't think he has your Irish number. He was trying to call you."

"I don't use that phone anymore. Is he okay?" Visions of him lying in a hospital bed fill my mind.

"He's fine. But he said he was—"

"Abby."

I spin around at my name, staring wide-eyed at the man on my sister's porch.

Tyler.

CHAPTER 28

Oh my God.

"—and it was the first I heard about it, so I wanted to make sure you knew because I figured you would have told me and I—"

"I've got to go, Jess."

"But—"

"I'll call you later." I hang up, sliding the phone into my pocket as I stare at Tyler.

Tyler who's here.

Tyler who's smiling at me.

"Surprise," he says, and his voice sends a jolt through me. "Not that I meant it to be one. I tried to call but you got a new number."

"An Irish one."

"I figured." He pauses, taking me in. "What on earth are you wearing?"

I glance down at my outfit, the now creased T-shirt over my summer dress. Louise's rubber boots caked in old mud. "I was at a protest."

"A protest?"

"With my sister. What are you doing here?"

"I wanted to see you," he says as if it's the simplest thing in the world.

Before I can answer, his gaze flicks behind me and I turn to see Tomasz's car pulling into the driveway.

"That's my—"

There's a whiff of cologne as Tyler strides past, his hand outstretched. "Louise!" he says as she gets out. "We finally meet."

I don't take in a word as introductions are made and pleasantries exchanged. I feel like I'm in shock and it's only when Louise steps on my foot do I realize she's invited everyone inside.

We head into the hall, where she quickly pushes a laundry basket into the kitchen before gesturing us into the living room.

"This feels expensive," Tomasz says cheerfully as he takes Tyler's jacket and hangs it on the banister.

I risk a glance at Tyler to gauge what he thinks only to find him looking at me. I catch his smile before I turn away.

What is happening what is happening what is happening?

I follow them into the front room where Louise and Tomasz sit on the old couch while Tyler and I perch on separate ends of the love seat. Somewhere outside, two children shriek as they play on the road and I am sure my life will never be weirder than at this moment.

"Tea?" Louise asks suddenly, breaking the silence. "Coffee?"

Tyler smiles at her. "A coffee would be great."

"It's Nespresso," she says, a slight edge to her words.

"Wonderful. The stronger the better." He tries a laugh. "To be honest, I think I'm running on caffeine at this stage."

She smiles weakly at him and makes a show of getting up, patting Tomasz's knee.

He gets the hint. "I'll help."

I can only watch them go as Tyler turns back to me. This time, he cuts straight to the point.

"I got you an interview."

I blink.

"A financial analyst at Hanson's," he continues. "I know it's smaller than you're used to but they had a few recruits drop out and I have a friend in—"

"I'm an associate," I interrupt.

"I wouldn't worry about it," he says calmly. "You know how they are with these things. It's a new company, a lot of competition. Give it a few months and you'll be able to move up easily."

"You flew all the way to Ireland to tell me you got me an interview?"

"No." He takes a breath. "No, Abby, I didn't fly over here just to tell you that. I thought we could—"

He breaks off as a cupboard slams, followed by a few words in Polish and the sound of the kettle heating up. It's as if Louise and Tomasz suddenly realized how quiet they were being.

Tyler smiles, unruffled as always. "Is there somewhere we could talk?"

Not in this house. "Do you want to go for a walk?"

"I'd love to," he says, and he looks so relieved that I feel a little bad.

I lead him back to the front door, letting him go ahead of me as I stick my head into the kitchen. "Louise?"

"*Go*," she mouths, her eyes wide. Tomasz gives me a sympathetic smile, eating a chocolate biscuit.

I bring Tyler without speaking down the street, past the kids and their skipping ropes, across the road and down the unofficial pathway to the river, where the grass is soft and wet under our feet.

It's always beautiful just after the rain and although I know Tyler's shoes must be getting muddy, he makes a point not to notice as we reach the weathered bench that looks out at the water.

"What does it say?" he asks, peering at the polished engraving.

"*Do Margaret, mo chara,*" I read in Irish. "For Margaret, my friend."

"I've never heard you speak Gaelic before."

"I don't speak it very well. Louise is fluent."

"Well, it sounds beautiful. And so is this river," he adds when I look away. "It must have been wonderful growing up here."

"It was alright," I say, watching him from the corner of my eye.

God, he looks good. The kind of good that money can buy. A decent haircut, a good skin regime, fitted, muted clothing that Tomasz was right about: it is expensive. I know it's expensive because my wardrobe used to be similar.

He glances at me and I look away.

"Sometimes there's a heron here," I say, turning to the heron-less river.

"Abby."

"They're pretty impressive close up."

"Will you look at me at least?"

I turn to him stiffly, focusing my gaze somewhere above his right shoulder.

"I'm sorry," he says.

"For what?" I'm unable to stop the note of tension that enters my voice. "For breaking up with me or for the timing of the breakup?"

"I don't expect for this to be an easy conversation," he says. "But I have a few days and if you have space in your heart to listen to me, I'd really like to talk to you."

"We're talking now."

He gives me a small smile. "Maybe when you don't have sand in your hair."

I frown at his words but before I can respond a loud engine cuts me off and we both look up the bank to see a red car speeding down the road.

Luke.

He does a double take when he spots me, one hand lifting in a wave before realizing I'm with someone. There's just enough time to see confusion flash across his face before he drives past.

"A friend of yours?" Tyler asks as he pulls in up ahead. I hear the car door shut and a moment later he appears over the crest of the hill, looking just as unkempt as I am. Or maybe I just feel that way standing next to Tyler. Luke's clothes are even dirtier than mine and he's thrown on the old hoodie he keeps in his trunk.

"Everything okay?" he asks, his eyes on me as he makes his way toward us.

"Everything's fine." My voice comes out too high. "Luke, this is Tyler."

And as always, he can't keep the shock from his face.

Tyler smiles. "Tyler Olsen. And you are?"

"Luke Bailey." He holds out his hand and Tyler doesn't hesitate to grip it.

The shake goes on a little longer than necessary.

Are they...

"Okay," I say. I've never been interested in a macho show off and I'm not about to start now. "*Okay*," I repeat when neither of them stops. They reluctantly let go, still sizing each other up.

"Tyler surprised me," I say to Luke, needing him to believe I didn't plan this, that I didn't know my ex-fiancé was coming and didn't tell him. To my relief, he nods.

He believes me because of course he does.

And now I have to deal with both of them.

"Luke's an old friend," I say as they stand on either side of me, a buffer to the wind.

"Well, that's great." Tyler's still smiling. "I was hoping you'd introduce me to people. But, if you'll excuse us, Luke. We were in the middle of a private conversation."

"Were you now?" Luke asks, equally as friendly. "I'm afraid you'll have to catch up another time. Abby's going to start seizing up if she doesn't get into warmer clothes and we have a lunch to get to."

"Lunch?"

"With his parents," I explain. "They're my next-door neighbors."

"Sounds great. Would there be room for one more?"

"No," Luke says before I can open my mouth.

"Alright," I say firmly. "Let me just..." I turn to Luke. "Give me five minutes. And then you're right. I need to take a shower. Could you let Louise know I'll be late?"

Luke doesn't move, looking at me as if he's trying to read my mind. But if I am trying to give him a secret message, I hope he tells me what it is because I sure as hell don't know.

"It was nice to meet you," Tyler adds.

Luke doesn't so much as blink at him. "I think I'll stay right here," he says, talking to me.

Tyler laughs once in disbelief, looking at me as if I know what to do. When I say nothing, his jaw tightens. "Fine," he says. "Sure, pal, do whatever you want." He turns fully toward me, essentially blocking Luke from the conversation. "The job is assured, Abby. The interview is a box tick, that's all. You're one of the smartest people I've ever met and you'll be moving up the ranks in a few months. You know you will. Take it."

"I don't—"

"Take it," he repeats, as Luke scowls behind him. "Don't worry about me. Don't even think about me. We can talk about that later. Do this for you because you know it's the right thing."

"But I don't think it is."

"I know you're mad at me, Abby, but you can't—"

"It's not that," I interrupt, trying to sort out my thoughts as I say them. "I'm not sure if going back to New York is the right thing for me."

"You want to stay here?"

"I don't know."

"To do what?"

"I don't *know*."

He's taken aback. He obviously expected me to be reluctant but not about this. Not about a job. But he's annoying me. Him with this "I'm here to save you" attitude. Him with his nice clothes and his charming smile as if nothing happened between us.

"You're angry with me," he says eventually. "I understand that, I do. And I'm sorry. But you don't have a job. You don't have your friends. You have nowhere to live and I know you want to move back because you've been applying to everything under the sun."

"How do you—"

"Because I have friends in the business and they tell me," he says, frustration starting to creep into his voice. "You still want to get out of here or else you wouldn't be trying so hard. Let me help you."

"I don't need your help. Maybe I want to stay here."

"You don't."

"I do."

"Why?" He rears back as my eyes betray me, flicking to Luke before I can stop of myself. "Because of him?"

"I..."

"Abby." Tyler shifts to the left, drawing my attention away from Luke, who's now staring at me. "I'm not mad if you met someone else, but you need to think about this rationally. You want to get back at me? Fine. I deserve it. But turning down this kind of opportunity for some hometown rebound is not you."

"He's not a rebound."

"You need to think about your future. Your life."

"He's not a rebound," I repeat, annoyed.

"I had to pull some serious strings to get you this—"

"I'm in love with him."

Tyler shuts up, this time unable to prevent his surprise from showing.

"I'm in love with him," I repeat, not trusting myself to so much as look in Luke's direction.

I thought Tyler might be angry. Embarrassed even. But his expression gentles. He almost looks sorry for me. "You don't fall in love with someone after a few weeks, Abby."

I say nothing, mute. I can tell he doesn't believe me. I can tell he just thinks I want him to fight for me.

But that's never been his style.

"I can see this isn't the best time," he says finally. "I booked a hotel room in Sligo if you change your mind and would like to talk. I'll be there all week. If it's okay, I'd like to give my regards to your sister and then I'll let you all enjoy your meal."

Ever the gentleman, he nods at both of us before striding back up the bank, toward the house.

For a moment, Luke and I just stand there, not saying anything even as a drizzle falls around us.

"I didn't know he was coming," I say eventually. "Luke? I swear I—"

"I know," he says, but he doesn't sound very reassuring. He gazes at the spot where Tyler disappeared. "Were you just saying that? That you're in love with me?"

"No."

"Right." He takes a breath to speak, seems to think the better of it, and then tries again. "It's just you can't just go around making grand proclamations like that."

"I know."

"Words mean something."

"I *know*," I say. "I know they do. I wanted to tell you before now but I couldn't. I kept chickening out because this thing between us felt so new." I hate the expression on his face, like he's trying to hide his feelings from me. Or trying to figure them out himself. "I meant it," I say. "I didn't say it just because I wanted to get rid of him."

"But do you? Do you want to get rid of him?"

"*Yes*. How can you ask that?"

"How can I not? You were engaged to him."

"Before he broke it off, remember?"

"Does *he* remember?" He frowns. "Are you going to take that job?"

"I already said I wasn't."

"You said that to him. Now, I'm asking you."

"And it's the same answer. I'm not going to take it."

"But you'll go eventually." He shakes his head when I don't respond. "Do you even know anymore?"

"That's unfair," I say, a sharp note entering my voice. "A lot has happened and it's a big decision. You can't expect me to make it that quickly." I cross my arms as the rain falls heavier. "Are you just going to stand there or are you going to say something to me?"

"What?"

"I told you I loved you, Luke, or did you forget about that already?"

He watches me for a long second. "I didn't forget," he says finally.

Embarrassment rushes through me, swift and all-consuming. "Right. I just thought..." I stumble backward, slipping slightly in the wet earth. The sudden urge to put space between us is overwhelming. "Whatever. It's raining. I need to get back to Louise."

"You're not," he calls after me.

"What?"

He almost looks pained. "You're not in love with me."

"I'm not? Oh!" I laugh, sounding a little manic. "Great! Thanks for clearing that up for me."

"You can't be," he insists. "I know what I am to you."

"And what's that? A hometown hookup?"

"A distraction. One that, I admit, I'd hoped would go on a little longer than it has."

I can't believe what he's saying to me. "That's what you think?"

"That's what I know," he says firmly. "That's what this has to be because I can't give you anything more. I can't give you what you want."

"You don't know what I want," I choke out. "How can you when you clearly don't know me."

"Abby—"

"I have to go," I say, climbing awkwardly up the riverbank. My foot slips in the mud but I manage to right myself as I move as far away from him as possible.

He doesn't follow.

And for some reason, that's what hurts me the most.

CHAPTER 29

"How's your moping?" Tomasz lingers in the doorway of my bedroom the next day, eating an apple. "Going well? It looks like you're really getting the hang of it."

"Shouldn't you be grocery shopping?" I mutter, scrolling through my phone. "It's on the chore wheel."

"I'm going now. Do you want me to drop you to the village?"

"No."

"Are you sure? Louise said if you don't leave the house, she's going to tell your parents about Tyler coming."

I roll over to look at him fully. "She wouldn't."

Tomasz only shrugs.

She would.

I push myself off the bed. I've been in a mood ever since Tyler showed up. I couldn't even bring myself to go to lunch with Pat and Susan, though, from what Louise said, Luke didn't show up either. He hasn't messaged me. I mean, I haven't messaged him either but, the way things ended yesterday, the ball is firmly in his court.

Tyler messaged twice. He got my Irish number from Louise (there was some yelling about that) and he gave me his hotel details and a plea to talk to him, privately. I don't plan on replying. My plan instead is to lie low for a few days until he leaves and hope everything magically sorts itself out.

But hoping this will be an excuse to see Luke, I grab a ride with Tomasz into the village, and head to the café, where Ollie is getting ready to leave for the day. She sees me standing outside dawdling, but instead of just ignoring me like she usually does, she gestures halfheartedly toward the door, which for her is the equivalent to waving me inside with open arms.

"I'm just on my way out," she tells me when I enter. "Beth's sorting the recycling out back. Luke's not here. Heard your ex came to visit."

I pause. "He did."

"Awkward."

"Tell me about it."

She almost looks impressed. "So you've got two people after you now?"

"I wouldn't put it like that," I say but she's already grinning at me.

"That's cool," she says, grabbing her bag. "Hey, you should know that I'm leaving soon. I got into a creative writing program at UCD."

"You're a writer?" I ask, surprised.

"Didn't I tell you?"

"I think this is the first time you've actually spoken to me."

"Huh." She frowns. "Well. Beth will be in in a minute."

"Okay. Hey, Ollie?" I hesitate as she turns at the door. "You write... poems?"

"Novels."

"Oh." I think back to all the times she stood by the counter, typing into her phone. "You're not writing about me, are you?"

"Not unless you live three thousand years in the future on an alien planet about to be destroyed."

"No."

"Then no." She smiles. "See you around, Abby."

She leaves just as a noise behind me draws me to the door and a moment later, Beth emerges, blowing her fringe from her face.

"Oh, hi!" she says with her usual enthusiasm. "Since when do they make cardboard boxes so sturdy? I had to jump on it to get it to fit. Ollie gone?"

"Just now." I glance around what used to be the yoga studio but where Beth has since moved the bookshelves to so she can have more seating up front. Or maybe they're just shelves now considering all the books are piled on the floor. "What happened?"

"I tried to dust," Beth sighs, gazing down at the stacks. "Then I thought it might be nice to sort them by order of color. Maybe a rainbow for pride month? But then we had way too many blue and pink covers and not enough yellow and *no* greens, so I gave up and started putting them back. And then I got tired and now I just have books on the floor. What can I get you?"

"A latte if you have one," I say, taking out my purse.

"Put that away! It's on the..." She trails off when I glare at her. "Right," she mumbles. "I need to get better at not doing that."

I take a seat at the bench as she makes me one, humming to herself.

"Beth?"

"Abby?"

I didn't intend to tell her, but the words come out of my mouth before I can stop them. "I got the job."

Her head snaps up. "The one you interviewed for?" Her mouth drops open when I nod. "That's wonderful! Are you going to take it?"

"I don't know. No," I amend quickly. "That's a lie. I do know. I'm taking it. I have to. There's nothing for me here and it's the best opportunity I'm going to get. Maybe ever. I'd be stupid not to."

"Well, do you have to tell them straight away?" She smiles when I shake my head. "Then why worry about it right now? It's okay to be conflicted."

"I'm not sure I should be *this* conflicted."

"You don't want it?"

"I do want it!" I falter, trying to explain my thoughts. Trying to explain when I don't even know myself. "But what if I don't and I just don't know it yet?" I sigh. "I'm not making any sense."

Beth rounds the counter and takes a seat opposite me, crossing her arms on the table. It's a few seconds before she speaks. "Did I ever tell you my younger brother has a doctorate in physics?"

"No," I say, surprised.

"I'm not joking. He lectures in Munich and he's married with two kids. Meanwhile I'm a failed farm girlfriend and a soon-to-be failed business owner. So believe me, I know what it feels like to worry about what you're doing with your life. I have no idea if I've made the right choices. In fact, I'm pretty sure I've made a lot of wrong ones. But that's okay. That's life. And if I did make any mistakes, at least they were mine. What does your gut tell you?"

"I don't know."

"Yes, you do. Your gut always knows. That's the rule of the gut."

I straighten, blowing out a breath. "To go," I say, even as my chest tightens with the words. "Things are different now. Clonard is different. My family is..." I shake my head. "But I still need to go. I *want* to go."

"It's not like we're living in the past," she says gently. "You don't have to wait weeks for a postcard. You can come back and visit whenever you want to."

"It still won't be the same."

"No," she says. "But it doesn't have to be forever either." She reaches for my hand, holding it tightly between hers. "I'll miss you a lot. But I'd much rather miss you while knowing you're doing right by you, than have you here, always thinking about what could have been."

"I'm going to miss you too," I say, my voice barely more than a whisper and she squeezes my hand.

"And don't forget, I still need an excuse to visit New York."

"It's not actually in New York," I say as she gets up to hand me my coffee. My other piece of news. "It's in Toronto."

"Oh." Her face falls momentarily before she musters up a smile. "Is Toronto fun?"

"I think so."

"And they've got that big tower there, right?" She reaches over the counter to grab a cloth. "I love big towers."

"They do."

"Then we're definitely going up it when I come and visit. Plus a new city will be good for you! No bad memories. It will be like a fresh start." She pauses, an odd expression crossing her face. "Your friend's still in New York though, right?"

"Jess? Yeah, she's born and raised. She'll be mad about the move but it's better than being over here."

Beth nods, cleaning the glass case with admirable focus.

Almost too much focus.

No way.

"She seemed really taken with this place," I continue casually. "If you want to visit. I'm sure she'd love to have you. She keeps asking about you."

Her hand moves faster, polishing and polishing. "She does?"

"Uh-huh."

"I guess you could give her my email or something. If she wanted to chat."

"Sure, if you'd like."

She shrugs, abandoning the glass to start wiping down the trays but she barely lasts five seconds before turning back around.

"So what did she say about me?" she asks, and I laugh.

It's late evening by the time I get back. The car is in the driveway, meaning Tomasz is home from grocery shopping, but the house is quiet when I let myself in. I find Louise in the kitchen, looking over blueprints of what looks to be the hotel, a coffee cup in her hands.

"It's decaf," she says, when I sit opposite her.

"I didn't say anything."

"But other people will. I'm going to spend nine months with people judging me every time I so much as look at a bottle of wine."

"Mam definitely drank when she was pregnant with us."

"Yeah, and look how you turned out."

"Oh, you're so funny." I take a sip from her mug, glancing at the prints. "You're not planning on becoming an ecoterrorist, are you? Where did you even get these?"

"Ned got them."

"And where did Ned get them?"

She shrugs, suddenly innocent, and I roll my eyes. "Just because you're pregnant doesn't mean you won't get arrested again," I warn as she turns a new page of her notebook. "I got the job."

Her eyes flick up. "You did?"

"They want me in Toronto."

"Toronto," she repeats softly. "Wow." She hesitates, tracing a circle with her pen. "I thought maybe..."

I wait, nervous, but she doesn't continue.

"Did you tell Luke?" she asks instead. She doesn't ask me if I'm going to take it or not. She doesn't need to.

"I will tomorrow. I want to tell him in person."

"When will you need to move?"

"I don't know. Soon probably. It's not like I have notice to give." I pause. "I might come home for Christmas though. See the baby."

"I think we could manage that."

"And maybe you guys could come over and see me? Or I could come back and—"

"Abby," she interrupts. "We're only a flight away. We'll figure it out. We'll do it right this time."

"Yeah." I take a deep breath. "Okay."

She smiles at me. "Do you want to celebrate?"

"Not yet." I say. "But are you doing anything tonight?"

"No. Why?"

I watch as she makes a small x on one of the pages. "I need a favor."

CHAPTER 30

An hour later, we sit in her car outside the Green Hill Hotel. It's the nicest hotel in the area, a modern three-story building mainly used for conferences, as evidenced by the three businessmen having a smoke nearby still wearing their suits.

"Maybe this isn't the best idea," Louise says as I gaze at the sliding doors of the main entrance. "Maybe you should meet in a restaurant. Somewhere public."

"It's not like we're going to scream at each other. And he did come all this way to see me."

"The element of surprise," she mutters.

"I know this is you being on my side," I say. "But I also need you to be quiet."

She gives me a look as if to say *fine* and I turn back to the hotel, steeling myself.

"Let's get this over with."

Louise accompanies me inside, going to the lobby bar while I walk past the desk to the small elevators. No one stops me as I ride to the third floor, following the signs down the winding carpeted halls to the dark wooden door of room thirty-two.

Tyler answers seconds after my knock as if he'd been waiting for me.

He's just showered, as evidenced by his wet, slick-backed hair and the strong smell of aftershave emanating from him. He's dressed casually for Tyler in an expensive sweater and dark jeans. He looks nice. He always looks nice.

"Going somewhere?" I ask.

"Not anymore." He opens the door wider, gesturing me inside. The room is nice, elegant and understated. One of the more expensive ones in the building no doubt. The curtains are open but the lights are on, meaning I can't fully appreciate the view of the Irish countryside below. A dinner jacket is laid out on the bed.

"You got a hot date?"

He closes the door. "I thought I'd check in on my other girlfriend while I'm here."

"I'm not your girlfriend," I remind him.

A pause. "You're right. I misspoke."

I doubt it. Tyler always says exactly what he means to.

"Are you hungry?" he asks. "I'm told the restaurant here is good. Or we could order in."

He goes over to the closet. It's a casual move. A "look at us being normal, doing normal things" move. As if I've just come back from a drink in the lobby.

"I already ate," I say, drifting toward the window.

"Never stopped you before."

I can hear the smile in his voice but I don't turn around. In the reflection of the glass, I can see him standing by the room safe, looking at me.

I stare straight back and I feel... I don't know what I feel.

"Abby?"

I turn around, hugging my arms to my chest. I no longer care about my body language. I no longer care about what he can read from me. Let him read. Let him know. I have nothing to hide anymore.

"You always said I was bad at small talk," he says eventually.

"It's more that we're good at it."

"We?"

I make a vague gesture to myself and the world outside. My country. My people.

"Right." He swallows. If I didn't know him any better, I'd say he looked nervous. "Well, I won't try to compete with them. And I won't waste any more of your time."

And before I know what's happening he drops down on one knee.

"The box is empty," he says, holding it up. "I was hoping you still had the first ring."

I can only stare. "What are you doing?"

"Proposing to you."

"You already proposed to me."

"And now I'm doing it again," he says politely. "I didn't get any rose petals. I know you'd think it would just be extra work for housekeeping."

"Tyler—"

"I'm sorry, Abby. I'm sorry for ever doubting my feelings for you and I'm sorry I didn't realize that until I lost you."

"You didn't lose me," I remind him. The back of my knees feel funny. "You broke up with me."

"I did. It was a mistake. One that I'm trying to amend."

"But I don't want you to. I don't want any of this." I drop my arms, pacing the three steps between the window and the bed. Tyler doesn't move. "You broke up with me like I was some girl you'd been seeing for a few weeks. Like three years together meant nothing."

"I know."

"I was going to marry you!" It hits me then. Marriage. I hadn't thought about it before. Not really. Sure, I said yes. We bought the ring and we told our families but I hadn't pictured a wedding or a dress or flowers and food and a honeymoon. I hadn't thought about putting a *Mrs.* in front of my name. Hadn't thought about what it meant. How different my life would have been. "I was going to marry you," I say again. "And you left. You left and you didn't talk to me again."

"I tried to."

"Only when MacFarlane happened."

"What does that matter? You didn't answer my messages."

"Because I didn't want your pity."

"It wasn't my pity. It was my *help*." He rises, slipping the box back into his pocket. "Help because I still cared about you. Can't you see that? I shouldn't have cared so much for someone I chose to cut from my life but I did. That's when I knew how much I loved you."

"So because you pitied me you realized you loved me."

"You're twisting my words," he says calmly. And I am. I know I am. I want to make him the bad guy.

It would be so much simpler if he were the bad guy.

"You don't want to marry me," I say, feeling tired. "You think you do but you don't."

He smiles slightly. "You might have to explain that one to me."

"Number one, how about the fact you were barely around the last year we were together."

Tyler takes a seat in one of the low, beige armchairs, folding his tall form gracefully into it. "I was traveling for work."

"And has that work just magically disappeared?"

"No."

"No," I echo. "So how would you balance that with our relationship?"

"My workload has never been an issue before."

"Well, it is now. What we had before didn't work, so we'd need something different."

"Okay," he says. "We can talk about that."

Talk. Always talk. Talking without saying anything. "Number two, your mother doesn't like me."

"Of course she likes you."

"She doesn't. She doesn't think I'm good enough for you. She always had some comment about my clothes or my hair or my accent. And you never defended me in front of her. Not once. I just had to stand there and smile, which, thankfully, wasn't that often because you never brought me to anything with your family."

"You never brought me to yours."

"Because mine were an ocean away and I didn't see them either! Sometimes I didn't even know you were with yours until you told me afterward how bad a time you had."

"I did have a bad time."

"So don't go!" I exclaim. "Or bring me with you so it can be fun. You say I'm your partner but you never let me into your world, into the family I was supposed to marry into."

"I didn't know you wanted to go," he says, his hands upturned as though to show how open he's being. "You always said it wasn't your scene."

"But it was yours. It was yours and you shut me out of it." I perch on the edge of the bed. "I'm not trying to blame you," I say. "I'm not saying it was a one-sided thing but you need to see that maybe what we thought we had wasn't actually what we had. Maybe we were together because it was the easiest thing to do, because neither of us thought we had to pay attention to the other and maybe... maybe that used to work for me before but not now."

"That's a lot of maybes," he says quietly. "Maybe you're not sure what you want."

"Are you trying to be funny?"

"No, Abby. I'm trying to understand you. Something I don't think I ever had a problem with before." He leans forward, capturing my gaze. "It's not that my mother doesn't like you, Abby, it's that my mother is mean. She's mean to everyone. I know that. I'm used to it too and that's why I never said anything when she picked on you. I also said nothing because I know you can handle yourself and that it takes more than a few snide comments to bring you down. I didn't bring you to see my family because I thought you wouldn't enjoy it. I was trying to save you from wasting your few hours of spare time with a bunch of people you don't like, not because I was shutting you out. I don't know what I was thinking when I broke up with you. All I know is I was stressed with work and we'd been seeing so little of each other and one day your name flashed up on my phone and I didn't want to answer it." Tyler sits back, softening as I stare at him. "I thought that meant something," he says. "But I was wrong. I was so wrong, Abby. You have to believe me."

I don't answer. A room service cart rolls heavily along the hallway outside and I picture Louise waiting in the lobby, wondering what's happening.

"I think I want to have children."

He looks like I just slapped him.

"Not now," I continue. "But one day. Maybe."

"Okay," he says slowly.

"We dated for three years. Three years together and we never talked about that, not once."

"If you want children we can discuss it, Abby."

"But that's not the point." I fight the urge to drop my head into my hands. "Don't you think that's something we should have covered? Who marries someone without thinking about something like that? We never properly let each other into our lives. We don't know anything about each other. Not really."

"Excuse me?" He laughs a little. "Abby, you know me better than most."

"But not what counts. I know how hard you work. I know how you like your coffee in the morning and I know where you like to buy your suits and what cars you like to drive and where you see yourself professionally in five years but I don't know *you*. We talk but we don't *talk*."

"So let's *talk*. We have time, don't we? Talk to me. Learn me. Because I obviously need to learn more about you. I know you haven't forgiven me for what I did. I wouldn't forgive me either. But I'm asking you to give us a chance. I'm asking you to try. Come back to New York with me. You don't have to take the job at Hanson's. You don't have to move in with me. You can move in with Jess or I can help you find somewhere new. I'd like to do that if you let me. And maybe I don't really know you, but I know you don't do well sitting still. You never have. It's one of the many reasons why I love you. You can't stay here."

"Number three—"

"Abby—"

"I don't love you anymore."

My words ring out between us. I've surprised him again. For three years I was convinced he knew my every thought and twice in two minutes he looks at me like I'm a stranger.

"And," I continue, when he doesn't say anything. "The reason I don't need an interview at Hanson's is because I've got a new job."

His eyebrows pull together, but this is safer territory. This he can deal with. "Where?"

"Stewarts."

"They'd be a good fit for you," he says. "Smaller but... New York?"

"Toronto."

He blinks, ruining his poker face. "Have you said yes?"

"Not yet."

"But you will."

I nod. I will.

He watches me for a moment, analyzing me. "Toronto's a ninety-minute flight from New York."

"Tyler—"

"You loved me before," he says as if it's such a simple thing.

"You don't marry someone because you hope you'll love them someday."

"No," he murmurs. "I guess not." He takes a breath. "So that's it?"

That's it. I remove the ring from my purse. "I want to give this back to you."

"Keep it," he says, but we both know I won't.

I stand and after a moment he does too. We meet each other halfway.

"It's a nice ring," he says when I hand it back to him. "You have good taste."

"Expensive taste."

"That too."

"Do you think you'll be able to return it?"

"I'll figure something out." He slides it into his pocket. "Come here, Abby."

I let him hug me, let his arms come around me and pull me into him. Let him rest his head atop of mine while I press my ear against his chest. I do all of that and know I've made the right decision. I feel no love for the man holding me. Sorrow, maybe. Relief. Maybe even a little affection for what I thought we once had. But not love. Not anymore.

"I think you're making a mistake," he says softly, his voice just audible above me.

I open my eyes, gazing at our reflection in the window, at myself staring back at me. "At least it's mine."

CHAPTER 31

"Are you okay?"

"I think so." I rest my head back against the seat, gazing at the darkening sky as Louise drives us out of the hotel. "But I'm getting a headache."

"That's probably from the cologne," she mutters. "Did you tell him about the job?"

I nod, glancing down at my finger where the ring once was. "He seemed surprised."

"That you got it?"

"That I didn't need his help." I frown as I remember his reaction. "I always thought he saw me as an equal, but he made it sound like the only reason he wanted me back was because he thought I needed saving."

"And you told him to stuff it, right?"

"I wouldn't use that exact terminology, but yes."

"I think you made the right choice," she says as we approach a roundabout. "And the right choice isn't always the easiest one. It's okay if you feel weird about it."

"I don't feel weird."

"That's okay too. Are you hungry? You want food? Chinese food? You can have Chinese food. You can have whatever you want. Just say the word."

I want Luke. My heart pangs with the realization. Luke who would tell me that it's okay and I'd believe him. Luke who would know exactly what I'm feeling.

"Pasta?" Louise continues. "I can make you pasta."

"I'm not hungry."

"You say that now, but once I put something in front of you, you'll want it."

"Would you stop trying to mother me?"

"I'm being nice."

"You're *being* annoying and... what the f— Ow!" I straighten quickly, bumping my head off the roof as we pass a red car.

"What the hell is wrong with you?"

"That's Luke!" I exclaim, twisting in my seat to watch him go. "He just drove past!"

"What?" Louise's eyes widen as she glances in the rearview. "Are you sure?"

"Yes, I'm sure." I almost strain my neck as we miss our exit, going around again. "That's his car. Where's he going?"

"That's the road to the hotel. It can't be him."

"It is." I slap the dashboard in frustration. "We have to follow him."

"But what's he doing out here at this time of night? Unless he—" Louise breaks off with a loud gasp. "Do you think he's going beat up Tyler?"

"*What?* Why would he do that?"

"For your honor!"

"I lost my *honor* the summer before college, thank you very much."

"I mean the honor of *you*. He could be going to fight Tyler for—"

"No one is fighting anyone! Go after him."

"But you don't—"

"Louise!"

She swerves dangerously to meet the hotel exit and I grip the side of the seat to keep steady. At this time of night, he's the only other car on this stretch of road. And there's only one destination at the end of it. Luke's going to the hotel.

Oh my God. I sit back as Louise accelerates, trying not to freak out. "What if he *is* going to go beat him up?"

Louise glances at me. "Please don't tell me you find that attractive."

"Of course not," I say automatically. "That's so unhealthy."

"Right."

Right. "I mean, I guess a little part of me wouldn't *mind* if—"

"Abby!"

"Well, don't put the idea in my head then! He's probably just—"

Louise blasts the horn, cutting me off as Luke's brake lights turn on.

"He heard us," she says, waving triumphantly at him as he slows down.

"You think?" I glare at her. "We could have just met in the parking lot."

"Oh." She looks embarrassed. "Yeah."

I will my heart rate to slow as we pull onto the side of the road. "I'm telling Tomasz you almost totaled the car," I say as I open the door.

Luke's already standing on the grass, understandably very confused. "Abby? What are you doing?"

"Were you going to beat up Tyler?"

He stares at me like I've lost my mind. "No."

Oh.

"You thought I was going to go fight him?" he asks as Louise comes to stand beside me.

"No," I lie.

"Try not to sound too disappointed," she murmurs.

"You weren't answering your phone," he explains as I pinch her hip. "I dropped by your house, but Tomasz said you two had come here and I..." He glances at Louise, trailing off.

"Could you go please?" I ask her.

"How are you going to get back?"

"Luke will bring me home." Like he always does.

She hesitates but Louise likes Luke a lot more than she likes Tyler, so eventually she just nods. "I'll see you at the house."

I wait until she drives off, thankfully a little less manically than before. "It's been a busy few weeks for her," I say.

Luke watches me warily before his eyes flick down, taking in my outfit. I'd dressed up for my conversation with Tyler. Of course I had. Styled my hair and did my makeup, put on a nice dress. Little things. Me things. But a me he's probably not used to.

"I shouldn't have let you walk away the other day," he says. "I'm sorry."

"You were upset."

"I was furious," he says flatly. "But not at you. Well, kind of at you. I thought you were going to go back to him."

"I told you I don't feel anything for him anymore."

"I know." He closes his eyes, looking tired. "I know," he says. "I'm—"

"You have to—"

"Just let me finish," he says quickly. He looks at me then, and the intensity of his gaze almost takes my breath away. "I came here to tell you that I'm falling in love with you. Or maybe I've already fallen. I don't know. But from the moment I picked you up in that parking lot, I haven't been able to stop thinking about you. And I mean that, Abby. Every day. Every moment, no matter how hard

I tried not to. I can't bear the thought of you going back to him. Of you being with anyone but me. And I know how that sounds and I know it's selfish and I know you're not owned by anyone but I love you. I love you and I'm sorry I didn't tell you before. I was scared yesterday that you didn't mean it or that you didn't know what it meant. I was scared you would take it back."

"I'm not taking it back." The words come out as a whisper. It's all I can manage right now. "I gave Tyler the ring," I say. "I don't want to be with him. I don't want *him*."

I want you.

The words are on the tip of my tongue, but I don't say them. It wouldn't be fair to him. Not yet.

"There's something I have to tell you," I say, and he straightens at my tone.

"You got the job," he guesses, and for the first time I can remember, I can't read anything from his expression. "New York?"

"Toronto. They opened an office there last year so there's space and… I'm going to take it. I'm going to say yes."

He doesn't say anything for a long second, as though waiting for more. When I stay silent he glances away, his expression tightening.

"So that's it then?" he asks eventually. "Back abroad?"

"It's what I want. Maybe what I need. I wouldn't be happy here in the long run. Not really." Even if here there were things to make me happy. "I can't turn down this job, Luke."

"I know you can't. I don't want you to."

There's a burning in my throat that won't go away. "I just feel like everyone secretly expects me to stay."

"They *want* you to stay. That's different. But you have to live your life for you, not for anyone else."

They're the words I'd hoped he'd say, but now he's saying them I don't want to hear them. I don't want to hear them at all.

"I just thought you..." I try to stay calm, feeling a hint of annoyance at the resigned look on his face. "That's all you have to say?"

"What more do you want me to say?"

"I don't know—how about telling me not to go?" I ask. "How about remembering that you're in love with me. How about..." My hands go to my hips as frustrated tears prick my eyes. "I wouldn't have minded," I tell him, "if you wanted to beat up Tyler. I know that makes me a bad person, but I think I would have been flattered if I'm being honest. Maybe even a little turned on."

"By me fighting your ex?"

"By you fighting for *me*! You just told me you loved me and now you're like, oh, okay bye, have a nice life, Abby. If you don't want me to be with anyone else, why is it so easy to just let me go?"

"Because it's what you want."

"But I also want you!"

"Then ask me to come with you!"

Oh.

We stare at each other, Luke looking more and more pissed off when I don't say anything.

Oh.

"That's what you wanted me to...?"

He shakes his head, turning to face the road as if he can't bear to look to me.

"You want to come to Toronto with me?"

"I want you to *want* me to— Christ." He rubs a hand down his face as if to wake himself up. The burn is blocking my throat now, and it takes a few swallows before I can speak.

"I didn't think you'd... I mean, it's so far and we've only been together a few... It's nice," I finish lamely. "I went with Jess once. The move can be a bit of a culture shock and it's not cheap but there are lots of Irish people there. Clubs and bars and museums and..."

I shouldn't have said it. Because as soon as I did, as soon as I let myself voice what I didn't even know I desired, it became all I ever wanted. A picture of Luke and me in some new city where no one knows us. With the anonymity and the time to sort out whatever this is between us, to develop it together, to explore it together. To *be* together.

"But your parents—"

"Are my parents," he says, exasperated. "I love them but I don't need to live five minutes down the road from them for the rest of my life."

"Your exams—"

"Are finishing next month. The lease on the café is up in August. Beth already told me she's thinking about not renewing. I could sell up. Get some cash." His throat moves as he swallows. "I love you, Abby. And whatever this is between us, I'm all in."

My heart does a painful leap and then starts to beat in double time. A horrible nervous hope rises in me. "You'll go with me?"

"If you'll have me."

"Yes," I say. "I'll have you. I will definitely have you."

He starts to smile. "Yeah?"

"Think of all the injured ice hockey players you can help."

His smile widens and my tears fall freely then, which seems to amuse him greatly.

"I'm fine," I say as he moves toward me. "I don't know why I'm crying. I'm fine."

"Don't tell me you were hoping I'd say no." His arms envelop me and I close my eyes, the pit in my stomach lessening as he pulls me into an embrace. I cling to him, soaking his thin cotton T-shirt but he doesn't seem to mind.

"These are happy tears," I tell him.

"I know."

"I'm very happy."

He tightens his grip, burrowing his face into my hair.

"Are we really going to do this?" I ask.

"We can try," he murmurs. "Speaking in practical terms, you're the only person I trust to do it with."

"I am very good with plans," I agree.

Luke pulls away just enough to look at me, wiping my cheek with his thumb.

"Jess says I'm an ugly crier," I tell him.

"You're a beautiful crier."

"Liar."

He smirks, dipping his head to kiss me softly. "You're beautiful," he whispers. "And smart and ambitious and brave and I love you. I want to wake up to you every morning and talk to you every day. I want to take you to dinner and meet your friends and teach you to drive. I want *you*, Abby Reynolds. All of you. For as long as you want me."

My tears have stopped now, though they still make my vision swim as I gaze up at Luke, at everything he promises. And now I'm really getting a headache from all my crying and a stomachache from all my worrying but I don't care. After so many weeks of not knowing who I was, or where I belonged, I've never felt more sure of anything than of this moment and of all the ones to come.

I rise on my toes, kissing him again as his arms slide around my back, holding me to him.

I love him and he loves me and we're going to do this.

Together.

EPILOGUE

EIGHTEEN MONTHS LATER

"I thought we left Canada to escape the snow," Luke grumbles, peering out of the airport. He's been in a bad mood ever since we boarded the plane, delayed for three hours due to the weather. The Irish weather. The Irish weather, which I'm pretty sure every Canadian I know would either laugh or cry at if they could see it now.

"I don't think they'd call this snow." I raise a hand to catch the soft flakes but he quickly grabs it, holding it to his side. "I was trying to have a Hallmark moment."

"You'll be complaining about how cold you are in two minutes."

"But you love warming me," I tease. I don't pull away. I like it when he holds my hand, even when he's grumpy.

"They're not here," he says. "Let's go inside before you turn blue."

I let him tug me back into the arrivals hall, his free hand pushing our luggage cart as we find a space over by a Sunglass Hut.

The airport is decked out for Christmas, with large twinkling trees and strands of tinsel and baubles everywhere you look. On the opposite side of the floor, a choir of schoolchildren sings their way through carols, making up for each off-key note with sheer exuberance, and a surprising number of people, including their pets, have dressed up in festive outfits for maximum embarrassment of arriving relatives. I look upon it all with a huge smile. Last year, we'd only been in Toronto a few months when Christmas came around and Luke was only a few *weeks* into his job at the sports clinic. We agreed it would be better if we stayed and got settled, meaning this is my first Christmas home in seven years, meaning I'm allowed to be a little indulgent.

"Do you see them?" Luke asks, scanning the hall. Before I can answer a cheer rises from the crowd as the next round of passengers emerges from baggage claim.

We watch a woman scream as she rushes into the arms of a man wearing reindeer ears.

Luke shakes his head. "People are weird at Christmas."

"I think it's nice."

"Of course you do. If you had your way, we'd be wearing matching pajama sets to bed."

"If I had my way, we wouldn't be wearing anything to bed."

I look up just in time to catch his smile. "Cheer up," I say, nudging him.

"I'm sorry." He sighs. "I guess I'm a little nervous."

"Think you're getting coal this year?"

"It's our first Christmas home as a couple," he says ignoring me. "Both sets of parents. I just keep thinking about all the questions they're going to ask."

"Oh yeah?" I raise a brow. "Like what?"

His mouth clamps shut.

"Like what, Luke?"

"Never mind."

"Like when we're getting engaged?"

"You're enjoying this."

"Making you squirm?" I grin. "Always. And trust me, you just need to sit there and look pretty. Let me handle the questions."

"And why would I do that?"

"Because I know the answers," I say airily, and turn back to the crowd before he can respond. "Did you talk to Beth?"

"She did most of the talking." He grimaces. "I guess I'm not the only one who's nervous."

I smile, sympathetic. Once Beth finally plucked up the courage to reach out to Jess online, they quickly become firm friends before a weekend trip to New York established them as significantly more than that. Trying to be a little less impulsive after closing the café, Beth wasn't ready to leave Ireland just yet, but Jess had insisted on bringing her over for the holidays this year, so she could spend Christmas in the city. Knowing Jess, I doubt there's anything innocent behind her intentions. The little festive week away is clearly her ploy to convince Beth to move over, but seeing as she's the first woman Jess has been serious about in a long, *long* time, I'm curious to see it where it goes.

"They're dangerous together," I say with a sigh. "You need someone in a relationship to reign the other one in."

"Like me?"

"Uh, no. I'm the reigner."

"You?"

"Yes, me! I—"

"Abby!"

I turn at the shout to see Louise barge her way across the hall, striding through a family reunion being captured by a news crew.

"What are you doing all the way over here? We've been looking for you for ten minutes." She hugs me while she chides me, the chill from outside still clinging to her coat.

"We couldn't find you. Where's Saoirse?"

"With her father."

"You didn't bring her with—"

"Of course I did," she snaps. "They're coming now. Hello, Luke."

"Louise," he greets, trying to hide his amusement. "Happy Christmas."

She nods, her attention already back on me. "You look terrible."

"Because I've been on a plane for— Oh my God!"

I push past her, aiming straight for the little bundle in the stroller pushed by Tomasz. She's wearing an extremely fluffy hat, making it difficult to see her face, but Tomasz crouches down when I do, tipping it up.

Baby Saoirse is fast asleep, oblivious to the world.

My niece.

"Oh my God," I repeat, touching her nose with exaggerated care.

"She slept the entire way," Louise says. "Which means she'll be up all night. Don't, Abby."

"What?" I ask as I try to touch her again. "She'll want to see me."

"She doesn't know who you are. And if you wake my child, I will kill you." The wild look in her eyes makes me think she isn't lying.

"We'll steal her when they're asleep," Luke says to me.

"Please do," Louise mutters but her gaze softens as she adjusts the blanket around Saoirse.

"How are you getting on with Mam and Dad?" I ask as I hug Tomasz hello. Our parents flew back a few days ago to spend the holiday at home. Luke and I will be staying with Pat and Susan while we're here. Me in his old bed and him on the couch.

"As well as can be expected," Louise says. "You cut your hair."

"I did."

"Hmm."

Luke fights a smile.

"Thank you again for her birthday present," she says, not so subtly changing the subject. "We appreciate it."

"It was my pleasure."

Starting from scratch with my savings wasn't easy, but Luke and I were being careful, and the first thing I did when things were a little back to normal was set up a bank account in Saoirse's name.

"Do they still have you working all hours?"

"Unfortunately but I'm getting better at finding balance." I glance up at Luke, who squeezes my hand. A lot better. The hours at Stewarts were as tough as they were at MacFarlane and I was giving it my all, but I was no longer bending over backward just to keep myself in the game. I didn't want to. I had no desire to stay dramatically late in the office if I didn't have to. No desire to give up my weekends or keep my phone on all night. Not when Luke was at home waiting for me. Not when we had so much time to catch up on.

"And Luke, how's the... ah, crap."

Louise sighs as Saoirse stirs, blinking sleepily awake. I clap my hands as Tomasz takes her out of the stroller.

"Give her to me," I say, holding my arms out.

Louise shakes her head. "Abby—"

"I didn't wake her, so I get to hold her."

"I give you an hour before you're fed up," she warns but doesn't say anything more as I coo at her daughter.

"You know me," I say, bouncing her. "We play on the phone. Yes, we do."

She blinks at me, confused but pliant with a "let's see where this goes" expression.

"Do you have everything?" Louise asks, eyeing the crowd. "We better go if we want to get back before Christmas is over."

"It's grand, Louise."

"The roads are a nightmare," she says as Tomasz takes our luggage cart. "When you're the one driving, you can set the schedule."

I continue to sing nonsense words at Saoirse as we follow them back out into the cold.

"You're good with her," Luke says, slipping an arm around my waist. "What?" He laughs when I give him a look.

"Don't go getting any ideas."

He smiles. "I'm not."

"Good." But I look down at her in my arms and feel a tug at my heart. What I have with Luke still feels new. Sometimes it's like we're still getting to know each other. Our thoughts, our moods, where we want to eat, what we like to do. Luckily, I find the more I learn, the more I like. I was just teasing him before. I don't have the answers. But for once that's okay. It's enough now just to be with him. To take each day as it comes and not have my life scheduled out in advance. Enough now to just spend the holiday with him and my family and one or two emails.

Maybe three.

"When you're older, we'll get your ears pierced," I whisper to my niece as she reaches up to grab a loose curl. "And you'll tell me all the secrets you don't want to tell your mom. And I'll give you your first sip of—"

"Okay," Louise says, turning to take her from me. "You can hold her at home."

"I was only messing!"

"I lived with you when you were a teenager, Abby. No, you weren't."

Luke tugs the back of my coat, pulling me to him as Louise settles Saoirse in her baby chair.

"You cheered up," I say.

"I did. I remembered that I loved you."

"Well, that's good timing. Even with all the family arguments to come?"

"Even with that."

"Even if you have to sleep on your parents' couch?"

"I've slept on the couch before, remember? At least this time I won't have to hear you snore."

"I don't—"

"Hey, lovebirds," Louise says, shutting the trunk. "Hurry up."

"I love you too," I say, ignoring her. "And I don't snore."

"We're driving away now," Louise calls as she gets into the passenger seat.

Luke draws me close, brushing the snow from my hair before kissing my temple.

"Welcome back, Abby," he murmurs into my ear, and hand in hand we head toward the car, head toward home.

A LETTER FROM CATHERINE

Dear Reader,

Thank you so much for reading *The Rebound*! I hope you enjoyed Abby and Luke's story.

With this book, I set out to write a story about women with unapologetic ambition. I wanted to write about returning home and small communities and handsome men in cars. But to my surprise, my favorite part of the writing journey turned out to be something else entirely.

Abby's sister wasn't in the initial proposal for this book. In fact, she didn't exist until a few weeks after I started drafting it. I originally had Abby move in with her parents but I just couldn't make it work no matter how many funny dinner scenes I threw at them. Now I know it's because Louise was waiting for me, tapping her foot in the corner of my subconscious, irritable and unimpressed. I loved writing their scenes together. I loved watching them try to communicate and fail miserably. It reminded me of how strange families can be, but also that they can be strong and rooted in love, no matter the time or the distance apart.

Some families you're born with and some you find. Whoever yours is, I hope they're safe and well, and I hope if you're not together right now, you can be soon.

All my best,
Catherine xx

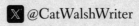 @CatWalshWriter

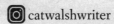 catwalshwriter

ACKNOWLEDGMENTS

My second pandemic novel! Words I never thought I'd say. I won't lie, one of the main reasons I was excited about Abby's story was because of the very vital "research trip" I was going to take to the west coast of Ireland. Lockdown had other ideas. Like my first book, *The Rebound* was written and edited during a time when I always had one eye on the news, and just like my first book, *One Night Only*, I'm so thankful for all those who saw me through.

A huge thank you to all the readers around the world who got in touch. Your enthusiasm and creativity blew me away and I'm so grateful for every review, rating, and comment you left. You've made the last few months a lot of fun and I've loved getting to know you all.

Thank you as well to everyone I know in "real life" who reached out with their congratulations. There are too many to list but please know how much I appreciate every one of you. For me, writing is a solitary activity, usually done at home so I can talk to myself and laugh at my jokes. To finally get to share something with people in my life was bizarre and wonderful.

I may write my books alone, but everything after takes a village. Thank you to Áine, JC, Jen, and everyone who read early chapters and/or listened patiently to my panicked ramblings. A big thank you to my editor, Celine Kelly, who immediately saw what I was trying to do and expertly paved the way for me. Thank you as well to Radhika Sonagra, Isobel Akenhead, and the entire team at Bookouture for your care, knowledge, and enthusiasm for both me and this story.

Finally, thank you to me. This journey so far has been a dream, but a stressful one. *The Rebound* came at a time when a lot was happening in my life and it was hard. I had a lot of quiet moments full of doubt and worry but I kept going and I kept working and I'm so glad I did. I'm so glad these books are in the world and I'm so glad I get to write them. Here's to many more.